Praise for Robin M. King's *Van Gogh Gone*

I loved everything about this bo  *ite heroine, and I can't wait to rea* *he and Daly will go on next. Rem* *ne are books I will recommend to a* *read. The next [book] can't come soon enough!!* —Amazon Customer

King has once again created a story that is impossible to put down until the very last page, and even then I left hoping for more. The twists and turns will keep you guessing . . . Two thumbs up!!! —Melanie Mason, author of *The Line That Divides* and *Crossing Lines*

Exciting! More adventures for Alexandra. You are all in for a treat with suspense, surprises, and relationships unfolding. Wait until you meet the bad guy! There were lots of twists and turns. I wasn't sure where the story was going to lead. I'm already waiting for the next in this series. I want to find out where Alexandra's next adventures takes her. And, most of all, where romance leads her. —Regency Fan

In Van Gogh Gone, *Alexandra's special ops become personal as she must travel to Barcelona and Paris to steal a Van Gogh painting . . . but she's really trying to save her family and those she loves from an evil enemy of The Company. We are left wondering who's telling the truth and who's not. But the real question is whether Alexandra can stay true to herself, especially with matters of the heart. Fast paced and exciting, yet poignant and heartfelt,* Van Gogh Gone *is a perfect follow-up to* Remembrandt *. . . oh please let there be more!* —Amy Martinsen, author of *Changing Worlds* and *The Secret Obituary Writer*

Van Gogh Gone *keeps you on the edge of your seat the entire time! The suspense, drama, romance, and danger of Alexandra's journey is absolutely riveting. Love love love!* —Robert Ahlstrom

Praise for Robin M. King's *Remembrandt*

Robin King debuts her first novel with an exciting plot line of teen spies and dangerous secret missions. The story . . . is thrilling . . . and the romance is simple and sweet. —Deseret News

With a tightly woven plot, great characters, and full of thrills and chills, you'll enjoy Remembrandt. —Michele Ashman Bell, author of *A Modest Proposal* (Butterfly Box series)

In this clever and fast-paced young adult novel, Robin King delivers a perfect mix of suspense and romance. . . . Alexandra's eidetic memory will reel you in, and her double life will keep you guessing until the end. —Brooke Hargett

Let's be honest, we've all dreamed of being one of those suave, oh-so-cool spies or secret agents, right? Well, with Remembrandt, *you get to be! Or at least, Alexandra gets to be, and the writing is so effortless you feel like you're right there along with her. And I'll just come right out and admit it: William is my new fictional crush. Oh William! Where have you been all my life?! And can Casey and I be real-life roommates? . . . Everything about this book rocks, and I already can't wait for book two.* —Caitlin Jacobs

When I read Remembrandt, *I didn't want the story to end. I loved the setting, intrigue, surprises, adventures, and romance . . . I'm happy to hear that the experiences and friendships won't end. I'm looking forward to what happens next. I recommend this book to the young and young at heart alike.* —Karen LuBean

What a great debut novel! Author Robin King keeps you intrigued as you try to figure out the puzzles Alexandra is faced with. . . . I would highly recommend this book to young adults and adults alike. —Wendy Mallatt

Memory of Monet

Robin M. King

WALNUT SPRINGS PRESS

Remembrandt Series

Remembrandt
Van Gogh Gone
Memory of Monet

Acknowledgments

It's hard to put into words the gratitude I have for the many people that helped me on the journey of bringing to life *Memory of Monet* and the whole Remembrandt series. But I'm going to try. At least doing it on paper lets me hide my teary eyes and shaky voice.

First off, I'm grateful for DeliciousReads.com and all the wonderful friends there that have supported me along the way. Our shared love of books has inspired and motivated me to grow as an author. It's nice to know there are fellow book nerds in the world.

I have the best beta readers and writing group. I gave them less than a month to polish my story and they did an amazing job. Alix Adams, Brooke Hargett, Mary Taylor, Cheryl Josie, Wendy Mallatt, Jared Dearth, Carina Heilner, Karen LuBean, Monica Parkinson, April Porter, Raelynn Zolman-Thorn, Heather Horrocks, and Rebecca Batty—I'm so grateful for your support.

Memory of Monet is my favorite book cover yet. I owe many thanks to Summer Bruford (www.summernicolephoto.com). She is seriously my favorite photographer. She listened to my ideas and helped me create the perfect book cover by making our model into a spy. The gorgeous girl on this book is Marli Sharp, who is such a doll (and could totally be a spy). I feel lucky that she agreed to be Alexandra. Marli, if we sell movie rights, you'd be my first choice as the star!

I'm thankful for my neighbors, family, and friends who have helped watch my kids while I've attended book signings, conferences, and writing groups, and while I hid away in my office, typing like mad. My hubby and six kids are probably the only ones who realize how much time it takes to get a book on the shelves, and I'm grateful they still want me around (at least I think they do). I need to give special thanks to my baby, Olive Grace. I was pregnant with her while writing *Memory of Monet,* and she lay patiently in my arms as I wrote the ending. She really was the reason I had the strength to finish. Thank you, baby girl.

Walnut Spring Press has been an easy publisher to work with and I couldn't be happier with how they've supported me in writing this series and helped me get my foot in the door of this crazy publishing world. Linda Prince is an editing genius. Everyone that reads this book should be thanking her for all the mistakes they don't have to read.

Lastly, I'd like to thank everyone who is still a spy at heart. I know that most of the time life is full of laundry that needs folding, bills that need paying, and spills that need cleaning, but we all have an adventurous side. Alexandra showed hers by traversing the globe in search of paintings and saving people. We can show ours by accomplishing something we never thought we could do — graduate from college, be a mom, run a marathon, record a song, or even . . . write a book.

1

Interrogation

I wiped my palms on my suit jacket and forced myself to breathe slowly. My stomach twisted under my pencil skirt and silk blouse. I smoothed back my long blond hair and tucked it behind my ears.

"I can't believe I'm doing this," I said, searching for pockets in my jacket, only to discover the flaps were just for decoration.

"Golkov only suggested it. You made the choice on your own," a voice said in my ear.

I peered around out of habit, but I was the only person in the hallway. The walnut floor and cold redbrick walls gave the space a feeling of foreboding.

"Shh," I said. "I'll lose it if there are any more distractions."

"I thought you liked distractions. You're the one who chose to wear your com unit. I was just lucky enough to guess you'd have it on." From hundreds of memories, Daly's cocky grin played across my mind.

Chose? I fought back the urge to laugh. I had a wireless nanochip nestled next to my eardrum. The Millard-enhanced earrings I normally wore on missions tended to fall off, and my handler, Daly, had insisted I try out this new communications device. The com unit was less an earpiece and more like a mini hearing aid, so small it couldn't be seen from the outside and had to be removed by Millard with a special magnetic tool.

"I'd rather be scaling buildings right now," I whispered to Daly.

"We can probably arrange that later today. For now just relax, clear your mind, and do what you do best."

"And what's that?" I closed my eyes.

"Dazzle them."

I could almost see his dark-brown eyes brighten as he smiled. Actually, that was a lie. In my mind, I watched that face and smile in images from my catalog of memories. James Daly had been there from the beginning—my first mission in Russia—and had stayed by my side even when I tried to push him away. There was a comfort in his presence that I'd never really understood until now.

My heartbeat had slowed to a steady rhythm. I didn't know how Daly did it, but he always knew the right thing to say.

"Alexandra Stewart?" A nasally voice interrupted my calm. "You may go in now."

I nodded at the woman, who stood at an open doorway. "Thank you," I said to her and to the man in my ear.

As my heels clicked across the floors of the Marston building's second story, I realized I was glad Daly was there. The last month since my unsanctioned mission in Paris had been a whirlwind of emotions, reprimands, makeup classwork, and planning. If it hadn't been for Daly's support, I might not have made it through.

Instinctively, I felt for The Company ring, the symbol of my work over the last several months. My right ring finger felt naked without the thick silver metal, and a part of me had felt empty since I'd given the ring back to Golkov and told him I needed time away from the spy organization he ran. That organization, referred to as The Company, happened to be housed in the basement of the building in which I now stood. It was a secret very few people on campus knew about. I had a decision to make about my role in The Company, but for now I had a different kind of mission to complete.

From the front of the room, an elderly woman with a bob of shiny gray hair commanded, "Ms. Stewart, take a seat." The rough Russian words were obviously spoken by a native.

Moments later, I eased myself into the single metal chair that rested about ten feet from a long table. Three people wearing suits and serious expressions sat across from me—a man in his forties with coppery-brown hair, the woman who had asked me to take a seat, and the dean of Russian Studies.

"My name is Elena Gulin," the woman said. "I am on the board for Russian Studies here at Brown University." She held up a hand with at least two rings on each finger and motioned to the men seated on either side of her. "You probably recognize Dean Matthews." He nodded at me but didn't smile. He began leafing through papers on the table in front of him. And this" —Professor Gulin indicated the younger man— "is Leonid Denisovich. He is part of our professor exchange program and comes from Lomonosov Moscow State University. We are lucky to have him as part of the board today." Denisovich's eyes never left my face.

"We have reviewed your scores and letters of recommendation," Dean Matthews declared, his Russian less harsh than his colleague's. "They are quite commendable. However, as you know, the verbal assessment will weigh most heavily in our decision."

"We'd like to begin by having you tell us a little about yourself," said Professor Denisovich.

I opened my mouth, but nothing came out. It felt as if a large hand was squeezing my neck. *What is wrong with me?* I'd jumped into the Kryukov Canal in St. Petersburg to escape terrorists. I had destroyed a biological weapon by blowing up a secret warehouse in Moscow. I had stolen a painting, albeit one that had been stolen previously, from a supposed philanthropist in Barcelona. I'd broken into the archives of the Louvre in Paris. I'd had the barrel of a gun pointed at my chest. Yet I couldn't sit in front of these Russian-language experts, two of which were obviously native speakers, without my throat seizing up.

"Ms. Stewart?" said Professor Gulin.

"Why don't you start by giving us some of your background," Professor Denisovich prodded. "Why did you choose Russian for your undergraduate degree?"

I can't do this. I shifted in my wooden chair.

"You've got this, Alex. Just . . . dazzle," Daly said in my ear.

He was right. If I could solve puzzles, break codes, and save lives, I could show these experts my knowledge of Russian.

I swallowed, trying to relax, and then said in Russian, "My grandparents came from Moscow, but they passed away before I could walk. While I grew up in Washington State, I realized I wanted a connection to them, since they were no longer living. I may have been born in the U.S., but Russian culture and language is in my blood." The words rushed out as I told of enrolling in college classes while still in high school and then transferring to Brown University at age seventeen. I explained my work with Professor Golkov—at least the above-ground work.

I didn't mention the car accident that had taken my mother from me, or my brother, Tanner, who lay in a coma due to injuries suffered in that accident. I couldn't tell the board that a secret Russian spy organization, Red Eye, had retaliated against my mom for not joining their ranks. Nor did I mention how their leader, Ivan, had threatened to harm my family and friends if I didn't steal a certain Van Gogh painting from the Louvre. Even though the events of the last six months had been traumatic, I managed to smile at the three professors in front of me. Despite everything, I was okay. I had hope. The brother I'd thought had died in the car crash last May was still alive. If he could somehow wake up and be okay, everything would have been worth it.

"If we accept you into this program, what contributions do you think you could make?" Dean Matthews asked. "What skills do you have that might set you apart from other applicants?"

My mind flashed to scenes from missions where I'd used my eidetic memory to complete my tasks. I knew I couldn't tell these professors how my mind recorded every experience I had in such detail it was like watching a movie in my head. They would never understand if I mentioned I had every Russian textbook in the Brown University Library engrained in my mind so vividly, I could recite every word of every page. No, there were many things I couldn't share with anyone outside The Company.

"Many students have a grasp on the Russian language and are quite proficient." I spoke my Russian now with ease. "But this language is my passion. When I visited St. Petersburg and Moscow last fall, the culture embraced me and I felt at home with the people. I may not have been born in Russia, but it is a piece of who I am." I sat up straight in my chair and focused on each face of the board that would decide on my admittance into their Slavic Studies master's program. "After my mother died last spring, I felt lost for some time, but the one thing that brought me back and sent me on this path was the knowledge that I could carry on her legacy."

Though I'd wrestled for weeks with the decision about returning permanently to The Company, speaking with these strangers began to sway me. My mother had been a spy, but I didn't know it while she was alive. She had spared my family the knowledge of her work with the CIA and, later, The Company, because she wanted us to have a normal life. She'd spent years of her life following her passion—rescuing stolen paintings. I couldn't turn my back on everything I knew now. I had to continue her work as well as carve a path of my own.

Once again I glanced at the empty spot on my finger—the place where The Company ring should've been. There was another conversation I needed to have soon that might be just as hard as this one.

"Well, thank you, Ms. Stewart, for your time. We will review everything and give you our decision within two weeks." Professor Gulin stood up and held out her jeweled fingers. I rose from my chair and moved awkwardly to the table to shake her hand and the hand of Dean Matthews.

"Your mother was a remarkable woman," the dean said.

"You knew her?" I barely managed to keep my voice from cracking.

"She was a TA of mine back in the day. Had to be, what, over twenty years ago? Time sure does fly." He squinted at me and tilted his head. "She didn't have you while at Brown, did she?"

"No, she didn't meet my father until after she graduated."

"Then that would make you . . ." Dean Matthews tapped his lips with a finger.

"Seventeen," I said. "But I'll turn eighteen soon."

"Pretty young to be vying for a spot in the program," said Professor Denisovich at our left.

"'A beard doesn't make a philosopher.'" I spoke the Russian proverb in my best accent.

"'Tis true, 'tis true." Denisovich nodded. He held out his hand and I walked over to shake it. He placed his other hand on top of mine. "You are such a surprise, Alexandra Stewart. I am hoping we see more of you in the future."

"Thank you." I pulled my fingers from his. His eyes held my gaze a little longer than necessary before I turned toward the exit, and I had a feeling he was watching as I crossed the room.

I closed the door behind me and made my way around the corner, then stopped to lean back against the wall. With my eyes closed, I rested my head on the rough brick. I didn't know if I'd really impressed the board, but I'd given it my all.

"Congratulations," Daly said in my ear. "I knew you could do it."

"I'm not sure I actually *did* anything, but thanks for getting me through that."

"So, what now, Alex?" he asked.

I released a long, slow breath. "Sometimes I wish I could just fly away."

"I think I could arrange that. Tahiti, maybe? I could have us there by midnight."

I didn't miss Daly's use of the word "us."

"Actually, I have something I need to do, and I'd prefer some privacy if you don't mind." The snippy edge to my voice was unintentional. I wasn't angry at Daly, just worried, and the stress of the day hadn't helped.

"You just have to switch the transmitter off on your phone if you don't want me at your ear," he said tightly.

"I know. I'm sorry. I wasn't . . . it's just. I'm going to see Tanner before . . ." I didn't have to finish the sentence. Daly knew about my brother's surgery the next day. I'd hardly talked of anything else since learning he was alive.

"I got it," Daly replied.

"But I could use a sparring partner later. You interested?"

"I'm always interested." The way he said it made my entire body warm. I knew he was interested in far more than a fighting match, but I wasn't ready for anything right now. Even though we hadn't had a conversation about it, he hadn't pressured me for an explanation. And other than the occasional flirting, he hadn't pushed me for anything more than friendship. Since the Paris mission and my break-up with William, only one guy held my focus—my brother.

"I'll see you later." I pulled out my phone and turned off the transmitter. Millard could probably override the switch, but I felt certain Daly wouldn't attempt it. Over the last month, I'd grown to trust him more than I'd ever thought possible.

Hurrying from the Marston building, I was tempted to visit the basement, but I hadn't been inside The Company headquarters in over a month. And right now Tanner needed me more than they did.

The lounge of Wayland House was unusually crowded for a Friday afternoon. A group of girls ran across the room, their arms filled with bags from what looked like a shopping spree. Another group of young women sat in the kitchen area, applying makeup to each other's faces. I managed to squeeze through the giggling chaos to the stairs.

"How did it go?" Casey asked when I walked into our room. Flat pieces of foil stuck out from her head like porcupine quills. She sat on her twin bed with a textbook laid open on her pillow.

"Is this some kind of fad I've missed out on?" I pointed to her head. "And what's with the craziness downstairs? You'd think the semester was over already."

"Not quite yet." She glanced at the oversized purple watch at her wrist. "Only five more minutes."

"Until what?"

"Until I can take these foils out of my hair and see if my new red streaks worked."

"Red?" I couldn't imagine bright red intermixed with Casey's gorgeous black locks.

"Yes. I have to look my best for the dance tonight."

"There's a dance tonight?"

"Seriously, Alex. It's all anyone has talked about for weeks. With that smart brain of yours, you'd think you could remember this." I nearly laughed. Casey didn't know about my eidetic memory. "And stop changing the subject, Alex. I have four minutes now. Tell me about the board review. How did it go?"

I pulled off my jacket, threw it over my desk chair, and fell onto my bed, which was surprisingly comfortable considering how old the mattress must've been. "I almost froze up but made it through in the end. I'm not sure how much I impressed them, but I did my best."

"I'll bet you blew them out of the water," Casey replied. "James is always saying how perfect your Russian is."

I blushed at the mention of Daly's first name. Casey had started dating Millard, The Company's gadget wizard, who was good friends with Daly. The four of us had hung out several times in the past month.

"Now you need to tell me." I pulled off my heels and let them drop to the floor. "Why red?"

"It's St. Patrick's Day," Casey said as if that explained everything.

"Um, shouldn't you be doing green then?"

"I'm *wearing* green, silly." She pointed to the tiny dress hanging on the front of our closet doors. "The red, well . . . the red is for J.R."

"Millard?" I still had a hard time calling people from The Company by their first names. I guess it was my way of differentiating them from my normal life.

"Don't you know anything? Red on St. Patrick's Day?" Casey looked at her watch and began pulling the foils from her head.

I searched through my mind. Had I ever seen anything about the significance of red on St. Patrick's Day? After a few seconds, the words from a teen magazine article surfaced in my mind. "You want him to kiss you?" I said.

A sneaky smile played at Casey's lips. "It's about time, isn't it?"

I seriously couldn't imagine Millard having the courage to kiss anyone, let alone my drop-dead-gorgeous roommate, who stood in front of a bed heaped in discarded party outfits. But I was happy for her and Millard. They were the perfect mix of awkward, smart, and quirky. "Yes," I finally replied.

"I'd better go wash this out. You coming tonight?"

"Maybe later. I need to do something first. I'll probably be gone when you get back. Just text me if you leave the dance, okay?" I sat up and started to unbutton my shirt.

"Sure."

"And good luck tonight. I'm going to want a full report."

Casey laughed. "I don't kiss and tell." I raised an eyebrow at her and she added, "Okay, I'll give you some of the details." As she left for the bathroom down the hall, I knew I was in for a thorough report of every look, every gesture, and every kiss.

I changed into black running pants and a long-sleeved shirt, then tied my hair back, slid on my running shoes, and grabbed my car keys. My body was due for a much needed run, but first I had something even more important to do.

2

Missing

Nothing had changed since I'd last seen my brother. Tanner lay in a hospital bed at the Providence apartment, machines humming at his side, a dark-blue blanket pulled up to his chest. His blond hair matched my own, though it was longer than he usually kept it and parted to the side in a style he never would've worn. The nurse, Rose, must have shaved his gaunt face, because it was clean and smooth. Tanner looked as though he could open his eyes any minute. Though he'd been fed intravenously, the bulk of his muscles from years of football training had disappeared, leaving behind thin arms and legs. He was my brother and yet I wondered if he'd really ever be the brother from my memories again.

I couldn't help thinking about what had brought him to this point. The terrorist organization Red Eye had been taken down, and the man who had caused the car accident that had killed my mom was locked away in a CIA prison. I fisted my hands at my side. Nothing could make up for the fact that she wasn't coming back and that my brother's life would probably never be the same.

"Alexandra?" A warm hand touched my shoulder. I looked back to find Elijah standing there with a look of concern in his eyes. A mixture of feelings swirled inside me until they settled on calm. I released my tensed hands and placed one on top of Tanner's. "He's going to pull through this," Elijah said.

"I know," I said out of habit, but I didn't really know anything anymore. I didn't know what was going to happen to my brother. I didn't know if I could go on without him again. And even though I thought I was ready earlier, seeing my brother made my resolve waver. Maybe I wasn't ready to reclaim that ring and my role as a spy for The Company. "When do you leave?" I asked Elijah.

"An ambulance will transport him to the hospital tonight. Shortly after that, Rose and I will prep him for surgery. By this time tomorrow the procedure will be complete, and in the next few days we should know if it succeeded."

I was aware of all these details. I had been to the room where the surgery would happen. I had met the doctors who would assist Elijah in the groundbreaking procedure that, if successful, would awaken Tanner from the coma that had silenced him for over ten months. I had read every manual and article on brain function I could get my hands on. I had watched as Elijah and his fiancée, Rose, practiced the surgery on models and cadavers. Still, I needed Elijah's reassurance.

If I'd told anyone that the man at my side had tried to push me from a ten-story building only five months before, they would have considered me crazy for trusting him now. No one could understand the pressure placed on Elijah to do what he did. Red Eye had been blackmailing him with the life of his fiancée. He'd had no choice. I'd forgiven him long ago. In fact, I felt indebted to him because he'd spent the past two months doing everything in his power to save my brother. Elijah's undercover experience working with comatose patients in Russia was part of the reason Golkov had called him after the accident. Elijah hadn't even hesitated when his expertise was requested. His work with my mom gave him a special connection to my family.

He walked to the other side of the room and checked the monitors on the machines at Tanner's side. Elijah didn't look like a doctor in his crisp black suit and gleaming cuff links, but there was no one else I would've trusted more with Tanner's life. I still couldn't believe the CIA had agreed to release Elijah before he was sent to a black-site prison. Fortunately my work in Paris, and handing over the leader of Red Eye, had given me some pull.

The light caught on something silver on Elijah's finger. "Is that—" I pointed to his hand.

He held it up for me to see. The silver flower—the bittersweet nightshade or *solanum dulcamara*—etched into the thick silver ring called out to me. He was wearing The Company ring again. It was a symbol for truth, a reminder of the bitter and the sweet consequences of always knowing all the facts.

He cleared his throat. "Golkov and I are finally on the same page again. I doubt things will ever be like they were. He'll never fully forgive me for what I did to you . . ." Elijah looked to the ground and rubbed a hand over his shaven head. Then his eyes found mine. "But he understands and trusts me again. That's all I can hope for."

I stared for a few minutes at the ring while Elijah worked at Tanner's side. "I know we talked about this, but I want to be there during the surgery," I said. "I need to be there."

Elijah shook his head. "Alexandra, if I was operating on anyone else, I'd want you by my side. You'd make an excellent doctor someday. But this surgery will take hours, and I'm afraid you being there will only make things harder for you."

"I need to be there, just in case . . ." I couldn't finish the sentence. I couldn't say goodbye again. I needed Tanner. He wasn't just a brother. He was my best friend. No one would ever understand me like he did. And maybe having him back would give me part of my mom back, too.

Elijah came to stand next to me again. "I'm going to do everything I can. The best doctors on the East Coast will assist me. If anything doesn't go as planned, I'll contact you immediately. Okay?" His Ukrainian accent seemed especially thick, as it usually did when he was tired.

"You should sleep before the surgery," I said.

"You and Rose worry too much. I'm only in my forties and already being treated like I'm eighty. Just because I shave my head doesn't mean I'm actually old and bald." He glanced up as if he could see his shiny head. "I will be well-rested and in top condition tomorrow. After working in the field for so long, with all this rest and the regular meals Rose is forcing me to eat, I doubt I'll ever be able to go on a full-scale mission again without feeling starved and sleep-deprived."

"You think you'll do missions again?"

Elijah took a deep breath. "Once I stepped into this life, I knew there was no turning back."

I recalled the words of André Berthiaume that Daly had quoted to me many months before, during the Moscow mission. *We all wear masks, and the time comes when we cannot remove them without removing some of our own skin.* My mind flashed to Daly's face when I asked if that meant there was no turning back from my joining The Company as a spy. He'd said that being a spy was already a part of who I was before I even knew about the organization.

Daly had been right; it was in my bones. I imagined that was what Elijah meant too. Even if I never again set foot in The Company headquarters, being a spy—searching for adventure, discovering truth, and helping people—would always define me in some way. Now I just needed to decide where to go from here.

I pulled my silver Jetta into the paved parking lot at the bottom of Neutaconkanut Park. I usually ran closer to campus through Blackstone Park, but I had stopped using that route since returning from Paris. It wasn't that I didn't want to run into William. I just wasn't sure what to say if I did. I'd heard people talk about how hard it was to break up with someone, but no one ever admitted how the relationship would change you forever or how you would always care for the person. The hurt look in William's eyes when I ended the relationship played in my mind now. I didn't need to experience it again in real life, and I was certain he didn't want to see me, either.

The grass at the park had yet to awaken from its winter's sleep, and the branches of the leafless trees curved downward like frowns. As I began jogging up one of the paved trails, my mind played movies in fast-forward of everything that had happened since I'd come to Brown—the missions, my first love, finding out about my mom's role as a spy, and discovering that my brother hadn't died in the car accident that had killed my mother.

I wished I could say I'd grown stronger or more sure of myself and what I should do with my life. In many ways I felt weaker and even more adrift. The only thing that kept me going was the chance of getting my brother back.

I hopped over a nearly melted pile of snow on the edge of the trail and made my way into a forested area of the park. Most of the snow that had covered Providence for months had dissipated along with the freezing-cold weather. A few remnants of snow dotted the forest, but soon all traces would be gone.

An unnatural rustling brought me back to attention. I slowed and had to blink my eyes to clear my vision. A man stood against one of the trees just ahead of me. I would've simply run past him, except he wasn't wearing hiking or running clothes. In fact, he had on a black suit and bright-blue tie. What was a businessman doing in the middle of a forested trail? Unease filled me the closer I got to the man. I recognized him. It had only been a few hours since the board review earlier that day. Leonid Denisovich's breath billowed out in front of him like smoke from a cigar, reminding me how cold it was in Providence in March.

"Ms. Stewart, how nice of you to meet me here like this," he said in his native Russian tongue.

I stopped about ten feet away and glanced around. There were no other runners out on a late Friday afternoon. It was just me, Denisovich, and an eerie feeling that everything was about to change.

"What are . . . why are you here?" I reached for the phone tucked in the zipped pouch on the back waistband of my running pants.

Denisovich held up both of his hands. "I'm here at the suggestion of Julia Helm."

Instantly, my mind took me back a few months to L'Arc de Triomphe du Carrousel just outside the Louvre museum. At my request, Golkov had sent me help in the form of a CIA tactical team stationed in Paris. If it hadn't been for them and the woman at their charge—Julia Helm—I might not have made it out alive.

"Ms. Helm sent you?" I held my phone at my side. Had it just been a phone and this man was a threat, a call probably wouldn't help. Luckily, my phone was more than just a means of communication. It also had a Taser that had come to my rescue at least a few times.

Denisovich slowly reached into the front of his jacket.

"Stop!" I yelled and held up my phone. It probably looked ridiculous to him with my hand positioned like I had a gun.

He paused and held his hands open in a sign of retreat. "Obviously, as a CIA agent, I do not have any credentials to show you. My job exists because of my anonymity. I was just going to inform Ms. Helm that I had made contact, so she can verify my identity."

I still clutched my phone tightly, pointing it in Denisovich's direction. My thumb and index finger hovered over the two exterior buttons that, if pressed at the same time, would send a shock through his body. Instead, I motioned to his jacket with my free hand. He retrieved a phone and typed something on the screen. A second later my phone vibrated in my hand. I kept my eyes on Denisovich while I pressed the answer button and lifted the phone to my ear.

"Ms. Laxer," said the female voice on the other end of the line. Dana Laxer, an anagram of Alexandra, was the name I used on missions. "I know I said I'd wait for you to contact us, but we need your help."

"My help?"

"We have a mission that requires someone with your . . . special traits," Ms. Helm explained.

Does she know about my eidetic memory? Only a handful of people had a clue what my brain could do. Even Golkov didn't comprehend the extent of my ability, though he knew I could bring back anything I had seen during a mission. If he understood how my mind played movies of everything I saw, how I remembered every experience right down to the smells and sounds, maybe he would press me harder to return to The Company right away. If Ms. Helm knew, it could change everything.

"What do you mean by special traits?" My eyes remained on Denisovich while I spoke to her.

"Agent Denisovich will provide the details. He is one of our best agents in the field and a great aid to the CIA."

"I understand," I said.

"So can we count on you?" asked Ms. Helm.

Denisovich slid his phone back into his pocket. His stare bore into me, his green eyes almost pleading. He seemed more vulnerable standing here than he had this morning, sitting behind the table in the Marston building.

The timing was anything but convenient. I had finals in a month. My brother was about to undergo a surgery that could go either way. I hadn't even committed to coming back to The Company, let alone joining the CIA on a mission. I could say no. Couldn't I? My blood pounded in my hand against my phone case. I hated to admit it, but I missed this feeling—the scary unknown that every mission brought with it. It had been too long since I felt that. Too long, or maybe just enough time to get back in the saddle and hurtle myself forward.

I licked my cold lips. "I'll do it," I said with resolve. It didn't matter what this mission entailed, as long as I was needed.

"Thank you, Ms. Laxer," Ms. Helm replied. "I'll be in touch again once Agent Denisovich briefs you on the mission."

I lowered the phone and examined the man before me. I should have known he wasn't just a professor. His eyes had that look about them, like he had something to hide. "Now tell me, Mr. Denisovich, why does the CIA need me? Why can't they just use you?"

"They already did. That's why I need your help." He slid a hand into his front pocket again. This time I remained still with my phone at my side.

With slow movements, he retrieved a wallet-sized paper from his pocket and held it up. I had to take a few steps forward to see the photo of the face of a teenage girl maybe a few years younger than me. Her dark-brown hair and the sharp curve of her eyebrows looked familiar. I glanced up at Denisovich. "Your daughter?"

"Yes." His Adam's apple rose and fell slowly.

"What happened?

"She's been taken." The fallen look on his face contrasted with the crispness of his suit. It pulled at my mind and ripped me from the real world to a memory I'd buried deep.

The sweetness of apple blossoms traveled to my nose, but this moment was anything but sweet. May in East Wenatchee was usually a time of awakening and renewal, the sun shining and greenery overtaking the mountains and hills. As we stood next to my mom's and Tanner's graves, I saw none of that. All I could see were memories of my family scrolling through my vision, while unshed tears welled in my eyes.

My dad stood next to me in a crisp, brand-new black suit, his face a mixture of grief and melancholy. Neither of us said a word after the graveside service. Friends had paid their respects, and the few distant relatives who had traveled to the funeral had already headed home. In fact, my dad and I had barely spoken since the accident. I'd only been out of the hospital for a few days; I still wore a sling for my broken shoulder and sported faded bruises on the side of my face. I hadn't even tried to hide them with makeup.

"I don't know what to do from here," my dad said. He still stared down at the place that would eventually be covered in dirt. My mom was going to be buried in the ground. She was gone. The thought sent another wave of sadness through me. I kept myself from looking to where Tanner was to be buried.

"Me neither," I said finally. School was ending in less than a week, I'd already been accepted to several universities, and I'd promised Tanner I would follow my dream of attending Brown. Now I didn't want to go anywhere.

"I got a call," my dad said slowly. "I've been offered a position. Your moth—" He stopped. "We weren't going to say anything until we knew for sure."

I kicked at a small clump of cut grass with the tip of my black heels. Was I really here? Had this really happened? I was having trouble focusing on the present as memory after memory bombarded my mind, something that often happened when I felt overwhelmed.

"Brown University has offered me an American History professorship." My dad's arms still dangled lifeless at his sides, but he turned to me. His green irises almost matched the brightness of the grass, the color even more pronounced with the redness of the whites of his eyes.

"You should take the job." I couldn't force excitement into my voice. If we'd had this conversation any other time, I would have been shouting and congratulating him. He had wanted to teach at an Ivy League school for years.

"I can't be here, not without him, not without her." Dad's voice faded to barely a whisper. "It's too much."

I slid my arm through his. "Me neither." I rested my head on his shoulder for several minutes, watching the breeze blow the pink apple blossoms in the orchard across the street. "I don't know if I'm ready to say goodbye." I paused to regain some composure and faced my dad. "Why do things have to change?"

"'There is nothing stable but Heaven and the Constitution,'" he quoted, a strength returning to his voice. He placed his hand on the side of my head. There was always something about history that transformed my dad into someone more confident and powerful.

I cleared my throat. "Should we listen to Buchanan's advice? I thought you said he was the worst president ever." I wiped my cheeks with the palm of my hand.

"He did have some redeemable qualities." My father's eyes glazed over like they usually did when he was formulating some new theory about our country's past.

"You're right, though," I said.

"About Buchanan?"

"No, about being here, taking the job at Brown."

"I don't want to pull you from your friends and school and . . ."

"Dad, there's only a week left. I have a scholarship to Brown. We can go together."

He stepped forward, put his hands on my shoulders, and studied my face. "Is this really what you want to do?"

I took in the balmy smell of the blossoms, then the green Cascade Mountains on either side of us, and finally let my eyes rest on the caskets. I would miss everything about this town I grew up in, but the things I missed most were already gone. Brown University had been my dream, and even though I didn't feel I could celebrate any kind of future for myself, it was time for a new chapter—a new memory.

Denisovich cleared his throat. The redness around his eyes hadn't left, though his brow now had a questioning arc to it. I knew what it felt like to lose someone. If I had it within my power to bring Tanner back, I would do whatever it took. If there was something I could do to save Denisovich from loss, I would do that, too.

"What do you need me to do?"

3

Just a Game

"The CIA?" Daly paced in front of me, running his fingers over his cropped brown hair. "When were you going to tell me about this? I thought we promised to be honest with each other now. No more running off to Paris to save everyone on your own. No more unsanctioned missions. No more secrets." He paused, looking every bit as flawless as a model in an aftershave commercial.

I bit down on my bottom lip and stared up at the back of the Sciences Library, where we'd met after my run-in with Agent Denisovich. Daly and I *had* promised each other. I'd told him everything that happened before Paris and while I was there — except for my conversation with Julia Helm where she told me I should work for the CIA.

"You can't keep doing this, Alex!" He stopped in front of me. "How am I supposed to protect you if you hide things from me?"

My guilt morphed into defensiveness. "Why do you feel the need to protect me? I can take care of myself."

His brown eyes blazed with intensity as he took another step forward. "Really? Who came to your rescue in Moscow? Who stayed overnight in a French prison to help you? Just this morning, I . . ." Daly's gaze drifted from mine to my lips. The motion distracted me from our current conversation and appeared to do the same to him. We stood just a foot away from each other, our exhales intermingling in the cold night air.

"I know." I looked down. My body and mind were torn between what they wanted to do and what I'd told myself I wasn't ready for. Truthfully, I didn't think Daly was ready, either. I dared to look up and found his face changed, the chiseled lines of his jaw softened.

He reached out and touched my face with his warm hand. Every inch of me wanted to lean into his touch and let it envelop me. Maybe it would make me forget everything. "Alexandra."

He said my name with such reverence that I played the sound over in my mind two times before he closed more of the distance between us. When I was about to give in and erase the space that separated us, he pulled me into an embrace, tucking my head into his chest. He sighed and held me close enough that I could feel his heart beating through his black overcoat. In his sigh I felt his thoughts were the same as mine—even if we were both ready, where would this lead us? What would happen to our partnership as operative and handler if we allowed ourselves to develop a romantic relationship?

I should've known Daly would be the responsible one. His arms encircled me for several more moments while his heart slowed. Finally, he let me go and took two steps back. He shook his head and muttered something to himself, then asked with a smile, "Is that everything?"

"What?" My breathing hadn't returned to normal, and my cheek still tingled from his touch.

"Did this agent Denisovich say anything more?"

"Only that they were making preparations and would be ready by tomorrow."

Daly frowned. "So his daughter was presumably kidnapped while he was working overseas? I guess I understand why they're involving the CIA, since he's an agent, but shouldn't they use the FBI or some other entity? The CIA is designed for collecting and analyzing data, not rescuing citizens."

"His daughter is not a U.S. citizen and neither is he. He's a foreign agent the CIA doesn't want to lose. Apparently they take care of their own, just like Golkov would do with any of us."

"But why was the girl in Mexico? I thought you said her father was a Russian professor." Daly motioned for me to follow him around to the front of the building. The library had closed and the campus had emptied; I figured most of the coeds were probably at the St. Patrick's Day dance.

"It's his undercover job," I explained as we walked. "He works as an adjunct professor in Russia and in Mexico. Apparently being fluent in both Russian and Spanish is a valuable asset in the CIA. Denisovich's daughter lived in Mexico City with his wife, and he spent about half his time there and half at Lomonosov University in Moscow."

Daly shook his head. "I guess I just don't get why they need you—not that you aren't a good agent—"

"Yeah, yeah, yeah, I get it. I'm not the most experienced." I tried to swallow my hurt pride.

"That's not what I . . . wait, do they know about your memory?" Daly was one of the few people who really knew how my eidetic mind worked, and how useful it could be.

"No, that's not exactly why they need me." My face began to grow warm, and it wasn't because Daly was walking close to me. At least it wasn't the only reason.

"Then why?" he asked.

"Because . . ." I stared ahead, remembering my embarrassment when Agent Denisovich had explained what they wanted me to do. "They need someone who is . . . someone who . . . they want someone who can attend the same art program as Amoriel—that's the daughter's name."

"Okay, and . . ." Daly looked at me questioningly.

I sighed. "It's an art school—for teenagers, like a high school."

My handler started laughing so hard he had to stop and lean over the back of a bench in the Sciences Park. Any other time I would have joined in his amusement, but tonight I wasn't in the mood. The reason Julia Helm has chosen me for this mission had nothing to do with the mission in Paris or my skills as an agent. She'd chosen me because I could pass for a teen. After all, I still was one.

"It's not funny." I plopped onto the bench and crossed my arms in front of me.

Still chuckling, Daly said, "Actually, it is pretty funny."

I stared up at the dark windows of the Sciences Library. The gray concrete building rose about two hundred feet into the night sky. The back of the library held eleven rows of windows—windows I was very familiar with. A few students walked through the square, glanced up at the windows, and then continued past, whispering to each other.

"You know, I wish I could've seen you in high school," Daly said, still standing at the back of the bench.

"You realize it's only been a few years. Technically I could still be there." If I'd followed the normal teenager path, I would have been a senior in high school, instead of here at Brown. But I'd opted to take college courses while in high school and graduated early to attend the university. I didn't regret it by any means—I'd never really fit into the "normal" category anyway.

Daly shrugged his shoulders and came around the bench. "Age doesn't mean that much to me. Growing up, many of my best friends were several years older. Heck, I consider Golkov a good friend and he's three times my age." At twenty-two years old, Daly could no longer pass as a teenager. Most of the time I thought the same was true for me. Apparently, Julia Helm thought differently.

"This is going to be a disaster." I leaned over and retied my running shoes.

"Why?"

"Let me guess." I double-knotted my laces and sat back up. "You played football, got straight A's, and were voted prom king. Does that about sum it up?" I didn't mention that part of the reason I didn't mind going to college early was because I'd had no real friends in high school and hadn't fit in.

"Actually, none of those are true." Daly put a foot up on the bench and rested his arm on his knee.

"Seriously?" I couldn't picture him as anything other than a popular jock in school.

"Well, yes and no. I didn't play football. I played rugby. And I did get high marks, but not straight A's. As for prom king, I still don't entirely understand what that is. Our high school didn't have prom, but most high schools in England don't."

"England?"

"Yes. You know—that country in Europe, kind of near France."

I rolled my eyes and hit his leg with the back of my hand. "How long did you live there?"

"My father started at the U.S. Embassy in London when I was five, and twelve years later, after I passed my college exams, I came to Brown."

My mind started moving a million miles a minute, scrolling through all my memories and conversations with Daly. How had I never known he'd spent so much time abroad? A few memories began to move to the forefront.

"The accent?" Whenever we hung out with my roommate Casey or anyone on campus, Daly always spoke with a British accent. I thought it was just his cover.

"After all your secrets, you can't really blame me, can you?" he said with a thick British accent.

"It's real?"

"Not exactly. I spent my first few years here in the U.S., but after living there for so long, it kind of became natural." This time his accent wasn't quite as thick and some of his words sounded more American than British.

"So what's natural for you? What's real?"

"Honestly, I don't know anymore. Like you, I learned Russian early on, so when I'm speaking Russian I have a Russian accent. If I'm in England, I speak with a British accent. If I'm talking with anyone at The Company, I usually speak with my American accent. Here on campus, I generally keep with the British one. I guess it's like my cover."

"Hmm," I said. "Can I make a request?"

"Sure." Daly sat down on the bench next to me with his eyes focused on the Sciences Library windows.

"If we are speaking in Russian, keep the Russian accent." We often spoke in Russian on campus. "But otherwise, just do what feels comfortable to you. I just want the real you."

"You do, do you?" Wearing his cocky grin, Daly continued to stare at the windows.

I replayed what I had just said and immediately wanted to erase it. "I didn't mean . . . ugh!" I threw up my hands. "You're impossible."

"Okay." He sounded more serious now. "I'll try to not think about it and see what happens." Many of his vowels still carried the more rounded British accent, but the rest of his words smoothed into American English. I didn't tell him how much I liked it.

"Why did you ask to meet here, anyway?" I said.

"It's the last night."

A flood of melancholy swept over me as my mind jumped to Tanner. His surgery was hours away, and I itched to be there. I didn't want to think it could be his last night. I'd told myself that this surgery was what my brother would have wanted. He was a risk taker, so he would have chosen the surgery if given the choice. But I wasn't ready to say goodbye. Not again.

"Alex?" Daly placed a hand on my sleeve. "It's Tanner, isn't it?"

I nodded, then glanced at Daly. His eyes held the comfort I needed. He understood.

A couple crossed the courtyard, heading in our direction. I would've recognized that bouncy walk from a mile away. Casey had her arm linked with Millard's, and they were chatting so loudly I could hear their conversation from over fifty feet away.

"But what about the space-time continuum? That would have affected it, right? Thrown it off?" Casey said. She tucked her red-streaked hair behind her ear, exposing large, glittery green earrings.

"Yes!" Millard wore a black T-shirt with the design of a gray vest and green bow tie screen-printed on front. He began to talk animatedly with his hands. "The temporal anomaly would have created an alternate reality, or at the very least it would have sent them back in time."

"So what you're saying is that if they entered the disruption, they could have changed history?" Casey asked.

Millard shrugged and stopped in front of us. "It's possible. In theory, there could be several people walking among us who are actually from a future timeline."

Casey poked his arm. Then she poked his cheek.

"What are you doing?" Millard asked.

She smiled. "Making sure you're real. Are you from the future?"

Millard glanced at Daly and me and then back at Casey. "You never know. But I assure you that this" —he poked her in the ribs— "is not a good scientific approach for testing your theory."

"Hey, guys." Casey twirled around in her green dress to face the Sciences Library. She spread out her arms. "You ready to make history one final time?"

Daly squeezed my arm and asked with his eyes if I was okay.

I nodded once. "How about we say we are making the future?"

"Ooooh, I like it," Casey said. "J.R., do you want to do the honors?"

Millard slid a bag from his shoulder and placed it on the bench next to us. He pulled out his laptop and began tapping away at the keys. About ten seconds later, a few windows on the top two floors of the Sciences Library lit up with a geometric "L" shape that began falling from window to window. Millard hit a key, and the shape turned ninety degrees. It continued to fall until the lighted shape rested on the bottom row of windows in front of us. Another shape, this one a squared "Z," began to fall. He continued to move shapes around until a solid line of windows lit up on the bottom row and then disappeared.

"Tetris!" Shouts came from behind us.

I turned to see a group of at least fifty students who had converged on the benches facing the library.

"I can't believe they haven't taken this down already," Daly said. "I thought security found out about it weeks ago."

"I think they like the publicity and wanted to catch the perpetrator first. It's too bad no one knows who it is." Casey winked.

Millard attached a wireless transmitter to his laptop and handed me a controller. "One last round before we let the crowd in on our game?"

"Of course." In my mind I watched movies of us carrying out Casey's latest prank—hauling frames and lights, then running wires through the entire building. That had been right after I returned from Paris. If it wasn't for Millard's genius, we never would have pulled off Casey's prank of an oversized Tetris game on the side of a university library.

I played a few dozen rows before handing the controller to Daly. When he finished playing, Casey took a turn until she lost. At that point, she carried the controller to the crowd. Millard and Casey and Daly and I squished together on the bench to watch other students play the game. We kept each other warm and chatted for about fifteen minutes until a streetlight began to flicker, then another. Millard looked between us. A loud pop rang out and a post lantern just to our left shattered, raining bits of glass onto the square. A few students screamed.

Millard picked up his laptop and began typing away. "The lights must be overloading the system. Stringing together this many Christmas lights was never a perfect plan."

Two more lanterns exploded with an earsplitting burst and the square went dark. No lanterns. No streetlights. No Tetris shapes on the windows.

Casey sighed loudly. "Well, I guess that's a wrap."

Applause broke out behind us, with students whooping and hollering. We joined in until someone yelled, "Campus Police!"

Everyone jumped from the benches and sprinted from the square. The security guards or police—I couldn't tell in the dark—moved close. Daly retrieved the controller, Millard grabbed the laptop, and we raced down the street.

"J.R., we could use a temporal anomaly right now," Casey yelled breathlessly at Millard as we crossed Brook Street. We slipped behind a group of trees along the back of Minden Hall. No one spoke for a few minutes as we waited for footsteps to pass.

Daly whispered in my ear, "I've missed this feeling."

"What?" I was still pressed between him and the brick wall of the building. I told myself that my quickened breathing was only caused by our quick getaway.

"The adrenaline of a mission. My heart beating so fast I could feel it in my throat."

"Why do you think I like it?" I smiled up at him.

"So, you're going to do it, then? The CIA mission?"

"Yes." Not that I wanted to go back on my word to Agent Denisovich, but I needed to understand all of the ramifications before I committed officially. "But there's something I need to do first."

"What's that?"

"I need to talk to Golkov."

"I understand." Daly took a step away, only to turn back to me. "No more secrets, then?"

I smiled. "No more secrets."

He peeked out from behind the trees, looked both ways, and gave a thumbs-up sign.

I spun around to tell Millard and Casey, but they weren't there. "Where are Casey and . . ." I let my voice trail off as Daly came to stand beside me. Millard and Casey stood at the side of the building, locked in each other's arms and lips.

My hand flew to my mouth and I slowly backed away, not about to ruin this moment for either of them. Daly and I moved to the sidewalk and began to walk casually toward my dorm.

When I could no longer hold in the laugh, it burst out of me. "I'm sorry." I bent over and rested my hands on my knees. It was ridiculous to be this entertained by Casey and Millard, but I let the emotion overtake me. Then the amusement began to change to something else. I still shook, but it wasn't with laughter. My mind was overcome with memories of Tanner and his boisterous laugh. Would I ever hear it again?

"Do you always laugh at displays of affection?"

By the tone of Daly's voice, I couldn't tell if he was amused or annoyed. I chanced a look at him. His crossed arms fell from his chest as he peered down at me. "Are you all right?"

Pulling in a deep breath, I vowed not to lose my composure in front of him. I just couldn't.

"Come on." He slipped his hand into mine and pulled me in the opposite direction from my dorm. "I think I know exactly what you need right now."

4

Superman

Ten o'clock on a Sunday night probably wasn't the best time to sneak into Marston Hall. Despite that, I followed Daly there. After the door handle read his fingerprints and the lock clicked open, he pulled me into the building. Nothing appeared extraordinary about the storage area at the bottom of the stairs. Stacks of molded plastic chairs filled an entire wall, while shelves held cleaning supplies and file boxes. The only thing that stood out as different from any campus building basement was the pristine concrete floor and the absence of dust. The electric humming of the building above accompanied us until we entered a hallway on the other end of the storage area.

Daly stopped at the end of the dimly lit space and entered his numbered code—one I could have easily punched in for him—and bent forward to let the retina scanner run over his eye. As the door clicked, I wondered if my own code and scan would have worked, or if Golkov had removed me from their system.

"Not that I mind a sparring session with you, but don't you think we should wait until Itosu is here to referee?" I asked.

Daly pushed open the large steel door and stepped through. "You do have a point, but we won't need the sensei. We aren't here to spar."

"Then what are we doing here?" I whispered as I stepped inside. It had been weeks since I'd ventured over this threshold onto the shiny obsidian floor of The Company headquarters. I would never become fully accustomed to the expansive space that boasted at least thirty offices, all separated only by perfectly clear glass walls. Each similarly sized room held a desk and chair, as well as computer screens in several shapes and sizes. Even though only about a quarter of the normal staff currently occupied the facility, it seemed strangely busy for a Sunday night.

My feet remained planted on the floor. "I'm not ready to—"

"Don't worry," Daly cut me off, looking back in my direction. "Golkov isn't here. He's on an assignment and won't return until tomorrow." My handler knew why I wasn't yet ready to see Golkov. "Come on." Daly's leather soles tapped against the floor. My running shoes squeaked a few times as I hurried to keep up.

An agent looked up from his desk and smiled at us as we walked by. Daly nodded to him and we continued down the glass corridor. Golkov's office came into view, the lights dimmed and desk empty. I told myself that my apprehension at seeing him was a result of my indecision, though deep down I knew it wasn't. I wasn't on the fence about being an operative again. Daly had been right. It was in my bones, a part of who I'd always been, even from the times as a child I hid under my mom's desk and listened to her conversations. No, I wasn't on the fence. I just wasn't quite sure which side I was climbing down and where I wanted my feet to land.

"Come on," Daly said for the third time. I hadn't even realized I'd slowed. He opened the door at the back of the offices and moved into the training gym. Reluctantly, I entered the gym behind him, hoping Sensei Itosu was sane enough to take Sunday nights off. I really liked the old man, but he could read me nearly as well as Daly, and I didn't need any more sympathy tonight.

A female agent in The Company workout clothes—black pants and fitted black T-shirt—ran on a treadmill in the corner. Two other female agents conversed just outside the women's locker room on the opposite side of the large sparring circle. Otherwise the gym was vacant.

Instead of going down the stairs to the black-cushioned floor, Daly headed up to the second level. I stopped when we reached the landing that overlooked the gym below.

"If we're not working out, what are we doing here?" I glanced down to the floor below us. I didn't mind spending time with Daly, but didn't want to study manuals or participate in complicated training simulations. "It's after ten. I know I'm not . . ." I wasn't sure exactly what I wasn't. "But I still have classes tomorrow and . . ."

"Just trust me." He glanced at the watch at his wrist. "We have to hurry." He held out his hand. I probably should've demanded more information, and the last thing I needed was his warm hand enveloping mine. But I trusted those soft-brown eyes more than just about anyone's, so I reached out my hand and let him pull me along the balcony, past Millard's office, to Daly's office on the other end.

He only dropped my hand when we arrived at his glass desk and he bent over to retrieve a black satchel underneath. "I was going to ask another agent to take care of this." He pulled a black cube about the size of a ring box from his top drawer. "But the sooner this gets done, the better."

"What?"

"I'll explain on the way. Right now, I just need some tools. Can you run to Millard's office and borrow one of his small tool kits?" Daly slipped off his dress shoes. "See if he has any black zip ties."

"Okay." I started for the door and then turned. "Is Millard okay with—" My words stopped in my throat. Daly's muscular chest was bare, his white dress shirt halfway off. He pulled himself free of the shirt and draped it over his jacket on the back of his chair.

"Yes?" His hands were on the belt at his waist, oblivious to my increased pulse and the heat at my face. *Can't he change his clothes in the locker room like a normal person?* I hesitated before turning around. There was nothing normal about those abs.

"Never mind." I waved him off and proceeded to Millard's office. It's not as if I hadn't seen a man without a shirt on—I'd just never seen Daly. I could have glanced back at any moment through the glass walls to get a second glimpse. Not that I needed to. My

eidetic mind had involuntarily started playing the scene on a loop—
or at least mostly involuntarily.

After I found the requested supplies in Millard's office, I walked
to the balcony and waited until Daly joined me.

"Got it?" He now wore a black hoodie and workout pants, not
seeming to realize that moments ago he'd nearly stripped off all his
clothes in front of me.

"Yes." I handed him the tool kit and zip ties.

He started toward the stairs, then stopped when he realized I still
stood motionless. "Coming?" The cocky smile on his lips told me
he had been baiting me. And apparently he'd done a pretty good job,
since I couldn't get the image of his bare chest out of my mind.

I raised my chin and made my way down the stairs and back
through the office doors. I didn't let him catch up to me until we
were outside the Marston building.

"Okay, where now?" *Mr.-Look-at-My-Abs*.

"To my car. I'm parked along Cooke and Manning."

I stopped in the middle of the sidewalk. I couldn't move.
William lived on Manning Street. Another person I didn't want to
see tonight. Why was it that the one human being I *did* want to
see—my brother—was the one I wasn't going to see?

Daly studied my face and realization hit his eyes. "Alex, sorry. I
didn't . . . I can go grab my car and pull up along—"

"No," I broke in. "It's fine. Let's just go."

"Okay." His stiff voice sounded foreign, and it wasn't because
he was speaking Russian again.

"Let's run there. My run earlier was cut short."

In response, Daly turned and sprinted toward Cooke Street. I
followed him, keeping in stride with him until we reached his black
BMW, both of us panting.

"You trying to tire me out" —he took a few breaths— "before
we even start the mission?"

"Mission?" If my heartbeat could've picked up, it would have.
That is exactly what my mind needed right now—a focus outside of
myself, something it could concentrate on.

"Why else would I drag you across town?" Daly opened the passenger door and motioned to me. "Now hop in. We need to get there before midnight."

"Where?" I slid onto the leather seat.

"The Superman building," he said before he closed my door.

During the six months I'd lived in Providence, Rhode Island, I'd gone downtown too many times to count, visiting my father at his apartment, and Daly and Millard at their place. Still, every time I drove into the city, I craned my neck to see the tops of the buildings. The tallest buildings in my hometown in Washington never reached more than ten stories. Providence was no mecca of skyscrapers, but many of its buildings reached high into the sky. The tallest one held twenty-six floors, all of them currently dark. Daly parked his car a few blocks away and we began to walk toward the building.

"That's the Superman building?" I asked.

"That's what everyone here calls it. I think it's called the Industrial some-thing-or-other. No one really cares now that it's empty."

"Why is such a large building vacant?" I stared up at the darkened windows. There had to be several hundred panes of glass. The building did remind me of the *Daily Planet* offices in Superman movies and shows. The old-school architecture was less skyscraper and more castle-like, with six wings stemming from its central tower. The peak of the building was actually a large dome that rose from the roof with a latticework of decorative windows and metalwork.

"I don't know," Daly said. "It was built back in the 1920s. I guess no one in Providence wants to live in a deteriorating building that is nearly a hundred years old. There's been talk of apartments or businesses taking over, but luckily, nothing has come of it."

"Luckily?" We stopped across the street.

"A vacant building is much easier to use." Daly pulled the strap of his bag up onto his shoulder.

I raised an eyebrow at him. Not that it would be my first time breaking and entering. In fact, it wasn't even my first time with him.

Only a month before, we'd broken into the Sciences Library to get our Tetris game going. This felt different, though. Brown University was a college campus. This was the middle of a large city.

"Why here?" I asked.

"It's the tallest building in Rhode Island, and we need the transmitter as high as possible. Millard can hack into satellites, but this little baby" —Daly patted his satchel— "transmits signals faster and picks up radio, TV, and cell signals as well."

My mind processed the information. I'd always known The Company had an ear out in all communication venues, I just hadn't realized how widespread it was or exactly how they obtained their information.

"Why not a higher place, like a radio or television tower? They are at least twice as tall."

"Not as easy to hide equipment or safely place it. This building might not be around forever, but its location and the fact that it's empty make it the perfect spot."

"So, we're just breaking in and taking the stairs?"

"Not exactly." Daly craned his neck toward the top of the building.

"What's that supposed to mean?" We crossed the street and stood on the corner of Westminster and Arcade. The Superman building was one building away.

"Despite what you may think, we actually try to stay away from breaking laws if we don't have to."

I rolled my eyes. "Oh, really?"

"Yes, really. Golkov might have connections with the CIA, but even they are bound by some laws."

"We're climbing it?" I could no longer see the top of the building from where we stood. The last time I'd climbed something had been a warehouse in Russia.

Daly shrugged his shoulders and smiled widely.

"Are we going to scale the building or are you really Superman under those clothes?" As soon as the words fled my lips, my cheeks started to burn. Once again, my brain betrayed me by flashing to the scene from earlier.

Daly tugged at his jacket collar. "You never know. But I certainly can't give you all my secrets, now can I?" His voice still hinted at the lighter British accent I wasn't used to hearing.

"Why?" I said. "You know all mine." That much was basically true. He knew about my eidetic memory, my brother, and my life as an operative. In fact, he was the only one that knew everything.

Taken off guard by Daly's gaze, I looked back to the Superman building and said, "So, scaling, then? Bring any rope?"

"Must you always do things the hard way?" He turned in the alleyway between the Superman building and a large bank. I jogged after him until he stopped about halfway down. He pointed up. "We could just take the stairs."

"There aren't stairs the whole way up." I stared up the side of the building. I could have totally climbed it. Maybe.

Daly pointed higher. "But the scaffolding makes a perfect ladder."

It was then that I noticed a network of wood platforms and metal beams leading up the side of the building, obviously to help in some kind of repairs or cleaning. They hadn't been visible from the street.

"Let's go. A new security crew comes in across the street at one and will do rounds then. I don't want to get caught. Do you?"

In answer to his question, I sprinted up the stairs, not waiting for him. Fifteen or twenty minutes later, I sat near the top of the Superman building, right below the final tower. I leaned against an air-conditioning unit, trying to catch my breath.

Daly arrived half a minute later, perspiration dripping down his face. "You training for" —he pulled himself over the edge of the building— "the Olympics or something?" He dropped next to me. "I don't think ladder-climbing is a recognized sport."

"It should be." Once my lungs calmed, I said, "So where are we placing this transmitter thing?"

Daly looked up at the last forty or so feet of window and stone that made up the final tower of the building. Large exterior lights on each corner lit up this part of the roof, making the tower glow.

"You can't be serious!" I stared up at the domed central tower, which had no ladders or scaffolding.

Daly unzipped his bag, grabbed the little square box, and held it in the palm of his hand. "*We* aren't placing it anywhere. *You* are." He reached into his bag and pulled out what looked like a handgun with a hook at the end of the barrel.

"Is that what I think it is?" I reached out. Daly gave me the gun.

"If you're thinking it's Millard's latest grappling-hook gun, you're right. I figured it would be good to finally test it in the field."

"Wait." I pulled the gun's aim from the turret above me. "It hasn't been tested?"

"It's either you or me. I can do it if you want."

"No. I got this." I raised the gun in the air with a hand on either side, cocked the triggering mechanism, and pulled. A whooshing sounded in the night air, followed shortly by a clang. I pushed a button on the side of the gun that caused the wire-like rope to recoil slightly until it came back taut. "What makes this different than your everyday-variety grappling hook?"

"It has something to do with the material of the rope," Daly replied. "I don't know all the specifics, but it lessens the friction on the line as it goes in and out. Other grappling guns get extremely hot, so the line does too."

I ran my index finger up and down the line protruding from the barrel of the gun. My finger glided against the gray-colored material that was smooth like silk.

"Looks like you're going to need these." Daly held out two thick leather gloves and the transmitter.

I relinquished the gun to him. While I slipped the gloves on and tucked the square metal box into my jacket pocket, he wrapped the grappling line around a metal pipe jetting out from the roof. Just in case, I grabbed some of the zip ties from his bag and put them in my other pocket. "So I just climb, huh? It's that simple?"

"I didn't say it was simple, but it could be fun."

My eyes followed the line from my position to the top of the building, where the grappling hook had lodged in the latticework that made up the metal dome. It was a good thing I wasn't too afraid of heights. I gripped the line with my two hands and began to pull myself up the building, using my black tennis shoes to grip the brick. Luckily there were several places to wedge my feet. It didn't take more than a few minutes to reach the next ledge. Since sitting was impossible, I held tight to the line and pressed my stomach against the building until the chill of the brick permeated through my running pants and jacket.

I wondered if anyone from below would have noticed me if it hadn't been so dark. I chanced a quick look to the city below. Most of the world around the Superman building had gone to sleep, but some windows were still lit, and tiny dots of lights moved down some of the streets. The entire landscape of Providence was visible from up here. I could even make out Waterplace Park below, the streetlights rippling across the water.

"It's beautiful," I said into the night air.

Daly's laugh sounded from the com unit in my ear. "Only you could stop in the middle of a mission to appreciate the scenery."

"What's wrong with that?" I probably could have yelled to him below me, but it was nice to just talk like he was right next to me. A few lights flickered off in a building to the west.

"Absolutely nothing." He laughed again. "I don't know how Golkov found you, but I'm glad he did."

My body warmed despite the cold night air. I'd tried not to think about it—how my feelings for Daly had changed over the last few months. Though we'd spent many hours together, focusing on Tanner had distracted me from thinking of Daly as more than my handler and friend. Most of the time. But there were times, probably too many, when I couldn't help replaying scenes in my head. The first time I saw Daly at the Mariinsky in St. Petersburg when he'd been shot. Seeing him alive at The Company, acting all cocky when he warned me that my life was about to change. Saying "Eew" after he kissed me when I was still dating William. Those memories flooded back until a final memory played on repeat—standing outside Daly's apartment door after the Barcelona mission. It was the first time he had admitted there was something between us. I had pushed him away—actually I'd run away. Looking back, I realized I'd been scared. Scared because for the first time in my life, someone almost knew me better than I knew myself.

"You okay up there?" Daly asked.

My toes nearly slipped off the edge as I repositioned myself. "Where am I placing this?" I reached for the cube in my pocket.

"Just find a hidden spot that allows at least one side of the transmitter to be in the open," Daly's voice rang out in my eardrum. "You can loop the zip ties through the holes at the top and bottom to secure it."

I searched around and found only brick and mortar, not a place to attach anything. I shoved the cube back into my pocket.

"Can you detach the line down there?"

"Sure."

I waited until the line went loose. "I hope this thing is secure."

"Why? What are you . . ."

Wrapping both gloved hands around the line, I pushed back from the building with my legs and swung a few feet to the right. I did it one more time before Daly's voice pierced my ear. "Wait!" he called loud enough that I heard it from below as well as through the earpiece. "The grappling won't hold if you go around the entire dome. You'll have to come back down and we can reposition it."

I searched my new location and said, "No worries." Above my head, the metal curved into the latticework of the dome. It would make the perfect hiding place. My biceps burned as I pulled my body a few feet higher. With my toes pressed against the metal grating of the vents below the dome, I reached into my pockets to retrieve the transmitter and zip ties. It took me several minutes to maneuver my body and adjust the ties around the cube, but eventually I was able to extend my arms above me and position the cube as Daly instructed. When I pulled the last zip tie tight, I let out a breath of relief.

"It's done," I said to Daly.

"All right. Climb on down. I just re-secured the other end of the line."

My eyes followed the grappling line from the dome to the place where Daly stood about thirty or forty feet below me. *There is an easier way down.*

I held a hand out in front of me. The palm of the leather gloves I wore appeared thick enough, and if Millard's line didn't create as much friction as a normal one, this might just work. It was fairly taut when I pulled on it. Throwing caution to the wind—or to the night sky, in this case—I grasped the line with both hands and used my legs to push myself away from the building.

The wind bit at my face and my feet dangled below me as I slid down my self-created zip line. I let out a free-spirited and slightly out-of-character scream as my body hurtled down the line. Anyone with open windows or standing on their balconies would have heard me. But all I cared about was the adrenaline rushing through me.

I tightened my grip as my landing spot approached. I was traveling too fast. Millard's frictionless line worked a little too well. Just when I thought I might face-plant or possibly fall over the edge, a dark figure stepped into my path and caught me in his arms. The force of my descent sent both of us to the floor of the roof.

Once I caught my breath, I raised my head to find Daly underneath me. I couldn't tell if he was laughing or choking as his chest moved against me, until a smile reached his eyes.

"You don't like to do anything the safe and easy way, do you." He said it more as a statement than a question, his words vibrating through my body as I lay on top of him.

"What do you mean? That was the easy way."

Daly opened his mouth to say something more, but then paused. Adrenaline still pulsed through my veins and my head felt light. Daly considered me for a moment, a mischievous smile forming on his lips.

"Alex?"

"Yes?" A barrage of heartbeats filled my chest.

"Iguazu Falls," he said.

"What?" I wasn't sure what I'd been expecting, but it hadn't been that.

"You said you sometimes wish you could fly away. You could escape to Iguazu Falls. I hear Brazil is beautiful there any time of year. I—" Daly touched his ear where his own com unit was hidden. A moment later, his smile disappeared and his hand fell to his side. I'd never seen the look that passed through his eyes, a darkness that shadowed the browns of his irises.

"What is it?" I asked.

Daly shifted under me and used his arms to lift me off him. Once he stood, he held out a hand and pulled me to my feet. He still didn't say anything. The serious expression on his face sent a surge of terror through me.

"James, what it is?" My hand tightened around his.

He swallowed, his jaw tight. "It's Tanner."

No more explanation was needed. I raced to the building edge, grabbed the ladder, and vaulted over the edge.

5

Miracle Worker

I didn't stop when I reached the sidewalk, even when I shed the leather gloves and tossed them on a bench, nor did I head in the direction of Daly's car. I raced down Dorrance Street and cut through the alleyways my eidetic brain pointed out as shortcuts. When I reached Eddy Street, I bolted down the straight homestretch, pushing my body harder than ever before. My lungs burned, and thanks to my injury from the Moscow mission, my leg screamed in pain. But with scenes of Tanner flashing through my mind, I couldn't slow down.

I burst through the doors of Rhode Island Hospital and pounded down the hall like my life depended on it—like Tanner's life depended on it. I didn't pause until I reached the surgical wing and saw Elijah close a door behind him. From the end of the hall, I watched him pull off his hospital mask and drop it to the tiled floor. The fallen look on his face told me all I needed to know.

"No!" I screamed. I ran to Elijah and gripped the front of his light-blue surgical gown. "No." I pounded on his chest with my fist, shaking my wet face. "No!" I hit his chest again. "You promised. You said it would be okay."

"I'm sorry," Elijah whispered.

My legs trembled beneath me. It was over. I couldn't go on without Tanner. I'd been lying to myself since last May when I said goodbye the first time.

There was no me without my brother.

"Alex." A gentle hand rested on my shoulder and I glanced up. *Daly*. I tumbled into him, letting his strong arms hold me up. I buried my face into his chest and let my emotions overflow. My mind flashed through scenes of my childhood with Tanner—games of hide and seek and climbing up hallway walls. Tanner hadn't been like the siblings of my friends, who bullied or teased constantly. We had been two sides of the same coin, attached by a force stronger than family or friends. We had been one.

". . . the anesthesia . . . heart rate dropped . . ." Elijah's words were muddled, disconnected. "Only the first stimulus point tested . . . blood pressure too low."

Another voice rumbled against my cheek. "I phoned their father. If Tanner still has time, I thought it was only right."

"Rose is cleaning up . . . be seen soon."

I pulled away from Daly's chest. "Time?" I looked up at Daly and then Elijah. "Tanner's not . . ."

They exchanged glances. "You didn't tell her?" Daly asked Elijah.

"I thought you . . ."

I stepped back. "What's going on?"

Elijah grabbed my hand. "We started the surgery and even stimulated the first synapses, but Tanner's blood pressure dropped too low and we had to stop."

"So he's . . . he's alive?"

"Yes," Elijah said solemnly.

Suddenly, all their words registered. I looked up at Daly. "You called my father? You had no right! What did you tell him?"

"I didn't say anything about your brother. I just told your father to come to the hospital and that it was important."

"You told him to come here? Why does he think he's coming?" The anger in my tone morphed to panic.

Daly rubbed his forehead. "I didn't give him a chance to ask."

I sighed in exasperation. "You know the last call he received like that? It was when he found out his family had been in an accident. That's when he lost my mom and my brother." My mind automatically flashed to the hospital in Wenatchee, the first time I woke up and saw my father's face. He didn't have to say anything—I knew Mom and Tanner were gone. I pushed back the memory. "You can't do that to my father." I sounded as hollow and tired as I felt.

"Sorry, I just thought . . ." Daly started.

"And not just that," I broke in. "I thought we agreed not to say anything until Tanner woke up."

Neither Daly nor Elijah spoke. Somewhere deep inside I realized it wasn't their fault—Tanner's life dangling from a thin thread, or my father's second heartbreak. Fault didn't really matter now anyway.

I turned and rested my hand against the beige-painted wall, leaning my forehead on my arm. I tried to breathe in slowly through my mouth and out my nose like Sensei Itosu taught me during meditation exercises. Scenes of the accident last year and recovering in the hospital afterward hurled through my brain. My heart still thrummed against my skin. I needed to see my brother.

A door opened near me and I whirled around to find a flushed-face Rose in the doorway of the surgical entrance. Elijah's fiancée stepped into the hallway and pulled the fabric scrub cap from her head to reveal her vibrant red hair.

"He's closed and stable," she reported.

My gaze shot to Elijah, who nodded and said, "Suit up."

I walked through the doorway into the outer room, where soap and alcohol permeated the air. Windows allowed a view into two separate surgical suites, but I didn't let myself look. Not yet. A nurse I recognized from Elijah and Rose's practice sessions draped a gown over me and placed a cap on my head. She handed me a mask, booties, and gloves. Once I'd put those on, she opened the door of one of the surgical suites and motioned for me to go inside.

Now that I was here, my impatience turned to fear. I inched through the doorway, my eyes cast down. It wasn't until the door swung shut that I raised my head. Two members of the surgical team stood at a hospital bed, one tapping an IV bag and the other pulling down a curtain from above the bed.

And there was Tanner. The beeping of the machines now registered in my ears in a slow rhythm. I moved to stand next to the bed, on the opposite side from the nurses. I sighed when I saw the tube coming out of my brother's mouth. All my medical reading and discussions with doctors about coma patients ran through my mind. The Glasgow scale was used to measure the consciousness level of coma patients. Tanner's score had never been high because whatever had him unconscious prevented any eye movement, motor movement, or vocal sounds. I knew what it meant to have him intubated. His chances of recovery had dropped drastically. But right then it didn't matter. He was still there. His heart still beat.

His head was wrapped in gauze and his face was paler than usual. I'd done this to him. I might not have caused the accident that sent him into a coma, but I'd been the one who pressed to have a new procedure done. He might have awakened on his own. He might have made it. I put a gloved hand on Tanner's arm. "I just wanted to give you a chance," I told him. "I'm sorry."

I don't know how long I stood there, watching the machine push oxygen into his lungs. It wasn't until I heard a commotion outside of the room that I pulled my focus from Tanner to the window that led to the outer room. My breath escaped when I saw my father's face. His bloodshot eyes locked mine, and neither of us moved as the nurse dressed him in a gown. He looked relieved, probably at knowing I was okay, until he saw Tanner. His brows knit together and he squinted like he couldn't believe what he was seeing. He stepped toward the window, nearly knocking over the nurse who had just placed a cap on his head and was tying it behind him.

Then my father's body began to shake. His eyes asked the question I couldn't have answered with my voice—"Is that Tanner?" I nodded and let the tears fall. My dad's eyes began to tear up, and he rushed to put on his mask and gloves. Within ten seconds, he was at my side.

My anger at Elijah and Daly hadn't subsided, but having my father there—having him know what I'd wanted to tell him for months—sent a wave of calm through me. Maybe now we could really say goodbye, and this time . . . this time we could do it together.

"How?" my father asked, the sound muffled by his mask.

"I don't know all the details," I said, which was the truth. "I just know that he's been in a coma all this time. They tried to save him, bring him out of it . . . but he doesn't have much longer now."

"It was them, wasn't it?" My father didn't look at me, but his eyes showed an uncharacteristic fierceness.

"Dad?"

"The same ones you've been involved with for months."

The world seemed to stop in that instant. The sounds in the room disappeared and my eidetic mind went blank. Because if my father was saying what I thought he was saying, it meant . . . it meant he knew what my mom had been. He knew what I was. *Has he known this whole time?*

"What are you . . ." I started.

"Don't." He put a hand on my arm. "Don't try to explain. Your mother wore that ring for years. After her death" —he swallowed— "when that man came to the hospital with the same ring, I knew there had to be a connection. But with everything that happened after the accident and leaving Wenatchee, I pushed it from my mind." He released my arm and reached up to touch the side of Tanner's face with the back of his gloved hand. Tanner had been my brother and best friend, but he had also been my father's only son. I should have told him as soon as I found out Tanner was alive. I couldn't believe I didn't see it until now.

"When I saw that ring on your finger last fall, I couldn't stop thinking about it," my father continued. "And then all those trips you were taking. You don't become a history professor at Brown University without a keen sense of deduction and reasoning. History is about finding out the truth." He turned to look at me then. Beneath the anger still simmering in his eyes was a quiet intensity that scared me. "I know you can't tell me everything, and honestly, I don't think I really want to know."

"Dad, I—"

He held up a hand to cut me off. "Just tell me one thing. Did they cause this?" He motioned to Tanner. "Was the . . ." He paused. "Was the car accident caused by them?"

"No," I replied. "It wasn't the group I'm with. It was another group, a bad one. The people with the ring have been trying to save him." It blew me away that I was talking to my father about The Company, though not by its name, and that this entire time he'd been trying to figure out what I'd been doing. *He must've spied on me!* I chuckled to myself. *I guess it's all in the family.*

My father's stance relaxed and he faced the bed again, then dropped his head and closed his eyes as if he was saying a prayer. Maybe he had the right idea. People and science had only gotten Tanner so far. What we needed now was a miracle. I held tighter onto his arm and closed my eyes, letting memory overtake me.

"It's less to do with strength and more to do with skill." *Tanner held the football in one hand and then sliced it through the air. It traveled from our position at the thirty-yard line and met with the metal at the bottom of the goalpost. The ball rebounded to the right. I raced to retrieve it and gave it back to Tanner. "Now you try," he said.*

I rotated the ball and spread my fingertips between the laces, turned my left shoulder to the goal, and glanced down to make sure my feet were far enough apart. Then I pulled my arm back and tossed the ball across the field. Or at least that was the plan. The ball lobbed awkwardly in the air and stopped about ten yards from the goalpost and over ten feet off center.

Tanner's laughter broke out next to me. "You're thinking too hard. You don't have to make it complicated. Sometimes the best way is the easiest way."

"Says the guy who can hit the post like a bull's eye every time." I stomped off to get the ball. The only illumination on the field now came from the large lights overhead. Tanner had convinced the janitors to leave them on for a few more minutes. When I joined him again on the field, he had his arms crossed over his chest and one brow lowered.

"What?" I said innocently.

"If you're not going to take this seriously, I'm going home." Tanner bent over to pick up his gym bag.

"No, I really want to do it right. Come on."

"Okay, fine." He let go of the strap of his bag. *"Give me the ball."*

I tossed it to him and it spiraled perfectly into his arms.

"See!" He pointed to the ball. *"You can totally do it. Your problem is the overthinking."*

"You try not to overthink it when you have millions of your brother's games flashing through your vision every time you try to throw the ball."

"Hmm. I wish I could replay every game." He smirked and rubbed at his chin. *"That would be so cool."*

I came to his side while he reminisced and punched him in the arm.

"Hey!" He rubbed at the spot I'd hit. *"Don't mess with the golden arm. This arm"* —he flexed his bicep— *"is going to be worth millions someday."*

"Yeah, and Dad will be a New York Times *bestseller while I cure cancer."*

"I wouldn't put it past both of you." Tanner tossed the ball high in the air above him and caught it in one of his large hands. *"Or me."*

"Okay, fine. You're going to be a star. Everyone knows that. Can you at least get me to the point where I don't totally suck?"

"Here." Tanner handed me the ball. *"Close your eyes."* I did. *"Now I want you to listen to my voice. Forget about where you are going or how far or anything in between. Just listen to my voice and point your body in my direction."* His voice moved away from me as he spoke until I was sure he was all the way across the field. *"Now I want you to think of the best batch of ice cream dad has ever made,"* Tanner yelled. I replayed the last time my father made ice cream with strawberries straight from the garden. My mouth watered, the sweet and tart flavor right there on my tongue. *"Now throw it."* Without another thought,

I pulled my arm back and threw the ball in the direction of Tanner's voice.

For about two seconds, the field was strangely quiet until a metallic thump resonated across the field. My eyes flew open to find the football bouncing away from the goalpost. Tanner stood directly behind the center post, his head shaking from side to side.

I raced to the goal and picked up the ball. Not only had I thrown it farther than ever, but I'd managed to hit my target.

"I don't know how I did that." Still stunned, I stared at Tanner.

He shrugged. "It's all in the teacher."

I turned and threw the ball toward his bag. Though it didn't hit it directly, the ball arched gracefully through the air before landing on the grass a few feet from the bag.

"You are a miracle worker," I said.

Tanner came up and put an arm around my shoulders. "You always had it in you, Lexie. You just needed a push in the right direction." And with that, he shoved me into the end zone.

My hand jerked in front of me and I nearly lost my footing. Had I fallen asleep standing up?

"Alexandra?" My father's voice sounded charged next to me.

"What?" I asked just as my hand jerked again. My eyes shot to Tanner's arm. It moved beneath my touch. "What's going . . ."

"Alexandra!" This time my father shouted. "Look." He pointed to Tanner's face. My brother's blue eyes were open and staring directly into mine.

"Help," I called to the surgical staff. "He's awake!" My voice cracked at the significance of the words I'd wanted to say for ten months. "Tanner's awake."

6

Awake

Chaos broke out in the surgical room. My father and I stepped back as Elijah and Rose burst into the room, followed shortly by Daly, now wearing the same blue surgical clothes as the rest of us. Rose managed to calm Tanner's flailing arms before he ripped out his IV or the tube coming from his mouth.

Blood pounded in my ears, drowning out every other noise. I just stared at Tanner, waiting for him to look at me again. Even with his open eyes and muscle movement, there were so many other variables that could still mean he wasn't out of the woods.

I looked away as they began to remove the tube from his mouth. *My brother is moving. His eyes are open.* I would concentrate on that. After about a minute, I glanced at the bed again. The tube was no longer in Tanner's mouth.

I tuned in to the voices in the room. ". . . hard for you to speak right now," Elijah said to my brother. "Just nod or shake your head in response. Do you understand?"

Tanner's head moved up and down. My fingers flew to my mouth and pressed back a scream of elation. My father gripped my other hand. Tanner understood Elijah. Tanner could recognize speech and respond to it.

Elijah continued. "Do you know where you are?"

Tanner glanced around the room. His eyes only paused briefly on my father and me before he nodded at Elijah.

"Do you know why you're here?" Elijah asked.

A crease formed between Tanner's brows and he closed his eyes. I held my breath for what seemed like several minutes. If he remembered the accident, did he know what happened afterward? Had he regained consciousness? Did he know about Mom? My throat and eyes burned. Someone would need to tell him.

When my brother finally opened his eyes again, he licked his lips and choked out, "Water."

"You really should wait to speak," Elijah said. "Your throat was roughed up from the tube, and your vocal cords—"

"Water," Tanner repeated, trying to sit up. Elijah put a hand on his shoulder, then motioned to a male nurse to go to the sink. The man grabbed a hospital cup and began to fill it.

"We'll get you some water," Elijah told my brother. "Please lie still. You just had major surgery."

Tanner slowly lifted his hand to feel the bandages wrapped around the top of his head. He opened his mouth to speak, but nothing came out. The nurse returned with the water in a cup, which now had a lid and straw. Elijah held the cup and put the straw to Tanner's lips. My brother took a sip of water and then grasped the cup and pulled it from Elijah's hand. Tanner drank for several seconds until the slurp of the straw indicated he'd drained the cup.

"Did we win?" my brother asked, his voice scratchy and quiet.

Elijah looked to my father and me and then back to Tanner. "I'm not sure what you—"

"The game. Did we win the championship?"

I bit down hard on my lip to stop the cry or laugh—I wasn't sure which—that wanted to bubble out of me. The first words out of Tanner's lips were, of course, about football.

I rushed to his bed. "Yes, you won the championship, 24 to 20. You scored the final touchdown."

A crooked, tired smile spread across my brother's face and he laid his head back. "Good."

"Is that the last thing you remember?" my dad asked, now standing next to me.

Tanner touched the gauze bandage on his head. "Must have been some tackle."

My father glanced at me and I was certain we were thinking the same thing: Tanner didn't know about Mom. From the look in my father's eyes, he wasn't about to tell him either.

Elijah cleared his throat. "Tanner, I'm Dr. Serben. You were in an accident and have been in a coma. I'm sure you have a lot of questions. We need to do some tests to make sure that everything is okay. Do you feel up to that?"

"Sure." My brother's voice was starting to sound closer to normal.

Elijah checked Tanner's eyes and reflexes. Though weak, his arms and legs moved properly. I watched Tanner's face during the examination. When he saw his arms and legs, he seemed surprised at the condition of his muscles, which had deteriorated significantly. Articles about long-term coma patients and treatments scrolled across my vision as Elijah listened to Tanner's heart. I knew giving my brother too much information too fast could be detrimental to his healing.

"Okay, Tanner. I'm going to ask you some more questions," Elijah said, holding a tablet in front of him. "I'd like you to answer as best you can, but there's no pressure. I just want to see how your mind is working."

Tanner nodded but didn't smile. I could tell he was nervous.

"What's the date today?"

Tanner glanced down at his body and then back up at Elijah. "I know the game was December 5. But I'm pretty sure that date is long past. What happened? How long has it been?"

My stomach clenched and I thought I might throw up, but I tried to hold myself together. Could he not remember anything after the December championship game? That was nearly six months before the accident.

Elijah's eyes found mine. We'd talked about this before in case Tanner woke up. Even though it would be traumatic for him to learn he had been in a coma for over ten months, we had decided it was important to tell him right away. "Why don't we let your family explain?"

"My family." Tanner's brows furrowed and he bit his bottom lip—a sure sign he was confused and trying to concentrate. "Yeah, they should come in."

"Tanner?" my father and I said at the same time.

My brother turned and looked at us. That's when I realized what had been nagging at me since the moment his eyes opened—something I hadn't even really considered. Tanner had never really acknowledged me the whole time he'd been awake.

"I'm sorry. I know I should recognize you," Tanner said, squinting at my face. "Everything is just . . ." His voice faded away.

My throat closed off and my vision blurred. My father squeezed my hand.

"Tanner." My father's calm voice suspended the tears that wanted to fall. "This is your sister, Alexandra. And I'm . . ." His composure threatened to break. "I'm your father."

I waited for a few seconds for Tanner to finally make the connection, to realize who I was. I was his sister. We had been best friends our whole life. Just as my feet were about to carry me from the room, he did something unexpected.

He laughed.

His eyes lit up and his body began to shake in a fit of boisterous laughter. Elijah peered down at Tanner in concern. The surgical staff looked to Elijah as if waiting for him to give them some guidance.

Daly stepped to the bottom of the bed. "He's pulling your leg, people. And from the looks of it, he's done a brilliant job."

I frowned. "What?"

Daly shook his head. "Alex, you told me a lot, but I didn't know your brother was a prankster too. He's good. Really good." He joined in with Tanner, whose hoarse chuckles still reverberated from his body.

My father released my hand and asked Tanner. "You're okay? You know who we are?"

Tanner threw out his arm. "Sorry." He laughed between his words. "I just . . . couldn't resist . . . too serious . . . can't believe you fell for . . . ridiculous Hollywood amnesia . . ." He looked at my father. "Dad." Then he turned to me. "Lexie."

Tanner's nickname for me brought a smile to my face. His memory was intact. He hadn't forgotten who we were. I couldn't believe I'd fallen for his selective-memory story, considering all I knew about comas.

Daly patted my left shoulder. "Don't worry. He even had me going for a second there."

"So you're really okay?" I asked Tanner.

"Yeah. At least I think so." He grinned sheepishly. Then he stared at Daly. "You, though. You, I don't remember. Are you a doctor too?"

Daly put out his hand. "Daly. James Daly. I'm a friend of Alex, but I think you are my new favorite person." Tanner reached out and shook Daly's hand, a wide smile on his face. My brother's face sent a wave of relief through me.

Then Tanner looked at Dad and me, his smile fading. "Where's Mom?"

Just like that my relief disappeared, replaced by memories.

I sat on a couch in the hospital waiting room, my body slumped into the cushions. Everything had been drained out of me — my physical energy, my mental strength, and my emotional fortitude.

Daly stopped in front of me and held out a Styrofoam cup. "Hot chocolate?"

He looked as tired as I felt. Without a word, I accepted the cup. The hot liquid nearly burned my tongue, but only felt warm down my throat. I was so spent I couldn't even taste the chocolate flavor.

"I don't ever want to do anything like that again." I set the cup on the end table.

Daly sat on the couch next to me. "I know."

The last thing Tanner had remembered was going to the grocery store with Mom and me to get ingredients for homemade brownies.

He hadn't remembered the drive home, or the accident. Worst of all, he hadn't known what happened to Mom.

My mind flashed to Tanner's stricken face when my father told him that Mom had died in the crash. The sight of my brother sobbing reawakened all the feelings I'd shut away over the last year. The doctors and nurses had left the room and allowed my family time to grieve together.

Later, my dad and I had answered Tanner's questions about the accident and the funeral. We'd had no choice but to tell him that we had thought he was dead, too. The news had confused him, but fully explaining the situation would have meant telling him about The Company, which I couldn't do. Besides, he'd already been given enough new information for one day.

When Elijah had entered the room, insisting on some brain scans, I didn't want to leave my brother's side. At the same time, I wasn't sure how much longer I could stand on my feet. So, when my father had said he would stay with Tanner, I'd escaped to the lobby.

"Do you need anything else?" Daly asked me now.

"No, I just need a minute, that's all."

Early morning sunshine streamed through the window and touched the side of my face. I let it warm me. My brother was alive. Not only that, he was awake. Everything that had happened up until this point had been worth it.

I smiled to myself. Hearing Tanner's laughter and even his cries had awakened something in me that I never thought I would get back. My brother had returned, and I couldn't help thinking that now I could really live too.

7

Something More

I paused outside Golkov's office at Brown University. I'd stayed with Tanner for most of the day, alongside my father and Daly. In the early afternoon, when Tanner's eyelids started to droop in exhaustion, my father had encouraged me to go home. He'd promised to stay with Tanner and call me as soon as my brother woke up. I hadn't wanted to leave, but when Daly said he would remain at the hospital too, I decided I could use a shower and a change of clothes.

I'd driven Daly's car to campus but hadn't gone to my dorm right away. I knew Golkov would be in his university office, and everything that had happened with Tanner had given me the nerve to finally talk with him. My courage only wavered for a moment before I knocked on the door.

Through the window, Golkov motioned for me to come in. His grandfatherly smile calmed me as I entered the room. The space was much smaller than his office hidden several floors below. Where The Company offices were all glass and technology, this one was like a home study. Dark wood, thick books, overstuffed chairs, and the distinct scent of cedar gave the room a warm, comfortable ambience.

"It's been a while, Alexandra."

I thought back to the last time Golkov and I had spoken—after the Paris mission, when I'd already given back The Company ring.

Golkov's connections with the CIA had helped me survive the Louvre incident and apprehend Ivan from Red Eye, but part of me still resented him for not telling me about Tanner. For six months, Golkov had let me believe my brother died in the car crash with my mom.

While I was debating what to say, Golkov spoke again. "I heard the good news about your brother. Elijah called me."

"You should have told me," I burst out. I hadn't realized how angry I really was until the words left my mouth. "You should have told me the truth about Tanner right from the beginning."

Golkov laid his pen down on his mahogany desk and stared at the paperwork in front of him. "I know that now."

"Why didn't you? You could have."

He smoothed his nearly white beard before he focused his gaze on me. "We all make decisions based on what we think is right at the time. Sometimes those decisions are right, and sometimes they are wrong. Despite what most of my students think, I do make mistakes." There was a sadness on Golkov's face then, and regret that seemed to go deeper than his decision to keep Tanner from me.

"There's something I need to tell you, something that I think you have a right to know," I said.

Golkov's posture straightened and he waited for me to go on. I moved to the chair across from his desk and sat down. I'd wracked my brain the entire drive from the hospital, but I couldn't put it out of my mind. Despite everything, I wouldn't keep this from him. "Julia Helm from the CIA . . . after the mission in Paris, she asked if I would work with them."

Golkov's lips tightened slightly.

"I initially told her no, that I already had a place, but we kind of made a deal when she got Elijah released from their custody."

"I see." Golkov placed his elbows on his desk and rested his two pointer fingers in a steeple over his lips.

"The CIA contacted me yesterday and asked me to help with a mission. I accepted."

Golkov's face was expressionless. He was so good at masking his emotions.

I leaned forward. "But now that Tanner's awake, I don't feel I can leave him. This mission they want me to go on is time-sensitive. I'm thinking of contacting them and backing down."

"Alexandra, as you well know, I left the CIA years ago for many reasons," Golkov said. I nodded, recalling our conversation the first time I visited The Company headquarters. "I mentioned bureaucracy, but it was more than just that," he went on. "The CIA's power doesn't just reach from the top to the bottom. Their control can extend to the personal lives of their employees."

"Meaning?"

"Meaning, once you make a commitment, you had better well follow through."

"You can't actually be saying that the CIA, an organization that is part of our national security, would go as far as to hurt me or anyone I know personally because I broke a promise."

Golkov put up his hands. "They would never do anything physically to harm you. I am just saying that it is critical to keep commitments with them."

I wanted to ask more questions, but the grave look in his eyes told me that he wasn't going to say more.

I started to get up.

"Alexandra." Golkov's voice moved me back into my seat. "I have been meaning to ask you a question." He fidgeted with two connected metal rings he'd picked up from his desk. "I know you are still making a decision about your future."

That statement was truer than he could ever know. Tanner, The Company, the CIA, the Slavic Studies Program—all those things pulled me in different directions. Daly's face ran through my memories. I hadn't made any headway in that department, either.

Golkov cleared his throat. "When your mother worked for me . . . the work we did together . . . What I'm so ineloquently trying to say is that her work is the kind of thing that I wouldn't mind duplicating."

"You mean like recovering art?" I said.

"I know cracking codes, catching terrorists, and spying seem to be what most of our missions are about nowadays."

Thinking about my most recent pseudo-mission with Daly atop the Superman building, I nodded, still not sure what Golkov was trying to say.

"That may be what the CIA is mostly about as well. But when your mother was here . . ." Golkov lowered his voice almost reverently. "When she was here, she brought a vibrancy to our work. She rescued what was lost. She brought back to life things forgotten. She helped us remember why I formed this organization in the first place."

He peered at the ring on his finger. The bittersweet nightshade etched into the thick silver metal called out to me. "Truth." He let out a long breath as if still searching for the right words. "I think you should go on this mission, Alexandra. For the CIA. Do what needs to be done for them, learn from them. But when you finish, I am asking that you consider taking your place back here." His solemn tone caught me off guard. He glanced behind him at the Rembrandt painting hanging on his wall, the one where my mother had discreetly painted her face in the crowd of people on the boat floating on the Sea of Galilee.

I swallowed back the emotion in my throat. Clearly, Golkov had loved my mom like a daughter, and maybe he had sought me out because he didn't have family. Maybe that was the regret I saw in his eyes. I thought of my dad and now Tanner, the brother I thought I'd lost. I had been willing to do anything to save them—even steal a Van Gogh painting from the Louvre, of all places. But that mission had taught me a great deal. I learned I was willing to do anything for my loved ones. I also discovered that no matter what, I would be true to myself and wouldn't compromise who I was for anyone.

While I didn't have my future sorted out yet, I had to trust my instincts. And at that moment, I wasn't ready to promise Golkov I would come back to The Company. It pained me to see that look in his eyes, a pleading even he couldn't hide. One word could have brought back the light I missed in his face. But I wouldn't lie to him again.

"I'm thankful for everything you've done for me, Professor Golkov. I have some decisions to make. When I'm ready, I will let you know."

He nodded as if he had expected that response. Realizing I hadn't surprised him was a huge relief.

"You know where I will be." He stood at the same time I did. I wanted to hug him, to reassure him that I would always consider him a friend and mentor. Instead, I just smiled at him.

He lifted his hand and held out something for me. At first glance, I thought it was The Company ring, but then I recognized the metal rings he'd been playing with earlier. The pieces clinked against each other when he placed them in my extended hand.

"What's this?" I said.

"A puzzle. For old times' sake." Golkov gave me a tiny bit of the smile held in my memory. A spark of mischief reached his eyes as he opened his office door and led me out. "Just keep it until you solve it" was all he said before he ushered me into the hallway and closed himself back in his office.

I paused in the hospital hallway, nearly gagging at the smell of antiseptic and cafeteria breakfast food. I wasn't sure why I was scared to see Tanner. I'd spent most of the previous day with him. But my father and Daly had been there too, and half the time Tanner was undergoing tests. Today was different. My father had things to do on campus, so Tanner and I would be alone.

Despite my hesitance, a good night's sleep and shower had rejuvenated me. I would need that strength today. I forced myself forward down the linoleum-floored corridor to the recovery wing of the hospital. They'd just moved Tanner from the ICU.

You spent half your childhood and teen years alone together. How different could it be? Actually, I was worried about the questions Tanner would ask. Though he'd never told me face to face, with what my brain had pieced together from before the accident, I was sure he'd known my mom was a spy. During his coma, I'd shared everything with him. But now I wasn't sure what to say to him or how to answer when he asked what I was up to. I'd always been open with him, yet somehow this was different. Did I really want him a part of it all? Had my mom been right?

My throat felt dry as I stopped outside his door. I hadn't made a decision yet.

The door swung open before I could pull the handle or make up my mind. "There you are." My father's bright, smiling face met me in the doorway. Where Golkov had appeared older when I saw him the previous night, my father seemed to have gone back in time a few years. The dullness of his eyes had been replaced by a lively glow emanating from his entire being. His lost son had returned. "Tanner was wondering where you've been. He says he has several months to catch up on."

"*Sí*. I mean yes." My mind often translated my thoughts in different languages, especially when I was under stress.

"Have you heard back from the Slavic Studies board?" my father asked as we stepped into Tanner's room.

"Not yet." I'd nearly forgotten about my application for admittance into the Slavic Studies Program. At least it was no longer up to me. Either I got in or I didn't.

Dad patted me on the back. "Everything will work out."

At a mumble from Tanner's hospital bed, my heart began to race. Had he regressed?

His chin was smudged with what looked like banana pudding, and he held up a spoon like he'd just won the Heisman Trophy. "I did it. The nurse didn't think I could swallow and they wanted to keep me using this G-tube thing." My brother pointed to his stomach where the feeding tube was still attached. "He said if I could swallow this and keep it down, they would consider removing it today and also the . . ." Tanner's face grew red, and I realized he was talking about his catheter. "Well, anyway. I'm well on my way. If I can help it, I'm going to be out of here by the end of the week." He slowly shoved another spoonful of pudding into his mouth.

I looked to my father, whose unsure expression probably matched my own. Tanner's enthusiasm was catchy, but maybe a bit too hopeful. He'd been in a coma for nearly ten months and had just undergone brain surgery. From what I'd read and seen, it often took weeks for a bedridden coma patient to gain back enough muscle to even hold his or her head up. The nurses had propped up Tanner with pillows on either side of his body, and his head seemed to be moving just fine. All the joint and muscle movements Elijah had prescribed during the coma must have helped. I would always be grateful to Tanner's nurses for how well they took care of him.

"Don't push it, Superstar," I said. "I know you want out of here, but give your body time to heal. You've been through a lot."

Tanner swallowed the pudding in his mouth. "Yeah, says the girl who insisted on leaving the hospital the moment she woke up from surgery for a broken arm."

"How do you—"

"Dad told me, Lexie. He told me everything."

I gave my father a questioning glare. If he'd told Tanner about my injury from the accident, did my brother also know about The Company?

My father placed a hand on my shoulder. "I only explained how you tried to pull out your IV, leave without a splint, and refuse pain meds. We nearly had to cuff you to the bed."

I'd forgotten about that. Not forgotten—that was impossible for me. I just had pushed it from my mind.

"I'm going to run home for a second and to campus for a few hours. Can I trust you to watch this kid?" My father turned to me. "Every time a female nurse comes in, he flirts with her mercilessly. I requested the male one, just to get Casanova to hold still during some of his tests."

"I believe that," I said.

Tanner grinned. "I have to make up for lost time."

My father and I shook our heads before he made his way out of the room.

"See you, old man," Tanner called after him as he shut the door. Apparently nothing had changed with their relationship.

I turned back to my brother, who spooned another bite of pudding into his mouth. It took him several seconds to swallow, and it appeared to be painful.

"Take your time, Tanner." I moved to the chair next to his bed and sat down.

He left the spoon in his bowl and picked up a napkin to wipe the pudding off his face. He hadn't quite mastered how to aim the spoon. After he put down his napkin, his expression grew serious. "I don't have time, Lexie. If I want to be ready by June, I need to up my game. Which means getting moving as soon as possible. I need to walk out of here by the end of the week."

I scooted forward on my chair. "June? What's in June?"

"James might be able to get me into the coach's exclusive camp in June. Fifty percent of the team's roster once attended that camp. If I want a chance at them looking at me, I need to start somewhere."

"Are you talking football? At WSU?" I stood up, unable to believe he would even consider it.

"Yes, football. But not in Washington. Here, at Brown."

"You want to play at Brown?"

"Yeah. James says with my grades and all-state status in high school, he could at least get me an interview. Since admittance is the first step, there's no harm in trying. Right?"

"You're going to go to Brown?" My voice wavered. Before the accident, we'd both been willing to sacrifice to be at the same college, but in the end Tanner had signed me up for classes at Brown, and I had made him promise to accept the scholarship at WSU, his dream school.

"What about WSU?"

Tanner sat up a little higher, his neck muscles straining at the effort. "What I always wanted was to play football. So what if I'll have to tryout as a walk-on and hope for some playing time. Playing for Brown is way bigger than playing for WSU."

"But you love WSU."

"No, I love football. I don't care where I play." He leaned his head back and rested his arms over the hospital blanket on his lap.

"Besides, I have another reason for wanting to stay here." A sly grin formed on his lips.

"And that would be?" I sat again and crossed my legs in front of me.

"Well, there's this nurse I think is pretty hot."

"Tanner!" I kicked at his bed.

"Hey, watch it. I'm an invalid here." He shifted positions. "Ugh. I'm sore everywhere."

"Are you sure this is what you want to do? You haven't had much time to make a decision."

"I want to be with family and I want to play football." My brother shrugged. "Seems like a pretty easy decision to me."

"But why the rush? You could take a year off to heal and regain your strength."

Tanner looked at his hands like he didn't recognize them as his own. "I've already lost enough time. Besides, James says you're rushing off to do new things even though you haven't been here a year."

Panic rushed through my veins. "Daly said what?"

"Something about a master's program in Slavic Studies." Tanner pushed his food tray to the side. "What's with that, anyway?"

"Slavic Studies? I've always been interested in Russian, and since it's part of our heritage, I want to learn even more."

"No, not that. The name thing. Why don't you just call him by his first name, like a normal human being?"

It was true that I rarely used Daly's first name. Perhaps I wanted to keep distance between us. As Daly, he was my colleague—someone I worked with, even a good friend. But as James? As James, he could've been something more.

"I know that look." Tanner pointed a finger at me. "I totally thought it when he talked about you, but I wasn't sure."

"What?" I traced the grains of wood on the chair armrest.

"You like him."

"Do not." I said. Suddenly the room felt warm. "He just works with me, is all."

"Don't worry. I won't say anything." Tanner scratched at the edge of his gauze bandage. "But you should probably know, he's totally whipped. Do people still say that?"

"Is that what he said?" Now the heat in the room was making me sweat.

"Nah. Just something a guy just knows."

I resisted the urge to open a window or run from the room. This wasn't news to me—I knew how Daly felt. I just didn't realize anyone else could tell.

"So you going to help me or just sit there blushing?"

"What?" I asked.

Tanner strained to lean forward. "If I'm going to get out of here in good time, I've got to start my own physical therapy regimen. My first order of business is to sit up all on my own." He put out an arm. "But I need some help. It's going to take months to get my abs of steel back."

"Do you really think you should be doing this now?" I stood by the side of his bed.

"The doc told me I can do whatever I want, as long as I stay in bed the next day. Sounds like the perfect time to me."

"Fine." I reached an arm around Tanner's shoulders. "But if Elijah gets angry, I'm blaming you."

"You wouldn't be my sister if you didn't."

My sister. I'd missed that phrase. I'd missed my Tanner. But he was back, and apparently he was going to prove he was the same cocky and strong brother I remembered.

8

Polyester

In the hospital cafeteria, I slid my tray down the countertop in front of the food displays, trying to decide which option looked the freshest. Surprisingly, the food smelled pretty good. Since I'd skipped breakfast, I couldn't argue when Tanner heard my stomach growl and told me to go get something to eat.

I settled on a fruit bowl, salad, and potato soup, then paid for my meal and found an empty table. I would've gone back to Tanner's room to eat, but he had insisted on enjoying his JELL-O uninterrupted before he took a short nap.

I checked my email on my phone while I ate the soup. No response from the Slavic Studies board. Waiting for their decision was killing me, since continuing to study Russian and getting my master's degree at Brown were the only things I knew for sure I wanted in my future.

Unexpectedly, there was an email from Agent Denisovich. It contained a series of numbers that made no sense. I tried to decipher them using keys I'd learned at The Company. When that produced only mumbo jumbo, I tried the Russian alphabet. A few minutes later a message emerged. Denisovich wanted to meet that evening at an address on the outskirts of Providence. I deleted the message and emptied my email trash. I'd taken Golkov's words to heart. Although I wanted to stay by Tanner's side while he healed, I felt compelled to help Denisovich find his daughter.

"Alex?"

I dropped the strawberry that had been on its way to my mouth. My whole body froze and my mind went blank. I knew that voice. I had *loved* that voice. I definitely wasn't ready to face the owner of that voice. *Not today.*

"Alex?" he said again.

The noises of the cafeteria blended together in a hum of nothingness. All I could hear was the echo of my name from the lips of someone I hadn't spoken to in six weeks.

"William." I raised my head. The dark curls that brushed his forehead hadn't changed. Neither had the beautiful eyes that could only be compared to the bright blue of a summer sky. I stared at him, then shook my head and tried to pull myself together. "What are you doing . . . why are you here?"

He cleared his throat and adjusted the tray in his hands. I looked at his sandwich and glass of clear soda—anything besides his face. He peered down at his own food. "Dr. Red wanted to meet for lunch." My mind flashed to William's goofy roommate. His real name was Aaron, but because he was in the middle of his medical residency and his hair was a brilliant hue of red, his nickname had stuck.

"Oh." I pulled my gaze from the rubbery cheese hanging off the side of William's sandwich. *What is wrong with me? We are both adults.* Well, that wasn't entirely true. William was twenty-two, but my eighteenth birthday was still several weeks away.

He glanced at my bowl of fruit. "How's your lunch?"

"My lunch?"

"Yeah, I hear the soup is pretty good. The sandwiches aren't too bad if you peel off the American cheese."

I looked at his sandwich again, but the image blurred as scenes from the last two semesters began to open up in my mind. The first time William and I met, when I knocked him over before class. Our morning running routes and Spanish tutoring sessions. In front of the Rochambeau fountain when he told me how old he was. The first kiss that could have melted the snow falling around us.

"Memory overload?" He set his tray down in front of mine but remained standing.

"Yes." Though William didn't know about my spy life, he was one of the first people I'd told about my eidetic memory. Now that very moment, in front of a large tree on campus, rushed across my vision. He'd been so understanding when he realized my memories haunted me.

"I'm sorry." His voice was so genuine, it broke through and brought me back to the present. I stared up at him. He really was sorry, and so was I. Not for breaking up with him. I had accepted my decision. I was just sorry things had changed. I missed our runs to Blackstone Park. I missed our tutoring sessions. Most of all, I missed our conversations.

"No need to be sorry," I replied finally. "My memories are a part of me. I wouldn't give up the best ones, even if it meant I could erase the bad ones."

William nodded and then glanced around the cafeteria. "Are you waiting for someone?"

"No, just getting some lunch before I go back to my brother."

One of William's brows lowered. "Brother? But I thought . . ."

My heart drummed against ribs. Why had I not thought this through? William knew my mother and brother had been killed in car accident. My roommate Casey knew it as well. Somehow she and I hadn't crossed paths since Tanner woke up yesterday, so there had been no need to mention it to her. What was I going to say? *Oh, by the way, the brother I told you was dead was actually saved by a spy organization my mom was a part of. He was in a coma for ten months, but now he's awake.* It sounded like the makings of a Hollywood screenplay.

I stared down at the finger on which I used to wear The Company ring. I owed William the truth.

"Yes, my brother Tanner is here recovering."

"He's alive?" William looked about as surprised as I'd felt the first time Elijah had told me the news.

"It's a long story."

William glanced at his wristwatch, which appeared just as vintage as his brown polyester vest. "Dr. Red's surgery must be going over.

But no matter. I'll make time for this." William motioned to the chair across from me.

I smiled at him. If I was going to have to share part of this story with others, I might as well start with someone who knew me well. "You remember me telling you about the car accident, back in Washington?" I focused on William's eyes—those beautiful eyes that still carried a warmth I probably didn't deserve. I could do this.

"Yes."

"Three of us—my mom, my brother, and I—were involved. My mom didn't make it." I moved a hand to my throat, as if to relieve the ache that would always be there, no matter how long she'd been gone.

William's eyes remained on mine while he waited for me to continue. I'd shared this story before, at least the version I thought was true at the time.

"Tanner, my brother . . . he survived the crash. But his body couldn't handle all the head trauma, and he's been in a coma for ten months." Now I glanced down at my uneaten bowl of fruit on the table. William and I might not have been together anymore, but I still cared what he thought. He must've thought I had lied to him about the accident when I said I'd lost my mom and brother. Yet I couldn't get into the details and explain that I had been lied to and that a spy organization had been keeping Tanner alive.

"He was in a coma?"

"He woke up on Sunday night." Saying those words sent a rush of exhilaration through me. I raised my head to meet William's gaze. "My brother woke up. And he's okay, William. He's really okay." I couldn't help the wide grin that filled my face or the misting of my eyes. It was the first time in the last forty-eight hours that I'd said those words aloud. My brother and best friend was going to be okay.

William's hand covered mine on the table. The gesture felt so natural that it took me several seconds to realize he was holding onto my hand. I slowly pulled away and grabbed for my tray.

"I should probably get back to him." I stood up.

"Alex."

The softness with which William said my name caused me to stop moving. I wasn't sure I wanted to hear what he had to say, but I needed to give him the chance to speak. He'd given me that opportunity when I'd broken up with him.

"I just wanted to say goodbye."

"Goodbye?"

"I'm leaving Brown," William said. "That's why I came to have lunch with Dr. Red. It's my last day in Providence."

"But what about your grant?" I asked. William had received a Fulbright grant to teach Spanish and study Mexican literature with some of the brightest minds on the subject.

"That's why I'm going. The school terms are on a different schedule in Mexico City. They want me there before their spring term begins. I'm flying out in the morning."

My heart pricked at the thought of William leaving. We weren't exactly a part of each other's lives anymore, but there had been comfort knowing he was still a Spanish professor, still going on morning runs, still on campus—like some things would always remain the same. Knowing his life was changing and that he was moving on made me feel . . . regret.

"Are you ready?" I directed the question to him, but it was almost like I was asking myself, too.

William stood up and pushed away a brown curl that had found its way over his eye. "It kind of took me by surprise, how fast everything happened. The Spanish Department wasn't too happy about finding a replacement professor with such short notice, but I think they're hoping that after my research and experience in Mexico over the next several months, I'll come back here. We've parted on good terms." He adjusted his brown-plaid tie before he picked up his untouched tray of food.

"So will you? Come back?" I cursed the hopefulness that came out in my voice. *Why should I care if he comes back to Brown? I don't even know if I will be here.*

William's head tilted and the fluorescent lights above us reflected in his eyes, making them glow like translucent sapphires. "I wasn't sure I had anything here in Providence drawing me back." He studied my face and then smiled that schoolboy grin from all my memories. "But I don't think Providence has seen the last of me yet."

With that, he turned and walked away as I stared after him, thoroughly flustered at the heat in my face and the fluttering in my stomach.

Tanner was asleep when I entered his private room at the hospital. I sat in the reclining chair that doubled as a guest bed, then pulled out my laptop and began working on my neglected homework. I had only missed two classes that day, and luckily the syllabus for each of them provided enough information that I could catch up using the textbook. I closed my eyes and leafed through the pages of my books for Chinese and Humanities. I hadn't even bothered buying the Humanity textbook but brought the Chinese one with me to class as a prop. After reviewing the new Chinese characters and vocabulary for the week, I read a chapter in my Humanities book on nineteenth-century Russian literature.

I had just started typing an essay comparing Tolstoy's *War and Peace* with Dostoevsky's *Crime and Punishment* when a movement in my periphery grabbed my attention. Tanner rolled from one side to the other and pulled his blanket up to his face. The motion caused me to smile. I was just so happy he could move. I went back to typing.

Several minutes later, a mumbling came from the bed. I set my laptop on the side table and stood. I wondered if it was the first time since Tanner woke up that he was having a dream he might remember when he woke up. He moved his head from side to side while he continued to mumble, like he was having a conversation, but none of the words made sense. His chest moved up and down a little more rapidly than usual. I glanced at the machine at the side of his bed. His heartbeat had increased to over ninety beats per minute.

Worry sent a chill through my body. I touched Tanner's shoulder and shook him softly. He didn't wake. *Should I call Elijah?* I shook Tanner's shoulder harder this time.

He shot up to a sitting position and gripped my arm, his eyes searching the room and his breaths coming quickly. "I have to remember. I have to get it," he said.

"What do you have to get?" I asked him.

He turned his head in my direction, but his eyes seemed to be looking right through me.

"Tanner?"

His tense shoulders sagged as he fell back against his pillow. His breathing calmed, along with his heart rate. His hand fell back to his side, but it left a white handprint on my forearm. I stayed by his bed and watched the handprint fade from my skin.

I didn't leave Tanner's side until the nurse came in a half hour later and woke him to check his vitals and the spot where the G-tube had been feeding him. I waited off to the side until she finished.

"Were you dreaming?" I asked Tanner after the nurse left.

"I . . ." He looked to the ceiling. "I don't remember."

"You were mumbling something in your sleep. Then you said you had to remember to get something."

"I did?" Tanner pulled his blanket back up to his chest.

"I was worried about you for a second there. Your heart was racing."

Tanner tapped his chest. "It's good to know that this baby can still pound."

"I'm just happy you're okay. You sure you don't remember what you were dreaming about?"

"Nope. Not all of us have a good memory." He gave me a knowing smile and laid his head back on his pillow.

9

CIA

"I thought aces beat all." Tanner stared down at the two playing cards between us on the blue hospital blanket. My card was the king of hearts.

"We never agreed on that," I said, trying not to smile.

"That's how we always play." Tanner grabbed both cards. I started to snatch them from his hand but stopped myself. It would be like taking candy from a baby, and in this particular instance I didn't want to be the thief.

"I still win." I picked up my cards.

"Count 'em." Tanner started leafing through his cards one by one, his fingers moving more quickly than in the previous game. His dexterity was coming back just fine.

I picked up my stack and left it in my hand while I rewound the game in my head and fast-forwarded through each hand in our game of War. Twenty-nine cards. That meant that Tanner had —

"Thirty-three — I win!" he said.

"Dad, are you going to help me out here? He's won three games in a row." I turned to my father, who sat in the reclining chair at the corner of the room. He pulled off his reading glasses and thumbed his spot in a very thick book.

"I've found it's best to stay out of any war." He gave me a look that basically said, "Take it easy on your brother."

"Fine. I concede." I tossed my cards into Tanner's lap. "You are the true champion. Hurrah, hurrah." I couldn't help the bit of sarcasm in the last "hurrah." I hated losing.

"Alexandra, 'in the time of darkest defeat, victory may be nearest,'" my father said, then opened his book again.

I didn't need him quoting presidents to me. I tossed a card in his direction. It barely hit his arm. He eyed me over his book.

"Come on, Lexie. Dad's right, and so was William McKinley."

"You knew that was McKinley?" I asked. *Maybe Tanner got some memory genes too.*

"Are you kidding me? Dad has quoted that to me every time the team was losing. Got me through several games." He lifted his chin to our father.

"Well, I think you cheat," I said. "How can you win every time in a game that is basically chance?"

Tanner shrugged his shoulders. "It's a gift."

"Do you guys need a referee?" Daly stood at the door with a large soda in one hand and a stack of magazines in the other. He came into the room and gave the soda to Tanner, then set the magazines on the side table. "By the way, if a nurse comes in, that's my drink," Daly said.

"Thanks, man." Tanner took a long sip. "Exactly what I needed."

"The latest *Sports Illustrated* is under the others."

"Awesome!" Tanner put down his drink and grabbed for the first magazine, with "College Football" written in big red letters on the front. "Thanks. I've got nearly a year of players and rankings to catch up on."

"Looks like I am no longer needed here." I stretched my arms above me and yawned.

"But I just arrived." Daly sounded disappointed.

"You guys don't have to babysit me 24/7. I'll be fine spending a few hours on my own," Tanner said.

"I wasn't here to babysit," I replied. "I just wanted to hang out."

"And skip school? Ha! When was the last time you didn't attend a class?" Tanner flipped open the magazine.

I wasn't about to get into the specifics of how many classes I'd missed earlier in the term because of the Paris mission. "I do have a few things I need to get done tonight."

"And I have some reading to do," Tanner put in. "So you guys can all go. James, you and I will need to have some serious discussions once I'm caught up. Tomorrow?"

"Deal." Daly nodded and put out a hand in my direction. I let him pull me to my feet.

Things were oddly quiet on the drive to meet Agent Denisovich. Daly had insisted on driving me, and since I wasn't sure what to expect, I had agreed. I didn't know what Daly was thinking about, but he seemed to be in his own world. He kept his gaze on the road in front of us, and I stared out the passenger-door window at nothing in particular. My mind kept replaying William's face from the cafeteria. I hadn't seen it then, with the wriggling nerves in my stomach, but now, in my memory, I noticed the strength in his gaze, a different kind of intensity. I wasn't sure what it meant, but it had me curious.

I half expected to see a CIA seal or sign on the front of the building where Agent Denisovich had told me to meet him. Instead, Daly drove into the industrial district of Providence, which was filled with warehouses and a shipping yard. Steam rose from the stacks of one of the largest warehouses and then dissipated into the clouds.

"Maybe I got the address wrong," I said to Daly.

"Have you ever remembered anything wrong?" He pulled to the side of the back street and turned off his car.

The gray metal building to our right appeared run down, large bolts rusting in several places on the seams. My stomach dropped. This was nothing like The Company.

"I'll be right outside. Holler if you need me." Daly lightly touched my ear, where my com unit was located, leaving a tingling warmth where his fingers had grazed.

"You don't have to stick around. I'm sure it's just last-minute details or something. I can make it home on my own."

Daly looked up and down the darkening street. "You might be Supergirl when it comes to solving puzzles and climbing buildings, but I have a feeling a gang of hoodlums or a serial killer might get the best of you."

"I think you're underestimating my training." I winked at him. Half of my physical training had been done under his watchful eyes or with him as my attacker.

"Even so. I'll remain here."

I didn't argue as I opened the car door. I was independent, that was for sure. But I had come to realize that the best spies let someone have their back. Having Daly there reassured me. It was like knowing you could walk a tight rope, but remaining steady because you felt certain the net was there to catch you.

"I'll be back soon," I said.

Gravel crackled underfoot as I made my way to what appeared to be the entrance of the building. More rust ran down the hinges and edges of a thick metal door. *What kind of meeting place is this?* I frowned. A camera above my head, almost out of my line of sight, caught my eye. At least they had some kind of security.

The door creaked as it opened in front of me, revealing Agent Denisovich with a solemn expression. "Ms. Laxer" —he looked around me— "come inside."

I stepped into a dark hallway, lit only by glowing red lights on either side of the walls. The slamming door sent a pulse of adrenaline through my veins.

I turned back and asked, "What is this place?"

Denisovich walked past me, and I almost had to run to keep up. After about fifty yards, he stopped and laid his palm flat on the wall. The spot he touched glowed green under his hand, and suddenly the space in the wall next to us slid open to reveal a doorway. I followed the agent through the opening and gasped at the sight.

The bright room, about the size of a football field, was sleek in design. Different sections were separated by ten-foot-high glass walls, similar to those in The Company Headquarters at Brown. The ceiling here must have been the height of the actual building, maybe forty or fifty feet. A woman in all black was climbing one of the charcoal-colored walls using tiny handholds and no rope, though the floor under her was covered with Rubix Cube-sized black foam pieces. To her left were other people dressed in black, one climbing using a rope, and another with what looked like suction cups. *Millard would love to get his hands on those. So would I.*

"I have an office set up this way." Denisovich motioned ahead of us. I walked forward, my eyes going every way at once. The central portion of the space was filled with computer screens, wires, and electronics I didn't recognize. I spied a gym-like room in the far corner of the space, with a young couple sparring using a combination of karate and kickboxing moves.

Denisovich passed by what appeared to be a lunchroom, though no one was eating at any of the sleek black tables. A few people looked up as we passed by three occupied offices and a large conference room.

"Has this place always been here?" I searched for clues of age, but couldn't tell if it had been around for a few days or a few decades. A few transparent office walls with data scrolling across made it clear that they had the latest technology.

"Take a seat, Ms. Laxer."

I crossed my arms and remained on my feet. "Are you going to answer any of my questions?"

Denisovich rubbed at a bloodshot eye and exhaled loudly. "This is a CIA training facility. There are several throughout the world. This one was built over ten years ago. The Providence location is perfect for European missions and is sometimes used in preparation for missions in Canada and Mexico." He opened a desk and pulled out a file. He pointed to a black rolling suitcase nearly hidden beside his desk. "The mission details we discussed are all here for your review. Your bag is packed and your flight leaves tomorrow morning at five."

"Tomorrow?"

"I think you can understand the time-sensitive nature of this mission." Denisovich cleared his throat. "We've done everything we can, and with no more leads we need someone on the inside."

"I just assumed I'd have more time." I'd planned to spend that time with Tanner, who had only been awake for a couple of days.

"We have contacts at Brown University," Denisovich continued. "Your absence will be excused and your classes recorded and sent to your location in Mexico. As far as anyone here is concerned, you are visiting a sick relative. We will ensure that your life as a regular college student isn't negatively impacted." He handed me the file. Though I wouldn't need to review the contents—they were already etched in my mind—I needed something to hold on to.

"Any last-minute questions?" Denisovich asked.

I shook free the flashes of memories trying to break my concentration. Daly's hand on my cheek. Tanner's smile during our game of War. William's comment about Providence not seeing the last of him. No. I couldn't think about any of those things now. I needed to direct my attention to the mission at hand.

"Do you trust your daughter, Agent Denisovich?" At his frown, I said, "What I mean is, do you trust that she would come to you if she could?"

He leaned back in his chair and placed his hands in his lap. "I adore Amoriel, and though I may not know everything about her, I am certain that she loves art and loved her school. Nothing would have kept her from pursuing her dream there, unless she was forced from it."

I brought the folder to my chest, then stepped forward and pulled up the handle of the suitcase. "I'll find her, Agent Denisovich. I'll bring her home."

He didn't say another word, but I caught a glint of moisture in his eyes before I left the office. Walking back the way I'd come, I studied the expansive CIA training site. When my eyes fell upon the center of the space, I paused. There, surrounded by computers and agents at work, was the CIA seal embedded in the floor. I stared for a moment at the eagle near the top of the seal. Like the bittersweet nightshade on The Company ring I once wore, the eagle meant something. It symbolized strength. That was a characteristic I was going to need.

Daly stopped near my dorm and turned off his car. Even though it was late and I had an early morning ahead of me, I didn't move.

"I'm coming with you." He continued to face the windshield. I'd spent the whole drive back from the CIA warehouse describing the interior and going over some of the mission details with him. He had listened and asked questions, but his usual energy had been off. "I'll get a hotel nearby and be there in case you need anything."

"I'll have a CIA handler, Daly. An entire team will be at my disposal." I still couldn't believe all the resources that would be within my reach.

"I know." He let out a breath. "But what if you need me?" There was a hopefulness in his voice that sent a whirl of commotion through me.

I faced him and said, "I need you here."

"Why?" He continued to stare at the building in front of us.

"I need you to take care of Tanner. I don't know how long I'll be gone. He's doing great and Elijah and Rose will be here." I bit the inside of my cheek. "But he likes you, so I think you could help him understand why I'm not there. Can you do that for me, please?" I looked down at my hands.

A finger touched my chin and lifted it until my eyes were upon Daly's fierce gaze. A heat wave traveled from my chin down my body, until it permeated to my core.

"You know I would do anything for you, Alex." His hand moved along my jaw and I leaned into it. His callused hands still felt soft against my skin as he brushed his thumb along my cheekbone. I didn't care about the boundary I'd tried to draw between us or the reasons why I'd held back. I just wanted him close.

I reached up and touched his face. The roughness at the warm skin of his jawline sent a fire through me. My racing heart told me all I needed to know. I closed my eyes and tilted my head until his lips met mine.

It was nothing like our first kiss—and everything I'd never allowed myself to imagine. He had been a protector, a friend, a support. In that moment, as his hand found the back of my neck and he pulled me into a deeper kiss, I realized something. He could really be everything to me if I let him. Finally, I crushed the wall I'd put between us and wrapped my arms around him, wishing against all odds that I'd never have to let go again.

Twilight cast a bluish glow across the inside of Daly's car. I lifted my head from his shoulder. After our kiss, we'd held onto each other, knowing it might be a while before we'd see each other again.

"I should probably go," I said quietly.

"Mmm." Daly put his hand on the side of my head and eased it back to his shoulder. If it wasn't for the center console, I had a feeling he would have pulled me even closer.

"No, really, I have a few things to pack before my ride arrives." It was still dark out and the sun wouldn't rise for a few more hours, but I needed to be ready in less than thirty minutes.

"Just let me savor this for a minute longer." He wrapped his arm around me.

I didn't need convincing. I'd never felt so warm, safe, and loved in my entire life.

10

Kiss and Tell

"Alex?" Casey mumbled from her side of our dark dorm room. Apparently, being stealthy wasn't one of my strongest spy qualities.

"Hey." I picked up my school bag, removed my textbooks, and slid them under my bed.

"Where have you been?" She sat up and peered out our small window. "What time is it, anyway?" The strap of her hot-pink tank top hung off her shoulder, and a dyed red streak of hair stuck out a few inches above her head.

"It's almost five. Go back to sleep." I didn't have time to explain everything to her.

"Were you with James?"

"Yes, but I really—"

"Alexandra Louisiana Stewart!" She used her made-up middle name for me. Her eyes were wide now. She was definitely not going back to sleep. "You must tell me everything."

I tossed some underclothes and toiletries into my backpack, along with a locked pouch that held my Dana Laxer passport, driver's license, and credit cards. "Case, we kissed. It was no big deal."

"No big deal? This is epic. J.R. so owes me. We kind of had a bet on how long it would take."

I stopped zipping my bag and stared. "You guys bet on when Daly and I would kiss?"

Casey pulled up the strap of her tank. "It was bound to happen."

If Tanner, Millard, and Casey knew about the attraction between Daly and me, I wondered if my father did, too. I cringed.

"It's a good thing, right?" Casey said. "You and Daly, I mean."

As I thought back to the past couple of hours, a tingling sensation spread through me. Even though the dorm room was only lit by a small lamp, I bent over to hide my flushed face and grab my favorite running shoes. Near my shoes, the light caught on the shiny surface of the metal-ring puzzle Golkov had given me. I hadn't yet found time to try to solve it. I threw it in one of the shoes.

Casey sighed. "Of course you think it's a good thing. How could you not?" She fell back onto her pillow.

I rose and tucked the shoes in the bag, then pulled it over my shoulder. "I'd like to talk more, but I need to go. My ride is waiting."

"Ride?" She sat up again. "You're not going to his . . ."

I threw up a hand. "No, no. I'm going to be gone for a while." I searched around the room to make sure I wasn't missing anything. I hoped Denisovich's team had packed the right clothes for me.

"Another Golkov trip? I thought you weren't his T.A. anymore."

"I'm not. My cousin is sick, which is why this is so last minute, and I need to leave right now to catch a plane. I'm sorry, Casey. I'll text you later, okay?"

"O—kay," she said, not looking satisfied.

My eyes caught the glint of my car keys on the corner of my desk. "Here." I tossed her the keys. "You can use her while I'm gone."

Casey eyed the keys in her hands, hugged them to her chest, and smiled up at me. "Providence Place, here I come."

"Go easy on your parents' credit."

She lay back on her pillows. "Don't worry. I'll get you something too."

I escaped from our room while she still dangled the keys in front of her face. If I'd known the car would have done the trick, I would have given her the keys before she asked about Daly.

I raced down the hallway and used my Millard-enhanced keycard to let myself out of the building. Without that card, I would have been answering too many questions from the resident advisor.

We didn't exactly have a curfew, but our RA was pretty good about keeping track of us.

A man in a dark suit leaned against the side of a black car with tinted windows. "Ms. Laxer, I presume?"

"Yes."

He opened the back door. At the sound of another car door shutting behind us, the driver and I looked down the street. Daly strutted toward us with the suitcase the CIA had prepared for me in hand. "You won't make it far without this," he said in Russian. I looked to my driver, who didn't seem to understand or care.

I accepted the suitcase and let my hand rest on Daly's.

"You nervous?" he asked, not moving his hand.

"No," I lied.

"Everything will go as planned and you'll be back in no time."

"What if I'm not?"

"You will be." Daly leaned forward just a little. "But if you're ever struggling, just imagine I'm at your ear." He touched my earlobe and his palm brushed the side of my cheek.

"And what would you say?" I whispered.

"I'd tell you, 'Don't give up. Fight. Push yourself. Alexandra Stewart can make a masterpiece out of any canvas.'"

"You're kind of cheesy. You know that, right?"

"It's part of my charm."

I looked down at our hands, my fingers now intertwined with his. When my eyes returned to his face, his warm smile and honest eyes had me convinced I could do anything.

"Thank you," I said. "For the suitcase and the pep talk."

"Cairo," he said with a grin.

"Hmm?" I had been staring at his lips.

"We could escape to Egypt. Giza pyramids, mask of Tutankhamun, camels . . ."

I glanced at the driver, who averted his gaze. Taking the chance, I pulled Daly to me for a soft kiss. I felt as if we were being watched, but I didn't care. A few seconds later, I brushed my cheek against his and whispered in his ear, "I don't really like the heat."

"Could've fooled me," he said under his breath as I stepped back. I hid my face behind my hair as I bent to retrieve the suitcase. Daly always knew what to say to throw me off balance. I couldn't have replied even if I'd had a comeback. I turned and rolled my suitcase toward my ride. The driver took the case from me and let me slide into my seat, then closed the door. I glanced back at Daly one last time through the rear window. He was rubbing the back of his neck, the look on his face a cross between want and worry.

When my driver pulled up to the main terminal of Green Airport in Warwick, I couldn't help feeling disappointed. On missions for The Company, I always flew in a private jet.

"I'm flying from here?" I asked the driver.

"Dana Laxer is a seventeen-year-old aspiring artist from Providence, Rhode Island. Agent Denisovich thought it wise that she travel the same way any other student would." The driver handed me an envelope. I recalled the mission details but had only glanced over the part about how I would get to Mexico. Now, with the paperwork open in my mind, I realized it had mentioned commercial travel.

The driver opened my door and held out my suitcase. I slipped my backpack onto my shoulders and took the suitcase. "Good luck, Ms. Laxer. I hope you find what you're looking for." He climbed back into the car and drove away.

Inside the envelope, I found my plane ticket and another coded message from Denisovich about a change in my housing arrangement. I had planned to stay in an apartment near the school, but he had found me an open spot in their on-campus dorms. He thought being closer to the students might allow me to obtain more information. I couldn't argue with that, but the thought of a roommate I didn't know, particularly one with a different language and culture, started a flurry of unease in my stomach.

The flight from Providence to Newark was uneventful and probably would have been forgettable if it wasn't for my eidetic mind. Every face I saw was recorded, along with the person's seat number—information I'd never need again.

I slept for the first two hours of the flight from Newark to Mexico City, which was only possible because I'd gotten a window seat and my backpack had worked as a pillow.

"I wondered if you would sleep the whole way," a voice said next to me.

The man to my left put out his hand. "I'm Erik. Erik Goldberg."

"Dana." I shook his hand and then discreetly wiped the sweat from his palm onto my ratty jeans.

"It's my first time to Mexico. Big client there." Erik's blond hair was thinning in front, and his outfit made me think he might be color blind.

"That's cool." I was thankful my clothing change and the streak of red I'd added to the front of my hair in the Newark Airport bathroom helped me appear my age or younger. Would a high school student talk with a businessman on an airplane? *I should've brought my headphones.*

"I do cyber security," Erik said. "Last month, *Forbes* ranked our company as one of the top-ten best small companies." At my nod, he continued, "Cyberity—that's our name. Get it? 'Cause we do computers or cyber stuff and security." He chuckled nervously.

If this was his sales pitch, I wondered how his company could receive a *Forbes* ranking. Giving him the benefit of the doubt, I asked, "What makes your company different than others that provide the same services?" He could practice his pitch on me.

"We're not the same as other companies. That's why I'm on my way to Mexico City. We just landed two big clients there, and part of our brand is that we aren't just a software someone downloads and hopes it will protect their information and privacy. We personally create an in-house system of security for each client using software and hardware. No one has broken through our security yet."

I feigned indifference by pulling at a loose string on the knee hole of my jeans. Inwardly, I was thinking Millard would love to chat with this guy.

"You going on vacation or something?" Erik asked.

I flipped my hair like Casey always did. It seemed a very teenager thing to do. Now it was time to sell myself. "I'm on my way to art school. My parents think I have talent or something. I'm just glad to be in a big city and do something I love."

"So you're an artist then? Got a portfolio?"

"I . . . uh . . . I'm still working on that." I cringed, realizing the CIA should have provided me with one. "Guess that's why I need art school." I shrugged.

Erik laughed as if what I had said was absolutely hilarious. The plane lurched and he stopped laughing. He gripped the armrests, his face paling. "First time . . . on a plane too." He closed his eyes.

I grabbed my barf bag, ready to push it in his direction. "I was eight the first time I went on a plane." I thought maybe a story would distract him. "Nothing scared me at the time. I think at that point I still wanted to be an astronaut and a tightrope walker. I hadn't discovered art yet." I'd nearly forgotten I was Dana and not Alex. "I insisted on the window seat so I could view the tiny world below. What I didn't realize was that my brother, who was sitting next to me at the time, was miserable. He hated confined spaces, and any kind of jerky movement made him sick."

"I know the feeling." Erik started breathing deeply, in through his nose and out through his mouth. My mind flashed to Daly doing the same thing on our mission to Barcelona. I forced the memory from my mind. I'd just said goodbye and wasn't ready to think about him yet.

I leaned back in my chair and looked over at Erik's white face. "I was too young to be much help," I said, continuing my story, "but it was my mom who knew what to do."

Erik peeked at me. "What did she do?"

"She told him to close his eyes and imagine the best place he'd ever been." I closed my own eyes as I watched the scene in my head. "Once he'd chosen the place, she told him to take himself there. First, he was to imagine the sounds he could hear. Since he'd picked the carnival that came to our hometown each year, he described the music and the screams and laughter coming from the rides. Then she said to remember the tastes and smells. My brother remembered funnel cakes sprinkled in powdered sugar and topped with strawberries and cream—how the dessert was crunchy and creamy and sweet and tart all at the same time. When Mom told him to think of the things he could feel, he described the soft and sticky cotton candy, the cool and smooth surface of the seat on his favorite ride, the cushioning from the grass below his feet."

Erik's breathing had slowed and his eyes were shut, but he still appeared to be listening, so I went on. "The last thing she told him was to take in the sights. What colors did he see? What things did he notice that he'd nearly forgotten, like the view of the Columbia River as the Zipper raised him high in the air? Or how they tried to hide the line of porta potties, but the blue plastic always seemed to be visible. Or the apple blossoms on the trees across the way." I continued to tell my fellow passenger of Tanner's memories of the carnival until Erik's hands relaxed on the armrests.

After several minutes, he finally spoke, "My grandpa's farm in Kentucky—that's my best place." He began to describe the expansive wheat fields and the horse ranch next door. About halfway through his description, he opened his eyes and continued.

I tried to think of my best place. Daly had suggested Cairo or Tahiti. Though I understood the draw to those places, neither would be my first choice. Seeing Russia and parts of Europe on missions had been amazing, and looking back at them as movies in my head was priceless. But still, I wasn't sure where I would want to escape to if I could. Maybe Mexico would be it.

By the time our plane began the descent into Mexico City, Erik's nerdy personality and quirky stories had grown on me, and I felt grateful for the distraction. He thanked me for getting him through the flight and handed me his business card. "Just in case you ever want to feel secure," he said.

I laughed at that. Hopefully the CIA would give me all the security I needed on this mission.

11

Security

"*Buenos días,*" said the gorgeous brunette who met me at the door of my new dorm. "*Me llamo Sofía.*"

"*Soy Dana.*" I put out a hand. "*Mucho gusto.*"

Sofía led me into a large living room and pointed to an open doorway on the other end. "That's your room," she said in Spanish. I wasn't expecting to have my own place to sleep, since Casey and I had shared a room for several months. Terra-cotta tile lined the floors as far as I could see, and a vibrant circular rug covered the area between a love seat and couch in the living room.

If this was Mexico's idea of a dorm, I could get used to it. It felt more like a five-star hotel room or apartment. La Academia de Arte de Santa Catalina was located on a small rise near the center of the city. With the dorms on the upper floors of the school, the view was unobstructed by nearby buildings.

"Sorry about the mess," Sofía said. "The maid doesn't come until tomorrow and I've been so busy in the studio, I haven't had a chance to clean up." My new roommate walked to the side of the living room, where I noticed a refrigerator and stove. Not that my cooking was any good, but I liked the idea of having a kitchen.

"You have a maid?" I asked Sofía in Spanish.

"We all do. She takes the laundry and does the deep cleaning. We're supposed to pick up our stuff, but she's amazing to have around." Sofía rinsed a glass in the sink. "Do you want some water?"

"No, thank you," I said, remembering that you weren't supposed to drink the water in Mexico unless you grew up there, and many natives still avoided it.

"Don't worry—it's filtered. Like you, some of our students come from other countries, and the school makes sure all the tap water is safe to drink. Really."

"Okay then. I guess I will have some." She filled the glass and I drank the entire thing. Though the temperature was in the forties and fifties in Providence, Mexico City had to be nearly eighty, and the sun was even starting to set.

"Your Spanish is amazing," Sofía said. "Did you grow up speaking it?"

"No, I've just been studying it for several years. I've had some pretty good tutors." I thought of William and all our conversations. If it hadn't been for him, I doubt I would have felt so comfortable speaking Spanish.

Sofía smiled. "Tomorrow, everyone is headed up to Teotihuacan for the spring equinox. It's kind of a big deal here."

"Yeah, I've heard about it. I've always wanted to see the Pyramid of the Sun. You can just drive from here?"

She moved to the living room and sat on one of the couches, then picked up a sketchbook from the coffee table. "They cancel morning classes and one of the teachers drives our bus. I know, the bus is lame, but we all get to stay together during the drive. It's only about thirty minutes away. If we get there as the sun rises, it's pretty great. There are tons of people there, and drums and dancing." Sofía took a pencil and started drawing. "You don't have to come. It's not mandatory or anything, but over the next week or two the teachers like to see, in our artwork, the things we observe at the equinox."

I cleaned my glass and set it in the drying rack next to the sink. "I definitely want to go." It would give me a head start at getting to know the students here.

"Great." Sofía continued to draw. "Well, you probably want to unpack. If you need to shower tonight, the bathroom is right there." She pointed to a door on the other side of the kitchen.

"We have our own bathroom?" I'd had to share a bathroom with an entire floor of girls for the past six months.

She raised her eyebrows. "Um, yeah. You and I will have to share it, but I'm sure we can work out shower times and stuff. I need to finish this drawing before Teotihuacan tomorrow, but I'd love to chat more. Maybe after you get your things put away?"

"Yes, I'd love that." I picked up my backpack and rolled my suitcase toward my new bedroom.

"Welcome to Mexico, by the way. I hope you like it."

"Me too," I said.

I stared at the ceiling fan as it spun slowly. The blades were made of a dark wood carved into leaf shapes. I'd stayed up for a few hours the night before with Sofía. She drew in her sketchbook while asking me questions about my life in the States. Though I'd had to stretch part of my story, I'd tried to stay true to the real Alex when talking of things I liked, and friendships and boys. She seemed to understand my dilemma about dating someone older. Apparently she had fallen for one of the construction workers who installed a pool at the dorms the previous year. He was four years older and now lived in Guadalajara. They kept in touch, but Sofía admitted that the fire in their relationship had waned after he left.

I wondered about Daly. Would we lose that fire now that I was gone? And what about William? If I cared for Daly, why did William's image flash across my vision when I least expected it?

I got up and made my bed. The fluffy white comforter was nothing like my old green fur one back at my dorm in Providence, but it fit in perfectly with the beachy feeling of my room. I wondered if I would fit in here too.

A light knock came at my door. "You up, Dana?"

"Yes. I'll be out in a minute." I looked in the full-length mirror beside the bed. I rarely wore a lot of makeup, but to go along with the red streak in my hair and the grunge/artsy image I wanted to project, I applied thick black liner to my eyes. My worn-out black jeans, combat boots, and fitted black T-shirt pulled together the look. I blinked at my disguise and tested an I-could-care-less smile. I frowned. Who was I kidding? I still looked like Alex.

"You ready to meet the sun gods?" Sofía filled a water bottle at the sink and tucked it into a backpack. The red silk scarf draped around her neck stood out against her white peasant top.

"I wouldn't be getting up this early for anyone else." Actually, that wasn't true. Early morning runs before sunrise were routine for me in Providence.

"You'll want to pack plenty of water," Sofía said. "There are always vendors up there, but they charge a lot and you just never know what you're going to get. The school will have packed lunches on the bus."

"Great." I filled my empty water bottle and accepted another from Sofía to put in my backpack. The CIA had given me plenty of cash, so I carried some with me just in case. The agency had said they would get in touch with me later that day to discuss communications and to receive any information I'd obtained.

When we arrived at the pickup spot, Sofía introduced me to a few girls before we found a seat in the center of the bus. Everyone looked in my direction as we sat down. I pretended not to notice. Alex might have been self-conscious at the attention, but Dana wouldn't have cared less.

A boy with a red scarf tied around his neck sat down across the aisle and faced Sofía and me. "Hi, I'm Enrique. You're the new student, right?"

"Of course she's the new student, Ricky. Now take your ego and white jeans and find another girl to harass." Sofía turned her back to him and told me, "Just ignore him. He's tried to date every girl at La Academia, and I'm sure he'd just love to conquer one more."

"Got it." I peeked over her shoulder. Enrique mouthed something like "I'll find you later" and moved up a few seats.

"Now him—him you can drool over. Everyone else does." Sofía nodded toward a guy now getting on the bus. His head almost touched the ceiling, and his silky black hair fell over one eye. "He was dating Amori . . ." Sofía's voice dropped and she looked down at her lap. "Anyway, he was dating someone, but he isn't anymore."

Blood pumped through my veins in a frenzy. *Amoriel*. I'd just arrived in Mexico and was hearing her name without even asking about her. Maybe this mission would be quicker than I'd hoped.

"Who was he dating?" I asked. I pretended to do a visual search of the bus, then waited for Sofía to point out the lucky girl.

"She's not here anymore," Sofía said stiffly and faced the window. The black-haired boy sat a row in front of us, and the rest of the bus filled with students. As the vehicle headed down the road, I noticed that most of the teens and even the teachers wore white shirts. Several of them, like Enrique, even wore white pants. They had accented the white with something red, like a strap of fabric tied around their waist or head, or a scarf or a red-beaded necklace around their necks.

"Why is everyone wearing white?" I finally asked Sofía.

She eyed my choice of clothing like she was just seeing it for the first time. "I guess I should have warned you. I was distracted this morning. Wait, is that a white tank under your T-shirt?"

"Yes."

"You're going to want to take off your shirt."

"Why?" I pulled on the hem of my black T-shirt. I didn't usually wear tank tops alone.

"The whole idea of the spring equinox is renewal. Everyone wears white, and when we get to the top of the pyramid, we let the sun's rays soak into us. It's a tradition. I think half of the people there don't even get it."

"Why the red?" I pointed to her scarf.

"Red and white are supposed to absorb the sun's good energy the best." Sofía reached down to her backpack and pulled out a beaded necklace. "Here." She handed me the beads. "Just take off the black T-shirt and wear the beads. It will look perfect."

I glanced around. When I was sure everyone was busy chatting or looking out the windows, I pulled off my T-shirt and donned the beads. Out of the corner of my eye, I saw the black-haired boy glance in my direction before he turned to face the front of the bus again. I replayed the memory in slow motion. He had been looking at me.

Sofía adjusted the rows of beads around my neck. "Wow. That looks great with the red in your hair. You may just absorb *all* of the good energy from the sun. Or at least all the stares from every guy that sees you."

"I doubt that." I tucked my black shirt into my bag.

My roommate smiled at me. "Learn to take a compliment, Dana. You'll find that talking about appearance is just a part of everyday language here. If someone is beautiful, we tell them. If someone is skinny or fat, it's not an insult, it's part of who they are. It's just how we are here—you'll have to get used to it."

"Okay." I'd read about the differences between our two cultures, but it was the first time I had actually experienced this aspect of Mexican culture for myself.

"Speaking of the male population of the school, Luca keeps looking at you," Sofía said quietly next to my ear.

"Luca?"

"Black-haired gorgeous boy, to our left. Of course he'd be interested in the new girl."

All this attention would have killed the real Alex. Even as Dana, I had to look out the window to hide the dark shade of pink I could feel rising up from my neck.

The timing of my turn was perfect. I nearly missed it as our bus drove past the Metropolitan Cathedral. It was a cross between a medieval castle and a Catholic church, with two large towers, and several turrets and domes. I hadn't read much about it but knew it was the largest and oldest cathedral in North America.

"Don't worry. You'll get plenty of chances to see it up close. One of my teachers takes the class there once a week to sketch the architecture and statues."

"Really? Doesn't it get boring?" That was a Dana comment. Alex was trying not to press her face against the glass to get a better look. My mom would have loved this place.

"I thought it would, except there are like fifteen chapels inside, and lots of artwork, too," Sofía said. "It probably doesn't come close to the Louvre, but it's like a museum inside. The exterior is even cooler in the daylight when you can see the statues and everything better."

We sat in silence as the rest of Mexico City passed by in a blur of old world and new. There were skyscrapers on one side of the street and beautiful statues on the other. I could have stared out the window all day, but I was meeting with the CIA later that night and wanted to have something to give them.

"Sofía, can I ask you something?"

"Sure, I'm an open book, though if you're asking about Luca, I should warn you he's hard to read."

"No, no. Not him. I know you had a roommate before me. I was just wondering why she left school in the middle of a term."

Sofía flinched. "Art school isn't for everyone," she said, not looking at me.

"So she just left?"

"Honestly, Dana, I don't know." Her words took on a bitter edge. "And I don't even care." She still kept her eyes forward as she pulled at her scarf.

"Sorry, I didn't mean to—"

"It's not your fault." Her breaths came out short and constricted. "I'm just mad at her is all."

I turned to face Sofía. "Mad? Because she left?"

"No. I mean, yes." Sofía looked at me, her dark-brown eyes glossy with anger and maybe sadness. "I just wish she'd said something to me. Her room was just cleared one day when I got home, with a little note that she was done with art school. She didn't even tell me in person. And she hasn't responded to my texts or calls. It's been over two weeks. We were like best friends."

"I'm sorry, Sofía. I didn't realize."

"No, it's fine." She shook her head. "If she wanted to talk to me, she would."

I touched Sofía's arm. I wasn't sure if it was a Dana thing or an Alex thing to do or why I felt the need to comfort her. Maybe it was because as far as the CIA and I knew, Amoriel had no way of contacting anyone.

Sofía looked to the road ahead. "That's why I need this today. My family used to go to the pyramids in Teotihuacan all the time, but especially during this time of year. God is watching us, and I believe that today he will bless us with the warm energy of the sun." My roommate glanced at me again. "And maybe some answers, too."

"I think we could all use that." I squeezed her arm and let go. I hadn't planned on making any friends in Mexico, but somehow this girl was quickly becoming one.

The view of the Avenue of the Dead right before sunrise was strangely serene and incredible at the same time. Photos and videos of a landmark could never replace the real thing, and this was no exception. We stood at the end of the ceremonial plaza the Spanish conquistadores had called the La Ciudadela—the Citadel. I couldn't take my eyes off the road flanked on either side with what looked like small pyramids. Stone stairs led up to a platform at the top, which was probably seventy or eighty feet high. I counted at least ten such platforms in the distance.

"The temple of Quetzalcoatl." Sofía pointed to a pyramid to our right. It wasn't the largest in the area, but its striking façade was adorned with a massive sculpture of what I'd heard someone say was a serpent and a rain god. "I like the look of this one the best," Sofía continued. "It's all the original stone and everything. The sun and moon pyramids had to be restored on some of the sides."

"You sure do know your stuff."

"My brother used to do tours here on Sundays before he graduated from college."

"You have an older brother?" For the first time in months, thinking of Tanner didn't make my throat constrict.

"Yeah, he moved to Guadalajara last year. My parents nearly flipped when I told them I applied to go to La Academia. They wanted me to stay at home and take art classes. I think they just didn't want to be home without me and my brother."

"Do you see them often—your family?" I asked. We walked with a concord of people down the avenue toward the Pyramid of the Sun. I recognized most of the group closest to us as students from the bus.

"Yeah. They insist we eat dinner together every week. Since they live in Mexico City, it's not a big deal to leave campus one night a week. You should come next time."

I smiled at her before taking a sip of my water bottle. The place of the main celebration was still about half a mile away. I squinted in the direction of the sun, which had yet to peek over the mountains in the distance. But the sky was turning from a dark blue to a light one. On the horizon, a faint orange hue began to color the sky.

Sofía had been right about the tank top and beads. Nearly every person on the road wore something white, and I would have felt out of place in my dark clothes. Luca started to pass in front of us. When he glanced back and saw me over his shoulder, he fell into step with us.

"*Hola, Sofía*," he said to my roommate and then turned back to me. "*Me llamo Luca*." I shook his outstretched hand. "You're new to La Academia, right?"

"*Sí. Me llamo Dana*."

"*Mucho gusto, Dana*. Are you from the south?"

I figured he meant south of Mexico, which I took as a compliment. Maybe all of William's tutoring had helped more than I thought. "No, I'm American."

"*Americano*? Guess I should have assumed that." He pointed to my blond hair.

"She's from the tiniest state in the U.S.—Rhode Island." Sofía linked her arm in mine.

"That's cool. So why come all the way from Rhode Island?" He tried to say the state name with an English accent but didn't quite get it right.

"Art school, obviously," Sofía answered for me.

"Plus I was looking for a change. I've studied Spanish for a long time. When I found out about La Academia and its focus on art, I couldn't pass it up." I fingered the beads at my neck. The idea of change resonated with me, not just Dana. Did I really want to work for the CIA? I had yet to hear back from the Slavic Studies Program and wasn't sure if I was disappointed or relieved.

"Is this your first visit to the pyramids?" Luca asked at my side.

"Yes." I stared toward the Pyramid of the Sun. We were still at least a quarter mile away. "I hope we make it there in time."

"We'll make it," Luca said with a teasing smile, "if we run." He grabbed my hand, pulling Sofía and me behind him. I could have easily released myself from his grasp, but I let him tow us down the dirt road and past all the ancient platforms. We zoomed by hundreds of people headed in the same direction. When we arrived at the base of the pyramid a couple minutes later, we were all panting.

Drums played by one corner of the massive pyramids, and a group of dancers moved in time with the music. The bare-chested men wore white wraps that resembled skirts. The women were in long white dresses. Intricate Aztec designs adorned the edges of the dancers' clothing. Some of the men sported large headdresses made of wood carvings and big feathers in various bright colors.

"Do we go up to the top?" I asked. Groups of people walked up the wide set of stairs leading to the pyramid's top platform. Thousands of other people stood or sat on the grassy areas surrounding the pyramid, while others gathered around the dirt-covered base.

Luca finally dropped my hand. "Yes, but no more running. The pyramid is like a chapel to many people here. People show a kind of reverence once they reach it."

"Why isn't everyone coming to the top?" I asked quietly as we ascended the steps.

"Not everyone can make it. There are 248 steps. Others have either done it before or don't know the significance," Sofía said.

We continued up the stone stairs, our heavy breathing not quite drowned out by the hordes of people and the drumming of the music below. A sheen of sweat showed on Luca's face, making me grateful for my tank top and for the physical training I'd done with The Company.

"Give me a minute." Sofía sat down on the step in front of her and wiped her face on her scarf. "I forgot how tiring this can be." She wasn't the only one resting. Several white-clad people leaned on their knees or took a seat on the steps. The pink tinge of eminent sunrise decorated the sky above us.

"Come on." I pulled Sofía to her feet. "If I've come this far, I don't want to miss the first rays of the sun."

Five minutes later, we arrived at our destination—along with several hundred other people. The music from below had faded, and so had the hushed voices on the pyramid. Everyone faced east, awaiting the sunrise. I found myself enthralled with the reverence of the participants. The expressions on their faces told me they truly believed the gods would send them good energy through the sun. The feeling of expectation was contagious. Just as the first rays peeked over the horizon, the crowd spread their arms wide, closed their eyes, and let the sunbeams reach into them. On either side of me, Sofía and Luca did the same as the crowd, their faces alight with sunshine.

I had started to close my eyes when an eerie, tingling sensation crept up my spine. I wasn't sure if it was The Company training or just an innate sense of awareness, but I knew if I turned around I would find someone staring at me. My training had taught me not to draw attention to my discovery. I stretched out my arms and let the sun warm my skin, though the heat couldn't penetrate the cold feeling inside me. After several minutes of silence, people around us began to move, so I took my chance and I peeked over my shoulder. Some people still had their eyes closed and their faces toward the sun. Others had their heads bent in prayer.

Suddenly, movement at the back of the crowd caught my eye. A dark-haired man with a billowing white tunic snaked through the crowd and disappeared from the platform. Not until he was no longer visible did I let out the breath I'd been holding.

Is the CIA following me? No, I was certain they would've let me know beforehand if they had a detail on me. A feeling of dread settled in the hollow of my stomach that I was sure trail mix and bottled water couldn't cure.

Luca and Sofía and I remained on top of the platform for another half hour. A few guys from the bus had found him, and they moved to the edge of the platform to talk quietly with one another. Sofía didn't move from her original spot, her eyes closed as the sun beat against her skin. I stared out across the valley and to the mountains. The familiarity of the scene pulled a memory from the deep recesses of my mind—an event I'd never recalled. Until now.

12

La Academia

"How much farther to the top?" Tanner dragged his eleven-year-old legs along the trail behind me.

"We've only been hiking a couple miles," Mom replied, joining me in front of Tanner and my dad.

"I think I just got bitten by a mosquito," Dad said. "I thought you said this bug spray repelled insects." He gave my mom a questioning glance. His orange hat blocked the sun from his face, and I could smell the coconut-scented sunscreen he'd spread over every exposed bit of his skin.

"Did you put it on under your sunscreen?" my mom asked.

I smiled. "You smell kind of yummy to me, Dad. I bet those bugs think so too. And your hat kind of looks like a pretty flower." I turned back to the trail.

"Next time we'll bring sunscreen with bug repellent in it. And I'll pack the hats." Mom winked at me, and we continued up the trail.

"Do they sell wilderness repellent too? Can't we just go to Disneyland like a normal family?" Tanner huffed behind us. Sleeping in a tent on hard ground without TV or running water wasn't his idea of fun. He loved being outdoors, but preferred his outdoors to include a swimming pool and ice-cold drinks.

"Once we get to the top you'll see it's worth it." My mom increased her pace. I tried to keep up.

"Race you to the next overlook?" she asked me.

I answered by running up the trail. Ten minutes later, we both stopped at a flat area with a sign that said "Freemont Lookout Tower: 1.3 miles." One side of the mountain path was covered in grass and shrubs, while the other side appeared desert-like, with barely a living thing in sight.

"Where are all the trees?" I asked.

"Don't worry. We'll be surrounded by them soon enough," my mom said. "But when we get closer to the top, they'll disappear again and we'll be hiking on rocks."

"Where's Dad and Tanner?" I glanced back.

"I'm sure they're close. Drink some water. We still have a steep hike ahead of us."

A few minutes later, Dad and Tanner trudged up the trail and dropped to the ground next to the path. "We're close now, right?" Dad asked. He removed his hat and wiped his sweat-drenched face on one of his shirt sleeves. Tanner poured some of his water over his own head.

Mom pointed to the sign. "Do you guys think you can make it another 1.3 miles?"

Tanner's eyes pleaded with Dad, who looked at the trail. Dad might not have been the most outdoorsy person, but he wasn't one to give up, especially this close to the goal. "We can make it." He put his hat back on. "How about this? If we all make it to the top and back to our campsite, with no complaints, we'll get a hotel tomorrow in Seattle and go out to dinner. How does that sound?"

Tanner jumped to his feet. "Sounds like a plan." He turned to me. "Want to beat Mom and Dad to the top?"

"Yes!" I chased after him along the trail. Dad yelled for us to slow down, but we continued racing to the top.

Twenty minutes later, Tanner and I sat on the deck of the lookout tower, dangling our feet below us.

"I wonder how much longer Mom and Dad will be," I said to my brother.

"I don't care as long as we get to rest longer." Tanner put his chin on the railing and stared at the view. *Everywhere I looked were mountains, some covered in evergreen trees, others still topped with snow. I recognized Mount Rainier from the pictures at the visitor's center and pointed out the peak to Tanner.*

"How do you know that's it?" he asked.

"Duh!" I tapped my skull.

"Yeah, sometimes I forget how you can see things." It was quiet for a minute before his head shot up. "Lexie, it's like a super power. You could be . . . you could be like a secret weapon. Or . . ." He threw his arms out to the sides, one of his hands barely missing my head. "A spy. You could totally be a spy."

"Don't they have to, like, kill people and stuff?" All I knew about spies had come from a James Bond movie we had watched in Mom and Dad's room when they didn't know we'd sneaked in.

"Yeah, you might have to do that, but maybe you could be a good one," Tanner said. "You could have a code or something, like how Daredevil won't kill anyone."

"Daredevil?"

"Don't you read anything cool?"

I was about to come back with something when we heard our parents' voices.

"You kids okay?" Mom asked.

I peeked over the edge to find her standing next to Dad, who was hunched over, fanning himself with his hat.

"Are you guys okay?" Tanner called to them.

"Just fine. All's good." Still breathing hard, Dad raised a finger in front of him. "I'll bet Captain Vancouver . . . never climbed this ridge before he named Rainier."

Mom patted Dad's shoulder. "I'm pretty sure these trails didn't exist in the 1700s."

"Right you are," he said. They both sat on a large flat rock about eight feet below us.

Tanner lay back against the wooden platform and closed his eyes. I continued to take in the scenery of the Northwest while Mom and Dad talked below.

"How's that project at work?" Dad asked. "The Monet one."

"It's not coming together as I'd hoped," Mom replied. "We're considering putting it on hold for a while. There are other things more pressing right now."

"Hmm. Anything I can help with?" Dad said.

"Unless you can go back in time, I think this one might be a hopeless cause. Besides, from what I've found, there is a strong possibility the painting was destroyed in a fire. I guess I was holding out hope that no one would let a painting like Waterloo Bridge go up in flames."

"A time machine, eh? I'd put all my money on someone who could invent that."

"Of course you would," she said.

"But Iolanta, maybe you shouldn't give up on the project altogether. If there's one thing I've learned about the study of history, and I've learned a lot . . ." Mom laughed at that before Dad continued. "Sometimes the pieces of history don't come together until years later. When we look back on things like the Civil War, we can see things now that they didn't see then. Maybe the missing piece isn't there because it's not ready to be found."

"Are you going to quote President Adams again?" Mom used a teasing tone of voice, but I sensed disappointment as well.

"Ah yes, the patience and perseverance mantra. But no, I wasn't going to say that."

"Really?"

"I was just going to suggest we run back to camp, pack up, and head into town. I know the mountain men of the past had patience with wilderness" —Dad paused to put on his hat— "but I'm beginning to think the inventions of running water and flushing toilets might be right up there with time machines."

"Are you okay, Dana?" Sofía asked when we arrived back at our dorm room, sweaty, thirsty, and caked with dust.

"Yeah, I'm good. That was really amazing. I think I'm just feeling the effects of traveling."

"I'm sure the teachers would understand if you skipped class today. You look like you could use some rest."

"Thanks, Sofía. I think you're right." I was tired, but more than that, I needed an excuse to meet with the CIA. Running off alone after dinner probably wouldn't go unnoticed.

"I'll jump in the shower real quick and then you can have it all to yourself," Sofía offered. "I will explain to Señora Lomez once I get to class. She's pretty lax. Just make sure you're on time tomorrow morning to Sketchbook Drawing. Señor Gonzales may be handsome, but he's a stickler for rules."

"Got it." I headed to the kitchen for a drink of water. "Thanks, Sofía. For today."

"*De nada*," she replied before disappearing into the bathroom.

After my own shower, I donned a pair of skinny jeans and a Bon Jovi T-shirt, then left our dorm and headed down the stairs. Somehow, I managed to leave the building without running into any students or teachers.

From the street, La Academia looked more like a mansion than a school. Set back from the street, it boasted a gated entrance and a large grassy field out front. A walk-through gate allowed me to exit with a key I'd received upon arrival, though the fence and the trees dotting the front yard wouldn't have been much of a deterrent.

I donned my large sunglasses and followed the sidewalk until it reached a street lined with cars and city buses. Clearly, Mexico City had their own problems with rush hour. It took me about ten minutes to find 16 de Septiembre, the street where the Gran Hotel was located.

While I didn't understand why the CIA needed to meet at a five-star hotel, after seeing the exterior of the place I certainly wasn't going to complain. It was like stepping away from Mexico for a moment and into old-time Europe. The hotel reached above me several stories, with concrete columns and large windows adorning the front. The center of the lobby was open all the way to the ceiling which was actually a stained-glass domed window that curved from one side of the room to another. I removed my sunglasses and stood in the center of the room for a minute before reminding myself I wasn't there to appreciate the architecture.

The black, cage-like elevator on one end of the lobby allowed the occupants to admire the open balconies of each floor as they traveled to the upper floors of the building. I made my way to the elevator, keeping a close eye on the people around me. The elevator stopped on each floor on the way up, allowing me extra time to view the Art Nouveau architecture.

I exited the elevator on the fourth floor and walked along the balcony until I stood in front of the room indicated in the CIA's instructions. Before I even raised a hand to knock, the door opened and I was quickly ushered in by a man in his thirties wearing a white shirt and navy slacks. The room was smaller than I had expected, with a large king bed in the center. The bed had been converted into a desk of sorts and was covered with laptops and computer equipment. A man and woman in business attire sat at chairs that had been pushed up to the bed, while three other people I assumed were agents typed away at laptops set up on a long table near the window.

"I'm glad you made it," Agent Denisovich said as he stepped out of the bathroom. His brown hair was shorter than when I'd seen him in Providence, and the bottom half of his face was still pink from a recent shave.

"I don't have much time," I said. "If I'm going to keep my cover, I need to be back before my roommate returns from classes."

"Understood." He went to the bed and picked up a necklace that had been lying next to a bundle of wires. "First off, we need you to wear this." He held out the gold chain with an arrowhead-shaped charm dangling from the center. "It has a camera so we can watch what you are seeing."

As I put on the necklace, I wondered if Casey would approve, but decided I probably shouldn't ask how much research the CIA had done on current fashion. Besides, I'd noticed that Mexican fashion didn't follow the same trends I was accustomed to in Providence.

"So you'll be watching me the whole time?" I asked.

"And listening. Of course we won't see you, but we'll see what you do. It will help us keep you safe, and we will use the footage to get clues as to Amoriel's whereabouts."

"Okay. What else?"

"We'd like a daily report on your findings. We have been unable to get an agent on the inside to pose as an administrator or teacher. Unless that changes, we will send an agent from this room to meet you near the school each night. A location will be texted to you when we feel it is safe and we can do it inconspicuously."

"Can't you just use the video footage?" I asked.

"We will be using that, but we would also like a face-to-face meeting where you can share anything you have learned."

"Anything else?"

"Don't forget the mission details. Interact with the students and teachers. Watch for anything that seems amiss. Ask questions."

I almost wished I could tell him that forgetting the details was entirely impossible for me. Instead I just nodded as I touched the necklace at my collarbone. The cool metal felt cool against my skin. The memory from the Pyramid of the Sun and the sensation of being watched shot through my mind. I glanced around the room again to see if any of the agents' hair color or shoulder width matched that of the person who'd been watching me.

"Have you already assigned agents to follow me?" I asked Denisovich.

"No, we wouldn't put an agent on you. It's too risky at this point, since we don't know who is involved and whether they would notice a tail on you. We haven't informed the school administration of our mission, though they were questioned when Amoriel disappeared and probably suspect she didn't just leave."

An arctic chill sped up my spine. *Did I only imagine the dark-haired man was following me?* Maybe being on a mission with so many possibilities and no real leads was messing with my head.

"You are a CIA operative now, Dana," Denisovich told me. "Everything you do and say must reflect that, meaning no one should ever know who you really are or what you are trying to find out."

I smoothed back my hair with its red streak and glanced down at the fringed black shirt, tight jeans, and combat boots Alex would have never worn. At least I was off to a great start at being someone other than myself.

Agent Denisovich's face grew solemn. He glanced around the room before moving a little closer to me. "Please find her."

I gave him a sympathetic smile before I put my sunglasses back on and exited the room. After the door closed behind me, I let out a breath. The CIA was counting on me to find more clues about Amoriel's whereabouts, and I needed to do it fast. Even more importantly, Denisovich was counting on me.

13

Daredevil

My phone alarm went off too soon, at seven in the morning. I'd spent several hours the night before on the phone with Daly, probably not the smartest choice since this was my first day of classes and I had to be at the top of my game. Over a gray tank, I slipped on a grungy black shirt with small tears and holes all over, then pulled on the jeans from the day before. It took nearly ten minutes to line my eyes in black to complete my look. I darkened the red steak in my hair with hair chalk, since washing it the night before had dulled the color.

Sofía was eating a piece of mango at the dining room table when I emerged from my room. "Up late talking to a guy?" she asked. "Which one was it—the one you worked with or the one who used to be your teacher?"

Having told her about both William and Daly, I couldn't help the flood of color to my cheeks that probably matched the red chalk in my hair. I'd even told her about seeing William before I left.

"The coworker," I mumbled, then found a mango in the bowl on the counter and cut myself a slice.

"So there's no chance for the curly-haired one with paisley vests?"

This girl doesn't miss a beat. I wondered if her memory was something akin to my own.

"I broke up with him." The scene played through my mind— me standing in William's living room right after the Paris mission, finally realizing the reason I couldn't be with him had less to do with protecting him from my spy life, and more to do with my feelings for someone else. I also hadn't told William about my real life outside of being a student. He didn't know about my agent work with Golkov, or anything about The Company.

"Yeah, but I saw your face when you talked about him," Sofía went on. "Are you sorry you broke up with him?"

I stuffed another piece of mango in my mouth and let the sweet juices run down the back of my throat. I couldn't lie to myself and say I had no feelings for William, but I also couldn't hold back the truth: he'd never known all of me. And that had been my choice.

"So this Señor Gonzales is good-looking, huh?" I asked.

"Nice segue, Dana." Smiling, Sofía studied my face. "Yes, he is *guapo*, but we aren't done with this conversation."

"If we don't leave soon, I might have to explain to this Señor Gonzales about the crush you have on him." I took one last bite of mango and picked up my backpack, which was filled with a new sketch pad and drawing tools.

"I do not."

"Then you won't mind arriving a few minutes early so you can come with me to introduce myself."

"Fine." She set her knife in the sink and tossed the mango cores into the trash. "But I don't have a crush on him."

"Prove it." I waited by the front door while she stuffed her things in her backpack.

We arrived downstairs two minutes later and entered a room with rows of chairs and tilted sketch tables. Bookcases lining the walls on both sides of the room were filled with an array of books, many of which looked like they were older than La Academia itself.

Señor Gonzales sat at the front of the room behind a dark-stained wood table. When Sofía and I walked through the doorway, he looked up from a stack of papers and grinned. I realized she was right when she'd called him handsome. Dimples on both sides of his cheeks accented his bright-white smile. He wore his wavy black hair nearly shoulder-length and tucked behind his ears.

"*Buenos días,* Ms. Isla. And this must be our newest addition, Dana Laxer?" He stood and offered me a hand. His eyes, in a light shade of green that almost looked silver, were so distracting that it took me a second to shake his hand. If he'd tried to kiss it, I probably would have let him.

"Yes," Sofía answered for me. "Dana is my new roommate."

"Good morning," he said in English. I still hadn't recovered from his mesmerizing eyes to speak.

"You don't have to talk to her in English. Her Spanish is *perfecto.*" Sofía looped her arm through mine.

"Where did you learn Spanish?" asked Señor Gonzales.

"Uh, high school and college," I mumbled.

"College?" he and Sofía said at the same time. It took me a moment to realize my mistake. I was supposed to be a high school student from Providence, not a college student. *What is wrong with me?*

"Yeah, I took Spanish classes at the college after I finished all the ones the high school offered. My parents really wanted to me to become fluent." At least that was partly true, about taking classes at the college, but I'd nearly blown my cover.

"Well, *bievenidos a Mexico.* I hope you like what you've seen so far. I had to miss the celebration at Teotihuacan yesterday, but I heard it went very well. Did you attend?"

"Yes. The pyramids were more incredible than I'd imagined," I said. "I feel lucky to have been here."

"I hope you both received enough good energy for the coming year."

"*Gracias,*" Sofía and I said together.

"Ms. Isla, why don't you show Ms. Laxer where she can sit? I have a few things to finish before our lesson begins." Señor Gonzales returned to a sheet of paper in front of him, which I now noticed was a drawing of the Pyramid of the Sun. He picked up a pencil and added texture to the background with a swift hand. I would have continued to watch as he added trees and even tiny people to the drawing, but Sofía pulled on my arm and led me to the second row of chairs.

"I like to sit close to the middle," she explained. "You can sit next to me if you like."

"Thanks." I pulled out a chair and relaxed into it, my eyes finding their way back to Señor Gonzalez.

Sofía lightly slapped my arm and whispered, "Told you. Now try not to stare too obviously."

"Sorry." I pulled out my sketchbook and a few charcoal pencils of differing thicknesses.

Sofía introduced me to a few of the other students. All the girls wore makeup and were dressed way too nice for school. I'd barely brushed my hair and added my Dana eyeliner. Luca got there just before class began. His side brushed my back as he passed by.

"As we discussed last time, we are going to concentrate this week on perspective." Señor Gonzales reached behind him and pulled out a six-inch replica of what must've been the Pyramid of the Sun. "I want each of you to look at this pyramid. When I hold it this way" —he turned it so the top faced us— "what do you notice?"

A girl wearing a red peasant top raised her hand.

"Yes, Ms. Rubia?"

"The top platform is much smaller than the base. From the bird's-eye perspective we can see that the pyramid is square at the bottom," she said.

"Now, what if I turn it this way?" Señor Gonzales moved the pyramid so the back faced us.

"You can see that the shape is triangular and that the pyramid is not quite as tall when looking straight on, because the platform cuts off the tip of the triangle," answered a guy in our row. "Since we are looking at the back, all the converging lines will lead to that side."

"Nice, Mr. Jarom. Good observation."

I pulled the memory of the real pyramid from my mind and studied the lines and shapes. The replica obviously didn't provide the same effect as the actual pyramid, but I didn't know how to explain the difference, especially using artists' terms. I made a mental note to get online and learn about perspective as well as anything else relating to sketching and drawing.

"Today, I want you to draw the pyramid from any perspective of your choosing," Señor Gonzales told the class. "But I want the whole sketch to follow that perspective. If you choose bird's-eye view, then everything needs to be from that perspective. If you choose a ground-level view, don't forget your overlap. Find your horizon and be certain your parallel lines converge at the vanishing point. Also, make sure you know where your horizon is. You can do two-point perspective or one-point. We won't focus on three-point until next week. Any questions?"

Um, yes. My mind was at a loss. Somehow I hadn't realized art school was more than knowing artists and paintings. Apparently knowing all about famous artists wasn't going to help me draw like one.

Señor Gonzales set the pyramid on the table. "All right. Let's get to work. You've got about thirty minutes here in class. The assignment is due at the beginning of class tomorrow."

Zippers opened and closed, papers rustled, and pencils began moving. The blank page stared at me. I didn't know where to begin or even how. Like any normal child, I had colored and drawn in grade school, but as I grew older other things became more interesting to me. Even with a mother obsessed with art, who could often be found in her small studio restoring pieces of art or creating her own, I had never picked up a brush or drawn anything besides doodles on the side of my school papers.

I peered again at the small model on the teacher's table. It was a perfect replica of the Pyramid of the Sun. All I had to do was press my charcoal tip to the paper. The room was quiet except for the sound of utensil against paper. Students around me were hard at work. Sofía's pyramid was already taking shape. She used the side of her pencil to shade in the back of her structure, making it appear three-dimensional on her page. Señor Gonzales was rounding the corner of our row and would be at my table in less than a minute. I forced myself to draw one line and then another, trying to capture the triangular shape of the model from the front.

"That's interesting, Dana." He leaned over my shoulder. "To create depth, you might want to imagine there's a focal point here." He touched a cool finger to my forehead, sending a shiver through me. "Have each of your lines move away from you like you have a string coming out of your head."

"Okay." I stared down at my attempt. The large triangle could've been drawn by a kindergartner. Señor Gonzales continued down our row.

Create depth. I could do that. I drew a line behind the pyramid, going away from me. Now my pyramid appeared to have some sort of antenna sticking out of the top. I spent the rest of class erasing and redrawing lines until my pyramid at least looked like a shape. Sofía and the other students near me had added the landscape, trees, and other pyramids to their drawings. As soon as class ended, I flipped my sketchbook closed, hoping no one had seen my work.

"Don't worry," Sofía reassured me on our way to our art history class. "It will take some time to get your bearings here."

I raised an eyebrow at her, not sure time could help me.

By the time lunch rolled around, I'd discovered two more things about myself. I might be able to break codes, climb ropes, and fight off opponents with my hands, but I couldn't make a recognizable shape out of clay. I also had no sense of artistic placement. Though I was pretty good on computers, graphic design was like a new language where I didn't understand the rules. I recognized when others' work looked good, but I had no idea how to get there.

By the end of a very long day, all I wanted to do was fall onto my bed, close my eyes, and not think about colors, perspective, or how to keep my clay moist. Unfortunately, I only had a few hours until my meeting with a CIA agent. And I had nothing to report.

"A few of us are meeting at a club tonight. Want to come?" Sofía asked as we finished our dinner of boiled chicken with a sauce that had a strange combination of poblano peppers, spices, and chocolate.

"I better stay and do homework. You should go, though, and have some fun." I picked up my plate and headed to the sink.

"You sure? I don't mind sticking around."

"No, I'm really fine."

"Okay. But this weekend, I'm forbidding you from doing any homework at night. I need to show you how we really party here."

I smiled at her. "Sounds good to me."

An hour later, she was teetering out the door in bright-red heels and a black dress even Casey would have called too short.

Ignoring my homework, I wandered about the apartment, making sure I knew everything I could about Sofía. Not that I didn't trust her. I just needed to start by taking everyone out of the equation who wasn't involved in Amoriel's disappearance. After a thorough search of Sofía's bedroom (lots of cute clothes, and amazing artwork she'd done), I decided that either she was a great actress or she was exactly who she said she was.

I'd met several other students that day, none of which seemed likely to be involved in anything, but maybe I could get more information by talking with them. I headed down the hall to the dormitory lobby on the third floor. Sofía had said the boys shared rooms on the west half of the mansion, and the girls were on the east half. The lobby was the central point where students often hung out.

"You should have seen his face," said a boy with shaggy hair as he pulled on a light jacket.

"I would have rather seen hers," Luca said, standing with his back to me.

The shaggy-haired boy stepped forward. "Hey, aren't you Sofía's new roommate? Dana, right?"

"Yes." I shook his hand.

"I'm Eduardo. You've met Luca, right?"

Luca turned to face me. "Yes, we met on the trip yesterday. You going to the club tonight? You can ride with us."

I considered his invitation. It would give me a chance to get to know them better, but I wasn't sure how much information I could get out of anyone at a loud club late at night. And dancing—for me that was never the best idea. "No, not tonight," I said. "I've got a few things to catch up on. I feel so far behind the rest of you."

"Don't worry. You'll get it in no time," Eduardo said.

"You sure we can't convince you to come? I could personally tutor you later in any subject you need help with." Luca's handsome, wide smile may have swayed any other girl, but knowing he had dated Amoriel put him on the top of my might-be-involved-in-her-disappearance list. Maybe I could find out more about him by snooping or asking around at La Academia while he was gone.

"Not this time. Thanks for the offer."

Eduardo looked at his phone and motioned to the stairs with his head. "The guys are just pulling up. Come on."

Luca bit the side of his cheek, like he was weighing his options.

"Luc, let's go."

"See you tomorrow in class," I said.

"Okay." He smiled and then rushed to the stairs to join Eduardo, who was already heading down.

The rest of the lobby was empty. Maybe everyone had gone to the club. This was the perfect opportunity for me to find some info on the boys at La Academia. I glanced around and listened. The girl's hallway was silent, but laughter and voices traveled from the boys'. I inched forward and peeked around the corner. A group of guys lounged about on the floor in the hall, playing a game of cards. I hid back behind the wall and listened. After about ten minutes of them talking of nothing but their poker-like game, and a few comments about sharing snacks, I was ready to leave.

"So why didn't you want to go tonight?" one guy asked another. "I thought you liked the club scene."

"I did." Someone shuffled a deck of cards. "I still do. Just didn't want to go if Luca was there."

"Why?" someone else asked.

"I don't know. Ever since that girl dumped him last month and left the academy a few days later—"

"You mean that cute Amoriel girl?"

"Yeah. He's been weird since then."

I wanted to look around the corner to see who was speaking, but I figured the conversation would stop if the boys noticed me.

"How weird?"

"Just not fun to be around. I almost considered going tonight. He did seem in a better mood."

"I wonder what happened to that girl. Her paintings were great."

"Yeah, she was better than me."

"Everyone is better than you."

"Hey! Well, at least I'm better at cards."

"Prove it."

As their game continued, I slowly made my way back to the lobby. I hadn't realized Luca and Amoriel had broken up before she left the school. I wasn't sure what that meant, but it cast more suspicion on Luca, especially if the breakup was Amoriel's idea.

I needed to find out more about Luca. The best way to do that would be to break into his dorm room. Problem was, I didn't know which one was his. I probably could have searched through some administration files or something, but there was an easier way.

I ran my fingers through my hair and shook it out. After I removed my black hoodie, I adjusted the torn neck edge of my AC/DC shirt to fall off one shoulder. Though I could have borrowed a pair of heels from Sofía's stash, I opted to keep on my combat boots. I tapped on the sign that read "Boys Only" and waltzed right into the hallway where the guys were playing cards.

One of the boys dropped his cards when he saw me. The other two just looked up and stared, no one speaking.

"Sorry, I'm new here. Can you tell me which room is Eduardo's? I just wanted to leave him a note." I pulled out a folded-up piece of paper—a receipt from the airport—and held it in front of me.

"There's a box in the lobby to leave messages. Girls aren't supposed to be in this hallway."

"Oh, I'm sorry," I said as sweetly as possible and twirled my hair. "Could I just put it under his door? It will only take a second."

The guys looked at each other. Finally the shaggy-haired boy shrugged his shoulders and said, "It's two doors down on the left."

No one spoke as I stepped over their legs and pretended their eyes were not on my painted-on jeans and the exposed skin at my shoulder. I pointed to the doorway. "This one?"

All three nodded at me, and I bent to slip the receipt under the door.

"You guys are the best." I gave them a flirtatious smile, one that neither Dana nor Alex would have endorsed. As I stepped back over their legs, I retrieved the fallen cards and placed them in the empty hands of one boy. I couldn't resist whispering in his ear, "Go for three of a kind."

I could have picked Luca and Eduardo's lock—Daly and I had practiced that a few weeks ago—but I couldn't enter the room from the hallway with the three boys watching. Luca and his roommate probably wouldn't return for at least a couple hours, but who knew how long the hall would be occupied. Plus, I had no idea when the CIA would text me to meet. There was only one way I could get into Luca's room.

It wasn't like it would be my first time scaling a building.

I put my hoodie on again, descended the stairs to the classroom section of the building, and exited through the back patio doors. Since each room had a balcony, I just had to use the schematics my mind had recorded over the last few days to find Luca's window. Since the mansion faced north, I walked to the left side and counted over a couple of rooms on the third floor.

Now, how to find my way up. The rain gutters on the corner of the house were too far away from Luca's balcony. The brick exterior didn't offer many toeholds or footholds, either. There were trees. I could climb a tree. I'd even done it on my unsanctioned mission in Barcelona.

The tree closest to Luca's balcony was tall and skinny, with a few thick branches near enough that I could reach the ledge of the balcony. However, with the bottom half of the tree bare, I didn't know how to get to the branches. Once more I studied the tree and the exterior of the mansion. If I'd had Millard's grappling gun, this job would've been easy. Without the gun, I would have to be creative.

I went back inside the house and up to the second floor. Sofía had informed me that the second floor had a gym, several studios that could be reserved for painting or drawing or sculpting, and a computer lab. I had yet to use any of those rooms, but a view from the exterior revealed they had balconies as well. I just needed the one below Luca's room.

I found it just off the computer lab. It seemed out of place to have a computer lab with a balcony that overlooked an expansive backyard and pool. It also seemed strange that the lab door was unlocked. I didn't see any security cameras in the halls or computer lab, but that didn't mean they weren't there. To play my part as a high school student, I stopped at one of the computers and did some searches on the internet on perspective drawing and all the art terms I wasn't familiar with from class earlier that day. If I was playing a part, I might as well make it useful. After about ten minutes I stretched my arms, then stood and slowly made my way to the French doors that led to the balcony. Once outside, I shut the doors and hoped the sheer white curtains blocked any camera view of what I was about to do. Just in case an exterior camera faced the tree, I pulled the hood of my jacket over my head.

The intricately tiled balcony was about six feet wide and four feet deep, with curved corners. The stone railing had thick ornate balusters that matched the columns on the front of the building. With no sign of anyone below, I stepped up onto the railing edge. The balcony above was still several feet higher than I could reach, but an extending tree branch would make a perfect balancing beam. I grabbed a branch above and stepped into the tree. The branch below me swayed with my weight. I tightened my grip and moved closer to the tree trunk, where the branch was stronger.

The climbing was actually easy, though my jeans weren't quite as stretchy as I'd hoped. The sleeves of my hoodie protected my arms from the rough bark of the tree. It took less than a minute to get to a branch only a few feet from Luca's balcony. Only two steps on the branch and a tiny jump would land me safely on his tiled balcony floor.

There was a loud crack as the branch I held onto above me snapped. I let it go and grabbed the trunk of the tree. With both arms wrapped around the trunk, I watched the broken branch drop at least thirty feet to the patio below. Once my heart rate returned to normal,

I faced the balcony again. Without a branch overhead for support, this wouldn't be easy, but the balcony was less than eight feet away. *You can do this.*

I put one combat boot in front of the other and inched forward. About halfway there, the branch jerked under me. I reached out for something to hold onto and only found air. I fell to my right, my hip slamming into a branch several feet below the one I'd been standing on. Pain blurred my vision, but not before my hand grasped a smaller branch another few feet down. I hung there for about ten seconds while my vision cleared. The second-story balcony was just feet away, the patio fifteen feet below. If only I could reach out and grab one of the balusters.

I filled my lungs with air and blew it out before I swung one arm forward. The tips of my fingers brushed the stone of the baluster right before my other hand slipped from the branch and I fell toward the concrete below.

Memories flashed in my vision. The black water of the Kryukov Canal. The shattering windows of a burning warehouse in Moscow. The cold metal of a gun barrel against my chest. Two headlights shining directly through Tanner's windshield.

A splintering pain shot up my leg. The world pulsated between pain and memory. Somewhere in my mind, I knew I should have felt the crack of my head against the patio. Instead there was a flash of light and a face above me.

Señor Gonzales.

Then the world disappeared.

14

Broken

The smell of antiseptic hit first, jumping into my nostrils and making my eyes blink open. Bright sunlight filtered through the blinds of an unfamiliar window. I was lying in a bed. A hospital bed. I groaned as my mind recalled, in slow motion, my fall from the tree.

"Alexandra."

I recognized that voice. Elijah?

My body screamed in pain as I turned in his direction. "What are you . . . why aren't you with Tanner?" I asked, barely able to focus my eyes on Elijah's face.

"Believe it or not, you're in worst shape than he is. Golkov and I fought over who would come, but apparently I can pass as more of a parental figure." Elijah's warm smile put me at ease.

"What's wrong with me?" My right side burned, my back hurt, and my leg ached.

"Fractured tibia and fibula, and a bruised kidney. Your bones didn't need to be set, and your kidney is going to be fine. I already looked at the scans."

"Wait. You're posing as my dad?" I asked. Elijah was in his early forties, but the thought of him as my father made me giggle. "Ow, ow!" I held onto my side.

"You're on some pretty strong pain meds, which might make you overly emotional. They should take away most of the pain, though. Are you comfortable?"

"Not entirely, but I'll survive. How long have I been here?" I just wanted out of the bed and back on the mission.

"Two days. It's Saturday afternoon."

"Two days?" I gasped. "What about the mission? I need to find Amoriel. What does La Academia know? How did you find out? How's Tanner?" I couldn't stop the flood of questions.

Elijah placed a hand on my arm. "Give yourself some time, Alexandra. The academy called Golkov, who was listed as your emergency contact. I'm not sure why the CIA had him on your enrollment forms, but it did make it quick for me to get here. I've been here since yesterday morning, overseeing your treatment. If at any moment I had thought your life was threatened, your father—your real father—would have been notified immediately. I thought it was best for him to remain with your brother for now."

"Good, good," I said. "So Tanner's all right?"

"He's out of the hospital, but I've put him in a treatment center where a therapist and emergency personnel can watch over him twenty-four hours a day. Daly's been by his side almost constantly."

I smiled. Of course I could count on Daly to do what I asked.

"As for the mission, the CIA is still working on some leads," Elijah said.

"What about La Academia? Do they know . . . ?"

"Mr. Gonzales saw you fall and reported it as an accident." Elijah pinned me with a stare. "What exactly *were* you doing on the second-floor balcony?"

"Recon on a student. Climbing a tree from the second floor to the third was the only way I could get into his dorm." My faced burned at the memory. "I wanted something useful to give to the CIA."

"Well, you will be released tonight, once we get a cast on that leg," Elijah said, "and there will be no more missions for you for several weeks. A jet is ready to take you home."

Home. My own bed with its warm, furry blanket called to me. I wanted to be in a familiar place with people I cared about. Tanner and I could spend time together while he continued to heal. The thought of seeing Daly tomorrow was tempting, too.

"No," I said finally and pushed myself up in my bed, a move that sent searing pain through my side. "I'm not going back yet."

"Alexandra, you suffered a potentially serious injury to an internal organ, and your leg will take months to heal. It's time to go home." Elijah turned his bloodshot gaze to the window. I knew he felt responsible for my safety, but I had a responsibility too.

"I came here to complete a mission," I said, "and I'm staying until it's done. I made promises to Agent Denisovich and the CIA."

Wearing his usual outfit of dark slacks and a crisp white button-down shirt, Elijah sat on the edge of the bed. "They'll understand, Alexandra."

How could I explain that this mission was not just about promises made to others, but also a promise I'd made to myself? Working with the CIA could help me decide what to do with my future.

I stared into Elijah's blue eyes. "I'm staying."

He shook his perfectly shaven head. "I should have known you wouldn't give up on a mission. Just like your mom." He had known her before I was born—he'd been her driver and good friend for years until Ivan had forced him to work with Red Eye.

Thinking about my mother sent a wave a nostalgia through me. "Can I ask you something about her, Elijah?"

"Yes, of course."

"Was she happy?"

He lowered one eyebrow. "What do you mean?"

"She seemed happy at home, but I didn't know about her spy missions to recover paintings. Do you think her years with the CIA and then with Golkov helped make her happy? I mean, would giving it up have changed who she was?"

Elijah leaned against the bed railing. "Your mother always knew who she was and what she wanted to do. There was a time, after she had you and your brother, that she didn't work for anyone. I believe she was content during that time, but when the opportunity came for her to resume her work in art recovery, for The Company instead of the CIA, she jumped at it. She never lost that drive within her. I think her happiness came from both her passion for her family and her passion for art. You couldn't have pulled her away from either."

Suddenly my lower back throbbed and I closed my eyes until the pain passed. "But what if she'd been forced to choose one life over the other, maybe before she had us. Do you think she would have given up The Company?"

In a fatherly gesture, Elijah found my hand, the one that no longer wore The Company ring. "Are you asking about your mother or are you asking about yourself?"

I should've known he would see beyond what I was saying and understand what I was really meant. "Maybe both?"

"I think that is the part you misunderstand. What I was trying to say earlier was that Iolanta didn't have to choose between them." Elijah squeezed my hand. "Neither do you. Sometimes you can have both—if that is what you want."

I looked at the ceiling. "How long before I can be mobile?"

"Let's take one thing at a time. We'll get that cast on in a few minutes. Then I want to ultrasound your kidney one more time. If all looks good, we can get you out of here tonight."

"And take me back to La Academia?"

Elijah released my hand. He got up and moved to the window, where he stood with his back to me. "I'll take you to the school on one condition."

"What's that?"

He turned to me and checked off a list with his fingers. "No climbing, scaling, repelling, swinging, jumping off or out of . . . anything."

I rolled my eyes. "Fine, as long as I get one condition too."

"Okay." He returned to the side of my bed.

"Can it be black?"

"What?"

"My cast, of course."

"Deal." Elijah put out his hand and we shook on it.

"You have created quite the buzz around here, Dana, " Sofía said, helping me into our dorm room. The hideous hospital-issue metal-and-rubber crutches keeping me upright were not black.

"That was my plan all along," I managed to say. "Trip and fall from a balcony to get attention from students and sympathy from teachers. I may have started a new trend."

Sofía laughed. "But really, I'm sorry about all of it, and glad you're okay."

"Me too." I hefted myself to the couch and sat slowly. Sofía took my crutches and leaned them against the couch. "Does everyone here think I'm the biggest klutz?" I wasn't sure I'd used the right translation for the word in Spanish. I'd never had the need to use it before, though I had a feeling I'd never be hearing the end of it.

"No. I think they were just all a little surprised. What were you doing on the second floor anyway?"

I'd practiced my response in my head several times. "I was using the computer lab and went to the balcony for some air before calling it a night. It was dark and I must've tripped over a chair. I honestly don't remember everything—mostly just falling and then seeing Señor Gonzalez before I blacked out."

"You saw Señor Gonzalez?"

"Yeah, he's the one who found me and called the ambulance. I thought you knew."

"No, I thought it was one of the security guards or something. I bet that was weird."

"I guess so. Honestly, I kind of want to forget it ever happened. If there was a way I could hide these stupid hunks of metal and this cast, I would."

"How long will you have those?" Sofía pointed to the crutches.

"At least a couple of weeks. Then I might get a walking cast."

"Maybe you should stay off all balconies until then." She winked and smiled. "Though I hear wheelchair races can be fun."

I started to respond, but my phone buzzed in my pocket. I held up my index finger and pulled it out. My brow furrowed as I looked at the phone screen, which showed a text message from the CIA.

They wanted me to meet an agent at a park a few blocks down the road. I couldn't believe they expected me to meet them less than an hour after I was released from the hospital. As far as I knew, they hadn't even tried to contact me while I was there.

"Sofía, I have to go."

"Now? Aren't you supposed to be resting?"

"Yeah, I know. There's just some problem with my tuition or something and I need to sort it out."

"On a Sunday?"

"I'm as perplexed as you are."

"Do you want me to come with you? I'm looking for any reason not to start that art history assignment."

"No, I need to learn to get around on my own anyway. I shouldn't be long."

She leaned back against the couch and put her feet on the coffee table. "Okay, but when you get back, you have to let me do some nail art on those toes of yours. If they are going to be exposed for several weeks, let's make them stand out."

"Sounds good." I picked up my crutches and got to my feet. I thought about taking a painkiller before I left, but opted to take my next dose right before bed in order to get more sleep.

I made it to the top of the stairs before stopping to rest my leg. *Why didn't I text the CIA back and tell them to come to me?*

Just then, a voice said over my shoulder, "Need some help?"

It was Luca. I refused his offer to carry me down the stairs but accepted his offer to carry my crutches. Using the railing for support, I hopped down the steps.

"We heard about the accident," he said, following next to me. "Sorry about your leg. That really stinks. I guess this means we won't be going salsa dancing."

"Dancing?" I almost choked on the word. I couldn't decide which was scarier: salsa dancing or going on a date with Luca.

"Don't worry. I'll come up with another plan. How about tomorrow afternoon? The teachers have meetings all day, and you probably haven't seen all the sights in Mexico City yet."

Cringing inwardly as I negotiated the last step, I couldn't respond.

"I'll meet you at the top of the stairs at . . . let's say three o'clock tomorrow?" Luca said, holding out my crutches for me.

"Wait, what?" It took me a minute to realize he'd just arranged for us to go on a date. His dark eyes gleamed, along with his unnaturally shiny hair.

"Don't worry," he told me. " I can even get a wheelchair if it will make it easier."

"No wheelchair," I said instead of what I really wanted to say, which was that I had no desire to go on a date with him.

"Okay." He started up the stairs. "See you tomorrow."

He was halfway up the second set of stairs before my flustered self was ready to turn him down. By then, it was too late. I'd have to come up with an excuse to get out of the date.

A dull ache had spread from my leg to my hip by the time I reached the park. Now I realized how foolish it was to be out and about so soon after the accident.

I found Agent Denisovich leaning against a tree in the same suit he had worn when he told me he worked for the CIA. Taking a deep breath, I pushed myself in his direction.

"We'll need your cell phone," he said in greeting.

"My phone?" I felt the weight at my back pocket where my specially enhanced Millard-created phone was hidden.

"It's not CIA-approved."

"You can't be serious." One of my crutches dropped to the concrete patio beneath us. I ignored it and gave him the iciest stare I could muster. I'd just had a nearly fatal fall and was in pain, and all he could say was he wanted my phone.

"The CIA might need your presence, but we're going to take it from here." He picked up my crutch but didn't give it back.

"What do you mean 'take it from here'?" I put a hand on my hip and then tried not to wince at the bruise still healing there.

"We'll give you instructions and use the video-feed necklace for information. You don't need to do anything else except keep pretending to be a student."

He reached out his empty hand. "Your phone?"

I didn't move. The Company cell phone in my back pocket wasn't just a communications device, it was a comfort. I wasn't about to just hand it and the entire mission over to him.

"We can't have anything else compromising this mission," he went on. "Your little stunt from the balcony almost blew everything. Just do what you're told and maybe we can still salvage your student cover at La Academia."

"My little stunt? It was an accident. I risked my life to get more intel on a lead and you call it a stunt? I was doing it to save your daughter." The anger I'd let into my voice began to subside when his expression wavered.

"I'm sorry." He ran a hand over the side of his face. "It's not my call anymore either, Dana. Once I turn over your phone, I'm being forced to sit on the sidelines. They've sent over a new team lead who is better equipped to handle a case like this." His words turned bitter at "better equipped," and I felt sorry for him. It was my fault he was being sidelined.

I pulled my phone out of my pocket and handed it to him. An emptiness filled me, not just at giving up the phone that had seen me through my other missions, but because it was the last bit of The Company I had. It felt as if I was letting them go, too.

"Thank you, Dana." Agent Denisovich handed me the crutch and ushered me to a nearby bench surrounded by trees. A grassy park lay in front of us with a few runners and dog walkers moving down the sidewalk. A couple sat on a red blanket eating from a picnic basket. All of them were oblivious to the tense conversation behind them.

Denisovich spent the next ten minutes passing along new instructions and giving me specific questions to ask several students and teachers. Each seemed more ridiculous than the next, like "When did you last see Amoriel?" and "Did she act strange the last time you saw her?" If they wanted me to ask questions like that, they might as well get the police involved. But I accepted the instructions without complaint or comment. Denisovich didn't seem to like anything he was reading to me either.

"Do you need me to go over them again?" he asked when he finished. I shook my head, where the memory of our conversation was recorded forever.

Denisovich reached into his jacket and brought out a thin black cell phone with no identifying logo or phone case. "This is only equipped to receive or send calls and texts to the CIA." He gave me the phone. "Keep it with you at all times." He pointed to the camera around my neck. "The same goes for the necklace. Make sure it is always on and visible."

I resisted the urge to give him a salute or turn the camera necklace around to my face and salute it.

He rose to his feet and stood in front of me. I remained seated, my leg throbbing, my body aching, and my emotions sagging.

"We'll be in touch," Denisovich said, holding out a hand for me to shake.

I looked at it and then his face. Unable to continue pretending I was okay with the situation, I kept one hand wrapped around my crutches and the other gripping the phone, which I was tempted to hurl to the other end of the park.

After a couple more seconds, he dropped his hand. "Again, I'm sorry, Dana." He turned and exited the park.

I watched until he disappeared through the trees.

15

.01%

The trek to the park had taken every ounce of my energy. If Luca had been at the bottom of the stairs, I probably would've let him carry me up. Instead, I had to pull myself and the stupid crutches along with me. By the time I got back to the dorm, I only managed a quick hello to Sofía before going to my room to sit down.

Just as I was popping a painkiller into my mouth, I heard a knock. "Dana?" My roommate cracked the door a few inches.

"Yeah?"

"A guy is calling for you. He says your phone isn't working." Sofía stepped inside with her cell phone tucked to her chest. "Do you know an Adam?"

I started to shake my head and tell her it was a mistake when I suddenly recalled Daly's code name: Adam Jesly. It was an anagram for his real name, James Daly.

"Yes. Do you mind if I use your phone for a bit?"

She handed it to me, whispering, "I want all the details later," then left and closed the door.

I put the phone to my ear. "Hello, Alex," Daly said.

"Is Tanner okay?" The words rushed out of me before I could even say hello.

"He's fine. I'm more concerned about you. Elijah said they kept you one more night because of the swelling in your leg. Are you sure you're okay?"

I'd spoken to Daly the previous night before bed, but I'd been on pain meds and didn't recall the entire conversation—amazing for someone with a brain that won't usually let her forget anything.

"I'm back at the school," I told Daly. "My leg will be fine. Are you sure Tanner is okay?"

"He's fine, Alex."

"Oh, good." I relaxed a bit. "Sorry, but I've been worried. He won't say much when I call. I don't know if it's because things aren't going as planned, or if he's doing good."

"He's doing great, but I think it's harder than he thought it would be. All I know is he's a warrior. He's even making his physical therapist sweat."

"Probably from all the flirting."

Daly laughed. "Yeah, that would probably be true if the therapist wasn't a guy."

"Oh, uh, yeah."

"Don't worry. He still keeps the female hospital staff on their toes."

Neither Daly nor I spoke for several seconds. Indecipherable voices drifted in from the background.

"What about you?" I said.

"Yeah, I keep them on their toes too."

"No, I mean, how are you?"

"I'm good. I've been with Tanner a lot, and Millard is working on some new gadgets. Until you get back, I'm the official beta tester. As long as he doesn't make me ingest anything, I don't mind."

Enjoying the sound of Daly's voice, I let him talk about the specifics for a few minutes.

"You're obviously keeping busy," I said when he finished.

He cleared his throat. "What I want to know is how you're really doing. I'm worried about you."

Could he sense the despair I felt? The homesickness? So far, the mission was a complete failure. I had no more leads than when I'd arrived, the CIA and Denisovich doubted me, and I didn't have a single artistic bone in my body. If the CIA didn't replace me, La

Academia would kick me out. I wondered if a student had ever been asked to leave the school due to lack of talent.

"I'm fine," I told Daly. "Just frustrated, I guess. And wishing I was there." *Or that you were here,* I wanted to say. I slipped off my one black combat boot and fell back onto my pillows.

A door closed on Daly's end of the line. "You going somewhere?" I asked.

"No, I stepped onto the balcony. Millard just got home."

"Oh." I let my mind play a memory of the view from Daly's apartment balcony, with the city of Providence surrounding him.

"You know, I traveled a lot when I was a kid," he said. "Living in Europe would have been a dream come true for many kids. Not me. I just wanted a place to call home—people I felt I belonged with. Maybe that's another reason I mask my accent or pretend it's stronger than it is. I've never quite figured out where I belong."

"Me neither. I thought I had it in Wenatchee growing up, but after my mom . . . I'm just not sure anymore."

"Guess all we can do is test the waters until our ships finally make port."

"Sounds like Itosu wisdom," I remarked.

"No. Not this time. Just James Daly for you."

"Do you think they'll ever be a place for us? I mean, do you think there's a place for someone who lives under the radar, someone who has to pretend, someone who is a spy?"

"Yes." Daly said it with such confidence that I sat up in my bed, my cast dangling over the edge.

"How do you know?" I asked.

"There has to be. I don't usually philosophize, but I do know one thing."

"What's that?"

"That even when we're pretending, even when we're hiding under wigs or accents or clothes that aren't our style, we can't hide our nature. Just like I knew from the moment I met you that you would choose this life. And just like I knew, when you told me about this mission, that you would agree to help the CIA find this girl. You would sacrifice yourself and your time with your brother to save someone. It's just who you are."

"I've already messed things up, Daly. What if I'm not good enough? What if I can't do it?"

"That's the thing, though. You'll find a way."

I lay back again and buried the side of my face into my pillow. "I'm just not sure how."

"If you continue to think as you've always thought, you'll continue to get what you've always got," Daly said.

I considered that. I wasn't ready to give up. At least not yet.

"That one is Itosu wisdom, in case you wondered."

I yawned into the phone. "It's good advice."

"I'll let you go. You should be resting. Don't you have school in the morning?" He said the last part in a teasing tone.

"Yeah, if I make it through another day at school. Maybe they'll get rid of me—kick me out or something. You'd think I would have inherited some of my mom's artistic genius."

"Can I give you one last bit of advice, Alex?"

"Sure."

"Throw it all out the window."

"What?" I stared at my open window. A slight breeze blew the gauzelike drapes in and out as if they were a living creature.

"Everything you've learned about art, the lines, the colors, the pictures in your head from other artists—just throw it all out. And throw out everything you've learned from books and simulations about being a good spy. Don't try to be like someone else. Don't force yourself to follow a set of rules that weren't meant for you. Those work for 99.99% of the people."

"You're telling me I'm the .01%?" I asked skeptically.

"No, I'm telling you you're not even on the scale." Daly's soft breathing traveled through the phone line. "With a mind like yours, you can't be put in a box. Or even expected to stand outside it. You were never meant to hold still, Alex. You have to stack all the boxes up and climb and keep climbing until you find you. I'm just saying that Alexandra Stewart will find her own way."

The cool night air brushed the skin of my arm and I wished it was Daly's hand instead.

"You sure have a lot of wisdom tonight," I told him.

I expected him to laugh. Instead, the line went silent for a moment. "Because I'm not there. Because I wish I was." His words were simple, but his message reached inside my heart and left a warmth—a warmth I needed.

"Thank you, James."

"Take care, Alex."

I wanted to say more, to keep him at my ear just a little longer. Yet the words itching to break free couldn't be said from over two thousand miles away. They needed to happen in person. I wasn't going home until I found Amoriel. Which meant I had to complete this mission. Not just for Amoriel anymore. I had to do it for me.

16

The Date

My mind was made up. I'd ask Sofía to tell Luca I wasn't feeling well. It wouldn't be a total lie, and then I wouldn't have to face him. As I lay in my bed, the arrowhead necklace on my nightstand caught my gaze. I narrowed my eyes at it. *CIA. Central Intelligence Agency. If they were actually intelligent, they would realize I am in the center of everything on this mission, because I'm on the inside.* Even though I wasn't about to turn an about-face on their instructions, my competitive nature pulled at me.

I groaned and threw off the covers. If I was going to do more, I probably needed to take a closer look at Luca. He had dated Amoriel and she'd broken up with him. In my book, that made him suspicious. Even if he wasn't involved in her disappearance, he might know something that could steer me in the right direction. That meant I had a date this afternoon.

Getting dressed proved to be a problem. My cast wasn't the removable kind, per Elijah's insistence—he knew me too well—which meant wearing jeans of any sort was impossible. I had survived the previous day in a pair of loose-fitting shorts, but I couldn't wear them again. There was really only one thing I could do, and it wouldn't fit with Dana Laxer's rebellious teen persona.

Ignoring my crutches leaning against the bed, I hopped to my door and peered out. Sofía lay sleeping on the couch, her sketchbook on the table and smudges of charcoal on her face. I wasn't about to wake her just yet. I needed to kill some time. I made my way back to my bed and sat down with my own sketchbook in hand. I wondered if Daly could be right. Maybe there was a little bit of my mom's artistic nature in me after all.

I stared down at my representation of the Pyramid of the Sun. It was even more awful in the light of the morning sun than in the classroom a few days ago. I ripped the page from the sketchbook, crumbled it into a ball, and threw it at a beachside painting on my wall. The painting didn't move, but the vibrant colors that represented the blues of the waters and the oranges of the sunset moved me. I studied the painting. Señor Gonzales wanted us to draw a perspective of the pyramid. The perspective I had been trying to mimic wasn't my own. I needed to go back to the source.

I closed my eyes and watched the day of the spring equinox from memory. The heat of the sun, the sounds of drums, and the colors filled my mind. I was there again, except this time I could take it all in more slowly. I studied the Aztec costumes of the dancers, and the fine grains of sand that filled the cracks in the stairs. I noticed how the smaller pyramids weren't all the same size, as I had previously thought. Some were slightly wider or taller. The symmetrical lines weren't as straight as I'd remembered, either.

Colors were always more vibrant in my memories, and this was no exception. The blues of the sky jumped out at me, with pinks, yellows, and oranges starting to appear above the horizon. The stone of the pyramid was no longer a boring beige but a mosaic of tans and grays with accents of browns and blacks. I paused the memory right when I was positioned near one of the corners before we reached the front of the pyramid. That was the perspective I wanted to show. Getting it on the paper would be a mission in and of itself.

"Dana?" Sofía stood at my bedroom door, rubbing her eyes. "Been awake long?"

"I couldn't sleep."

"You feeling okay?" Her eyes fell to my blank sketchbook and then the crumpled paper on the ground. "Looks like you're making some progress."

"I'm feeling fine. And I am making progress. I'm studying the negative space. Isn't that what Michelangelo did?"

"As long as you get it turned in by tomorrow, I don't think Señor Gonzales is going to care which artist you channel." She started to go back to the living room.

"Hey, Sofía," I called out to her. "I have a huge favor to ask. I'm supposed to go on this date with Luca this afternoon."

"Luca? Like, Mr. Serious Hottie Luca?" She arched an eyebrow.

"That's the one."

"And how can I help?"

"Well" —I rolled over and off the bed— "I don't exactly have anything I can wear over this." I pointed at the big black cast that went from my toes to just below my knee.

Sofía's face brightened. "You're going to let me be your stylist and pick out what you wear?"

"Sure. As long as I can get it over my cast and it's fairly comfortable, I won't complain."

"You might regret that. After art, fashion is my favorite hobby. Give me a few minutes and I'll bring in some options. It's a good thing it's prep day for the teachers. This might take a while." She spun around and leaped over the couch on the way to her room. If I'd known she'd been this excited about dressing me, I would've woken her up earlier.

Three dresses and two skirts later, I sat on a wobbly chair in the bathroom while Sofía played with my hair. She eventually braided it into a crown around the top of my head. Red streaks of hair accented the entire braid. I had to admit it didn't look half bad. It did nothing for my don't-care-how-I-look CIA cover, but I probably wasn't pulling that off anyway. Besides, this looked different enough from my normal Alex in T-Shirt and Jeans that it was its own disguise.

Lunch had come and gone by the time I was ready. I still had a few hours until my date with Luca. The blank page of my sketchbook on my bed taunted me; I just wasn't quite ready to mark it yet. Instead I joined Sofía in the lounge, where people had gathered to hang out, since no one had classes. I listened in on conversations and even managed to throw in a few questions about Amoriel without it seeming too obvious. As far as I could tell, she got along with everyone and was an amazing artist. In fact, it sounded as if she was an ideal student and friend.

Luca came from the boys' hallway a few minutes before three and found me on a couch with a group of girls. He walked straight over to me. "Your carriage awaits, my lady."

"My carriage?" I looked at the girls around me, who smiled their encouragement. Luca picked up my crutches and offered his hand. With everyone staring, I had no choice but to let him help me from the room. He carried my crutches again while I held the railing and hopped down the stairs.

"Now I want you to wait right here. I'll be back." He left me on the sidewalk near the circular driveway in front of La Academia while he jogged around the side. A minute later, I turned at the sound of a bell. Luca rode up on an oversized tricycle pulling a small, carriage-like seat on wheels. I couldn't help laughing. It was a ridiculous way to travel, but at least I wouldn't have to walk with crutches. And it wasn't a wheelchair exactly, so I couldn't be mad.

"What are you driving?" I asked, still laughing.

"You've never had the pleasure of a ride through the city in a *bicitaxi*?"

"I knew I was missing out on something."

Luca smiled as he helped me into the little seat.

"Where are we headed, chauffeur?" I asked.

"I was going to surprise you with someplace exotic, but I think it will be best if we stay closer to home. How would you feel about exploring historic Mexico at Zócalo?"

"I like history," I said.

"I know we drove past the Metropolitan Cathedral on our way to Teotihuacan, but we can see the plaza, the National Palace, Templo Mayor, and anything else you're interested in."

"I've always wanted to go inside the cathedral," I said.

"Then that will be our first stop." Luca pedaled to the front gate of La Academia, then hopped off the bicitaxi to let us through.

Excitement pulsated through me as we moved down the street. I tried to concentrate on questions to ask about Amoriel, but all I could think about were the places Luca and I were going to visit.

"So what do you think of Mexico so far?" Luca asked. He looked over his shoulder before focusing again on the edge of the road where he was pedaling.

"It's even more beautiful than in pictures. Teotihuacan was totally amazing. It's hard to imagine the people who built those pyramids and that some of their buildings are still intact."

"I agree," Luca said. "When my parents first took me there when I was about eight, I thought we were in Egypt. The pyramids are basically in our backyard."

"So you grew up in Mexico City?" I adjusted my position on the seat as we passed the Gran Hotel, where I'd met with the CIA.

"Yeah, born and raised," Luca replied. "Many of the students that live at La Academia have family in the city. I don't go home every weekend, but I go once in a while."

"That sounds nice."

"It's okay. It's just my parents and me. Unless I tell them I'm coming by, they are usually out and about. That's why I stay at La Academia most of the time. What about you? Why come all the way to Mexico? Don't they have plenty of art schools in the U.S.?"

"Guess I'm kind of like you—I wanted to get away. Plus I always liked the idea of Mexico, and working on my Spanish seemed like a good idea at the time." I carefully lifted my cast to stretch my leg.

"But you don't think so now?" Luca asked while we were stopped at a corner waiting for the light to turn green.

I motioned to my cast. "It hasn't exactly started out under the best circumstances."

"Don't let that keep you from doing what you came here to do," Luca said.

"I won't." I did have work to do. I ran over some questions in my head as he pedaled down the street.

"So . . . how long have you been at La Academia?" I asked, leaning forward slightly to make sure he heard me.

"This is my first year, but I'll still graduate in May."

"So you haven't been at the school as long as Sofía."

"Yeah. I've known her since the beginning of this year."

"Then you must have known her roommate too—Amoriel, right?" I tried to keep my voice casual.

"Sofía probably told you we dated for a while." He turned his head to the side, his lips turned down. "She was a sweet girl, but we weren't right for each other. It's too bad she left the school. Her art was amazing."

There was so much more I wanted to ask, but Luca stopped the bicitaxi, hopped off, and held out his hand.

"Are you ready to see some beautiful architecture and art?"

I glanced around and realized we had stopped right in front of the Metropolitan Cathedral. I'd been so focused on getting answers from Luca, I hadn't even noticed when we crossed the gigantic, paved-stone plaza. Hundreds of people walked about the square and on the side of the street. Several stopped to take photos of the church that looked like a castle. Seeing it from the bus had been great, but being this close was magical.

I allowed Luca to pull me out of the seat, but released his hand once I found my footing. He grabbed my crutches and insisted on helping me to the entrance.

When we reached the open doors, I found myself just a few feet from a handsome face, curly hair, and a vest that screamed 1970s.

"*Hola*, Al—"

"William?" I interrupted. "What are you? How . . . ?" My voice trailed off and my hands started to tremble. I grabbed for the crutches Luca held in his hand. It shouldn't have been a surprise. I'd known William was working at the University in Mexico City. He'd told me the day before he left, yet for some reason I hadn't put the information together. Or maybe I had and just didn't want to admit it to myself. His last words to me floated on the edge of a memory. *I wasn't sure I had anything here in Providence drawing me back. But I don't think Providence has seen the last of me yet.*

Luca cleared his throat and gave me a questioning glance.

"Sorry." I shoved back the memory of William at the hospital. "Luca, this is William. He's a friend from back home."

"Oh, *mucho gusto*, William. What brings you to Mexico City?" Luca said, eyeing William's plaid vest and his penny loafers.

"*La universidad.*" William stuffed his hands in his pockets.

"What are you majoring in? Are you an artist, like Dana?"

William's brows lowered and he stared at me. I bit my bottom lip and gave him my best don't-say-anything look. Everything would be ruined if he blew my cover, especially now that I was on the verge of getting useful information on Amoriel. *Not now. Please, William.*

"No." He pulled his hands from his pockets and straightened his posture. "I'm a professor and I'm doing research for a book."

"A book?" I said.

"*Sí.*" He relaxed a little when he turned to me. "I decided to use the grant to study North American literature and its influences from the Spanish and Portuguese. There are a few professors who are well-versed in Mexican literature, as well as an emeritus professor who is mentoring me. I've set up interviews with some local authors to broaden my research." As William spoke, the dimple on his left cheek became more pronounced.

"That sounds amazing, William."

Luca touched my arm. "We should probably go, Dana. The church closes soon." I started to pull away from him and then remembered the mission. I needed to keep near this guy.

"Sorry, William. Can I . . . you'll be here still, I mean." I swallowed. "I'll call you, okay?"

"Yes. That would be great . . . Dana."

The question in his eyes made my stomach flutter with worry. If I did talk to him, the story about my name change would have to be a good one.

As William walked across the plaza, disappointment washed over me. Luca had been a gracious date thus far, but all I wanted to do was find out more about William's book and his experiences in Mexico. If it wasn't for the mission, I probably would have followed after him, crutches and all, right that second.

"Are you ready to see the inside?" Luca asked.

I pulled my gaze from the back of William's head. "Of course."

My heart wasn't into the ornate gold décor that covered the entire front of the first chapel. It wasn't until we reached the towering organ pipes that I finally realized what was nagging at me. William hadn't acted surprised when he saw me or the cast on my leg. It was almost as if he had already known where I would be and what had happened to me. But how?

"Are you okay?" Luca stood beside me. "Usually people have more of an awe-like expression on their faces, instead of a grimace."

"Sorry. I was just thinking about something else."

"Your leg's okay?"

"Actually, it's a little achy. You mind if we sit for a minute?"

Luca led me into one of the chapels, where we sat on a pew. "Did you know this chapel is named after a saint?" he asked.

In my mind I pulled out the map I had seen earlier as we entered the cathedral. "San Isidro, right?"

"Yes. But did you know he was the patron saint of farming?" Luca ran his hand over the back of the dark-stained wood pew in front of us.

"Actually, no."

"I like to think he was the patron saint of work. He worked hard and he always had angels watching out for him and helping him because he worked honestly. There's a painting of him in his field with angels on either side of him, helping lift his plow."

I thought about that for a minute. Strangely, it made me think of Daly at my ear or by my side on missions—like my guardian angel. It made me miss home. It made me miss him.

"Do you believe in fate, Dana?" Luca turned so I had to look at him. He had a handsome face, but there was something about his eyes. I still couldn't decide if it was intriguing or conniving.

"I believe some things happen for a reason. I guess if you want to call that fate, then I believe in it."

"I'm glad you came to our school, Dana Laxer." Luca smiled. "You ready to see the rest of the church?"

Any other day the sculptures, ornately framed paintings, and woodwork would've captured my full attention, but the events of the week had drained me, and I felt like the historic building was crushing me.

"Actually, I hate to do this to you, Luca. But would you please take me home? I was pushing it to think I could do so much today."

"No. No problem. We can continue another time."

We exited the cathedral, neither one of us saying much. Luca asked me to wait while he pulled the bicitaxi as close to the front as possible. I winced as he helped me sit down in the little seat. The effects of the painkiller I had taken earlier must have been fading.

"Are you going to be all right?" he asked.

"I'll be fine. I just need to get back and lie down."

Luca hopped onto the main seat and began to pedal. "I will get you back as fast at this carriage can go."

17

All of You

When I got back to the dorm, Sofía made me go straight to my room, then brought me dinner in bed. Insisting I had overdone it, she said I should skip school the next morning. Since my sketchbook still had only blank pages for Señor Gonzales' class, I didn't argue. I spent the morning in bed reading Mexican newspapers online, hoping something might give me a clue as to how I could find Amoriel.

Around noon, a text came in on the CIA phone, asking me to meet at the café around the corner from La Academia. Since I didn't have much to share with the CIA, I figured I would make it back to the dorm before Sofía's last class ended.

The meeting with an operative I'd seen but hadn't spoken with before was nearly pointless. He had watched the video footage and said I should get to know Luca better and press him with more questions. I hated to admit it, but the agent was right. I couldn't skip class again or try to avoid Luca. It was time to up my game.

Just after I sat down on the couch with my sketchbook to try my perspective drawing again, Sofía got back from school. "Your friend called," she said, shaking her phone at me.

"D . . . Adam?" I said. *Oops, I almost blew Daly's cover.*

"No, someone new. His name was William. He sounded really nice." She wiggled her eyebrows at me. "Having you as a roommate is almost better than a telenovela."

"Hey."

Sofía shrugged and handed me her phone. "Maybe you should stop giving my number to boys and get your phone replaced."

"Maybe I will."

"As long as I can be here when you make the call, I don't mind at all. Wait, let me get a snack first."

I ignored her comment and dialed William's number. At least there was one use for my eidetic memory here in Mexico.

"*Hola*," he answered after the first ring. I wanted to ask him how he'd gotten Sofía's number, but decided against it since she was sitting on the couch next to me, listening to every word with a bag of *duros* in her hand. The wheel-shaped snacks had become a staple in our pantry. "How are you?" he asked.

"*Bien*. Fine."

"I'm wondering if we can meet tonight," he said. "There's this amazing ice cream place near La Academia. I could pick up some ice cream and meet you at the school, so you don't have to walk."

"Actually, I could use some fresh air." I gave Sofía a friendly glare. "What if we meet at the park to the west of the school?"

"Sounds great. At seven?"

I looked at the screen of Sofía's phone. It wasn't quite one o'clock. I had two classes and then time in one of the studios for what Sofía called "freestyle work." It allowed students at the school to use any medium they wished for their artistic expression. Sofía had invited me to come with her to get some ideas for my art.

"Okay. I'll meet you on the corner," I said.

"See you soon, Alex."

"*Adiós*, William."

I ended the call and gave Sofía's phone to her. She eyed me curiously and said, "Adam, Luca, and now this William guy. The drama just keeps getting better. Can I come to the park? I promise to hide behind a bush or something. You won't even know I'm there."

I rolled my eyes and tossed a couch pillow at her head.

"I have a confession to make." William looked down at his bowl of ice cream. We sat across from each other, at a café-style table on the edge of the park.

At his serious tone of voice, I set my spoon down. "Yes?"

"I didn't just happen to find you at the cathedral yesterday."

"What do you mean?"

"I was surprised when he called to say you were in Mexico City, and then when he said you'd been hurt . . . Well, I couldn't not see you and make sure you were okay."

"William, what are you talking about? Who called you?"

"James. He told me what had happened and that he couldn't be here, and he explained where to find you."

"He told you to find me?" A burning pricked at my eyes. Daly had asked William to come to me. But why?

"He said you were alone in Mexico and could use a familiar face." One side of William's lips pulled up in a smile. "Was he right?"

I picked up my spoon and took a bite of ice cream, letting the strangeness of the situation sink in as the cool dessert melted down my throat. I was sitting here with a guy I had broken up with because another guy I cared about had asked him to help me.

"No. I mean, yes. He was right," I said. "Things haven't turned out quite as planned."

William swirled his now partially melted ice cream. "Why are you here, Alex?"

I'd known the question was coming. I had rehearsed in my mind my cover about study abroad and an exchange program at an art academy. All I had to do was give him the lines. He would believe me, and we could go back to where things were easy and less complicated.

Memories of our runs together, study sessions, and dates began playing at the front of my mind. When the scene of our break-up forced its way forward, I let it play. I had been hiding my spy life from William to protect him. At least that is what I'd told myself. It took me an unsanctioned mission to Paris to realize my feelings for Daly had grown and that the real reason I hadn't told William was because I'd already given that part of myself to someone else.

Now, sitting across the table from William with his caring eyes, I came to a decision.

I pushed my ice cream bowl to the side, unclasped the CIA necklace, and tucked it in the bottom of my purse. Then I placed my hands together on the table between us. "There's a lot that you still don't know about me."

William nodded once. "I realize that."

I leaned forward and whispered in English, "The trips to Russia and Spain and France—they weren't just research trips for Golkov. I didn't cut my leg last fall or break my arm or my leg because I was clumsy."

"What are you—"

I put up a hand. "Please, just let me get this out."

William straightened and I checked my resolve. Was I ready for this? I'd never told anyone about my dual life.

"I'm a spy." The words fell off my tongue so quickly, I wondered if he heard them. "All those trips and injuries happened on missions. Right now, I'm working together with the CIA to find a missing girl here in Mexico."

"You work for the CIA?" William asked softly. He didn't seem as incredulous as I had expected. In fact, I could almost see things clicking in his head, like he was finally putting it all together.

"Yes, well, not entirely. I'm working with them now, but I usually work for Golkov."

"Not just as a TA, right?"

"No. All those missions before were for him. He is the director of the organization I was working for."

"And you've been doing this for how long?"

I sighed. "Since I met you."

"Paris?" William said.

"A mission too."

His face tightened and then slowly relaxed as he processed this information. He leaned across the table and said, "Start at the beginning."

Two hours later, William escorted me to the front steps of La Academia. We stood in silence for several seconds until he reached for my hand and squeezed it. "Thank you for telling me."

The warmth from his touch surged through me, and I felt peace for the first time in what seemed like forever. I leaned my head back and took in the night air. The sky above us was clear and dark. Despite the lights from the city, tiny dots glittered across the sky.

"I know it's the same sky, the same stars, but it feels so foreign here. Like an entirely different world. It's hard to feel myself here." I dropped William's hand and steadied myself with a crutch.

"Yeah. I think the only way I've made it this far is to remember what home really is."

"What's that?" I asked.

I thought about William's youth—moving to Argentina when he was a child, and the studies abroad he had done since moving back to the States when he was older.

"It's true what they say. Home isn't a place, it's the people." William's eyes caught mine. There was a comfort there. I understood what he was saying. It was just hard because not everyone I cared about could be in every place I went.

A light flickered on the porch of La Academia, a place I was sure would never feel like home to me.

"I'm sorry," I finally said, not exactly sure what I was sorry for. Maybe for not telling William sooner about my spy life. Or maybe I was sorry about how things had turned out between us. It was probably a combination of both.

"I know." He took a few steps back and stared at me and then down at my casted leg. There was that grin of his—the one that showed his warm-hearted nature and yet still had a mischievous edge. "Take care, Alex. If you need me, you know where I'll be."

He turned and walked down the path, a slight strut to his step, like he knew something I didn't.

"You have some serious explaining to do." I kept my voice quiet, in case Sofía was nearby. She'd left her phone on the counter for me when I returned from meeting William, but I wouldn't have put it past her to sneak out of her room and listen at my door. I lowered myself to my bed and rested my casted leg on a pillow.

"Before you get angry, just let me explain," Daly said.

"I'm not angry—I guess I'm just confused. Why would you ask William to check up on me?"

"I promised to stay and watch over Tanner. I wasn't going to break that promise, no matter how much I want to be there with you."

"I still don't get it." I grabbed a pen off my dresser and started easing it under my cast to scratch my leg.

"Elijah couldn't stay and I knew you didn't have anyone there . . . and I thought . . ."

"Thought what?"

"I just wanted you to . . ." He let out a low exhale. "Ugh. I hate stuff like this. I just wanted you to be sure, okay?"

"Be sure of what?" I set the pen on my dresser and lay back on my bed. I had absolutely no idea what he was getting at.

Daly's side of the line was quiet for a few moments. "Of me," he finally said, his voice low and intoxicatingly rugged.

I rolled onto my side as what he was saying registered in my brain. He knew me well enough to realize I needed outside support, even if I said I didn't. That was why he'd asked William to be there for me. But that wasn't the only reason. Daly also wondered if there was still something between William and me.

"James, I . . ."

"You don't have to deny it or explain yourself. I just don't want to be the choice that makes sense. The easy choice. If you're going to be with me, I want all of you, Alexandra."

My breath hitched. His message was so intense it was like each word caressed my skin. When my full name left his lips, I had to hold in a sigh.

"Okay." I sat up on the edge of my bed, my breathing slowly returning to something less than if I'd just run a marathon.

"You should get some rest," Daly said. "And a new phone. I'm pretty sure your roommate will be annoyed if I call you at her number again."

"Believe me, she enjoys every minute of it. But I don't. I'll pick one up the next time I'm out."

"Okay."

"Good night, Alex."

"Good night, James."

In my mind, I listened to our conversation a few more times. Why would Daly think I still had feelings for William? Scenes from seeing William in Mexico played through my mind. The peacefulness that had come over me as we conversed at the park had been real, as had the warmth that flowed through my body as he'd held my hand. But I had made my choice. How could Daly doubt that? And why would he want me to question the decision?

18

Tutor

In class the next morning, Señor Gonzales leaned over my chair to get a look at my drawing. "How is it coming along?" His exhale blew a few strands of my hair against my cheek. My blank page had come and gone and come and gone and was now in front of me again. I'd thrown my pencil across my dorm room at least three times that morning. I simply couldn't reproduce what I wanted on the paper. I knew it took practice, but practice wasn't helping.

"I promise I've been working on it. I just can't get it to look the way I see it in my head."

Señor Gonzales held out his hand. I relinquished my pencil, and he stepped to my side and leaned over my paper. With a few flourishes of his pencil, a pyramid emerged on the page. He added a few lines for the horizon and then a few more to make it look as though we were walking toward the pyramid. "Perspective is hard to capture," he said while he kept adding to the scene in front of me. When he stepped a little closer to draw something on the side of the page, his leg pressed against mine. I moved a little to give him more space. After another minute, his sketch was complete. He had done something in a few minutes that I'd spent hours trying to do.

Everyone else in the class had moved on to other sketches. Some of the students had more artistic talent than others, but at least everyone had something to show for themselves. I had nothing.

"I'm not sure what I'm doing wrong. I can see exactly what I want to put on the page, but as soon as my pencil meets with the paper, I lose it."

Señor Gonzales gave my pencil back and said, "Sometimes you have to step away from it for a while and then return when you feel ready. Why don't you take a break from this scene? I have some photography books up front. You can choose a scene you like and then re-create the perspective. How does that sound?"

"Better than what I've been doing."

"Here, let me help you." He put his hand under my arm and lifted me to my feet. I picked up my crutches and made my way to the front of the room. Señor Gonzales offered me the chair at his desk while he continued to help other students. Every time I glanced up from one of the photography books, he seemed to be staring at me, but I was too engrossed in the photos to care. After several minutes I chose a photo—an ocean scene with a lighthouse in the distance. The ocean water was clearer and bluer than any I'd ever seen before.

I returned to my desk and glanced over at Sofía. She was working on a sketch of downtown Mexico City. It was intricate and chaotic and absolutely amazing. Later, at the apartment, I would definitely ask her to help me.

Before my pencil met with the paper, Señor Gonzales dismissed the class.

Seconds later, Luca stood next to my desk. "I can take those to your next class if you want," he said, motioning to my bag and the book with the beach photo.

"Sure. Thanks." That would give me a few minutes to ask him more questions.

"Dana?" Señor Gonzales called from the other side of the room. "Can I see you for a minute?"

I looked to Luca, who shrugged sympathetically. Sofía winked at me and left the room.

"I'll meet you in the hallway," Luca said, then left me alone in the room with Señor Gonzales.

Using my crutches, I walked back to the front of the room, where the teacher was straightening his desk.

"Thanks for letting me borrow the book, Señor Gonzales."

"You can call me Miguel when class isn't in session. I hate the administration's policy about using our last names—it is so outdated."

I stared at him, wondering if other schools in Mexico let students address teachers by their first names. My high school in Washington wouldn't have allowed it.

"I noticed your struggle today and thought you might be interested in private tutoring," Señor Gonzales said.

It took everything I had to hold in a giggle. The last time a teacher had asked if I wanted private tutoring, he'd turned out to be the head of a secret spy organization in the basement of Brown University.

"Maybe. I know I'm still learning things around here," I said. Honestly, I didn't want to waste my time learning to sketch when I was here at La Academia to help solve the mystery of Amoriel's disappearance. The CIA wanted me to look into teachers, but others seemed more suspect than Señor Gonzales.

He folded his arms across his chest, accentuating his bronze biceps. "Tell you what. Why don't we meet in one of the studios during your freestyle time today, and I will help you with your sketch of the photo you chose. Maybe having someone to guide you would help you get off on the right foot. How does that sound?"

"Okay," I said, thinking I would ask him about Amoriel.

"Great." Señor Gonzales smiled, showing off perfectly white teeth. "I'll reserve studio 7 and see you there at, say, a quarter after four. Does that work?"

"Yes. Thank you, Señor Gonzales."

"Miguel," he prompted.

"Thank you, Miguel." I couldn't get over how strange it felt to call a teacher by his first name.

"See you then, Dana."

I hobbled out of the room and met Luca in the hallway.

"Lecture?" he said.

"Not quite. He says I need some extra work outside of class. I guess he thinks private tutoring will help." We moved down the hallway toward my computer-based design class.

"Who will be your tutor? I'm free if you're interested." Luca grinned.

"Actually, Señor Gonzales offered to tutor me himself. He must think I need all the help I can get."

"Really?" A flicker of jealousy or distrust crossed Luca's face. "When is this tutoring session?"

"During our freestyle time in one of the studios. Since I haven't decided on my medium for the final project, it's probably perfect. Who knows, maybe sketching will be my thing."

"It's definitely Sofía's," Luca said. "Did you see her cityscape?"

We stopped at the bottom of the stairs and he took my crutches. I hopped up the stairs, using the railing as a crutch.

"Yeah, maybe some of her talent will rub off on me."

"We could all use some of that talent." Luca handed my crutches to me at the top of the stairs and waited for me to get them under my arms. Then we continued down the hall to the computer lab.

When we reached the door, he handed me my bag and held the door open for me. "I'll see you later, Dana."

"You're not coming to class?"

"I've actually got a few other projects I need to work on. Señora Juana will understand."

"Okay. I'll see you later." I took a step across the threshold of the room. The other students had already taken a seat and were working on the beginning-of-class brain teaser.

Luca wrapped his hand around my upper arm and stopped me. "If you need anything, call me, okay?"

"I can't. I ruined my phone when I fell." Even though the lie was necessary for the mission, I felt guilty about it, maybe because he was being so nice to me. "I plan to buy a new one today."

"How about I pick one up for you?" Luca said. "No one should be without a way to communicate these days. What type of phone do you want?"

I told him that a small prepaid phone with international calling would be perfect. I watched him walk down the hallway. Maybe my first impression of him had been wrong. Perhaps I would make a few friends here in Mexico after all.

Señor Gonzales met me just outside of studio 7. "*Buenos tardes*, Dana." He opened the door and we walked into the room. I'd expected a tiny space only a few feet wide, but this studio had to be at least a couple hundred square feet. Light drifted through a small window at the back. An artist's easel faced a side wall. A counter and cupboards lined another wall, each door labeled in Spanish with names of supplies. A pottery wheel and painting pallet lay on a small round table at the center of the room.

The door clicked closed behind us, and I propped my crutches against the table to take a seat.

"First of all, please tell me what it is you want to accomplish here at the school," Señor Gonzales said. "Is there a specific medium you are drawn to?"

The metal chair squeaked as I shifted my weight. "Well, I'm not sure if sketching is my passion, but I'd like to learn." I figured honesty was best if I wanted to make it through this tutoring session. "My mom could paint, so I guess I'm drawn to painting. I like how the paint isn't just color, it's texture, too. I love how every artist I've studied has a different way of representing a scene. Sometimes it's impressionistic, like Van Gogh or Monet, and other times it's so real you can feel like you can touch it, like with Goya or Rembrandt."

"You sure do know your painters."

"I just love color. Maybe that's why I'm having a hard time sketching." Suddenly I regretted mentioning painting. I didn't want Señor Gonzales to suspect I hadn't painted with anything other than watercolors, and that was in grade school.

"Let's get you a canvas. At this school we like artists to branch out to other mediums, but maybe we need to have you start with something you are passionate about." He squeezed my shoulder before opening a cupboard and pulling out a blank white canvas about the size of a textbook. From another cupboard, he produced a clear plastic box filled with tubes of acrylic paint. He set me up near the table with an easel and brushes, then stepped back.

"Start with something that moves you."

I picked up a brush but had no idea what to do with it. I also didn't know what I could paint that "moved" me. Color. That's what I needed to start with. I picked out six colors and squeezed a bit of each of them onto the palette. With Señor Gonzales looking over my shoulder, I was afraid to mar the canvas with my strokes. But I couldn't just sit there.

Once again I pulled from my mind the scene of the pyramids. I studied the vivid colors and how the lines connected. *Here goes nothing.*

The room was silent except for our breathing and the occasional creak of my chair. I dipped my brush in orange and a bit of yellow and swiped it across the horizon of my canvas. My hand moved in slow and steady strokes as I blended the sky from orange to blue, picking up a new brush when I added a different color. I waited for Señor Gonzales to give me instruction, but he remained silent only a few feet behind me. When I had finished the sky, sand, and grass, I added the mountains and rolling hills in the background, using a bit of water in places to blend some of the colors together. I watched a panoramic movie in my head of the scene over and over, adding trees and bushes exactly where they belonged.

I don't know how long I worked, only that my stomach began to growl as I added the finishing touches to the Pyramid of the Sun and Pyramid of the Moon. My hand ached and my painting palette was a mess of colors when I finally set my final brush down and leaned back in my chair.

Señor Gonzales moved behind me and set his hands on my shoulders. "It's exquisite. How you blended the colors and how vivid they are. It's almost exactly as I remember it, yet somehow different—like you captured the emotion of the scene as well."

"Um, thank you?" My cheeks burned from his praise of my work. "Wait, you were there? At the spring equinox?" I hadn't seen him on the bus or anywhere at Teotihuacan. I turned to look up at him as he stood behind me.

His dark eyes bore down into mine. "No . . . I've just been there many times before."

"Oh." I faced my painting again. It was just as I'd seen it in my head. I'd never created anything I was genuinely proud of. I had tried to be musical but couldn't carry a tune. My attempts at cooking usually involved Tanner coming to the rescue to turn whatever I'd made into something edible. I'd excelled at karate and sports, and written papers and given presentations that could have been deemed as well done, but that was about it.

"I can see why art school is definitely for you." Señor Gonzales' hands were still on my shoulders, and his thumbs moved across my shoulders until they reached the skin at my neck. My stomach tightened and my hands froze in my lap. He continued to stroke my skin. Every part of me wanted to lean forward out of his grasp, and yet I couldn't move. What was he doing?

"There you are!" The door to the studio slammed up against the wall on the other side, probably leaving a mark. "I thought we were meeting at six." Luca's frame filled the doorway, his eyes narrowing at Señor Gonzales, who had finally dropped his hands from my shoulders. My body relaxed.

Luca took a few steps in the room and peeked over my shoulder. "You did that?" He pointed to the painting in front of me. I nodded as he came nearer and Señor Gonzales stepped away.

"I should probably get back," the teacher said. "I have some things to prep for tomorrow. Well done, Dana. If you don't mind, I'd like to show this to our painting teacher. I think we need to adjust your classes a bit and make sure you are involved in at least one of her courses this term."

"Okay." My voice came out so quiet I barely heard it.

"I'll see you both in class tomorrow," Señor Gonzales said before he hurried out of the studio.

Luca waited for about thirty seconds before he spoke. "I seriously hate that guy." He held out a hand to help me to my feet. Ready to get out of that room, I took it.

"You hate him?" I asked.

Luca found my crutches against the table and handed them to me, but his eyes kept returning to my painting. "I don't know. I hate how everyone woos over him and listens to his every word. It's not like his sketches are that great." Luca peeled his eyes from my painting and looked at me. "And he's too touchy-feely."

I nodded but didn't expand on the awkwardness Luca had rescued me from. Then I remembered what he had said when he entered the studio. "Were we supposed to meet tonight?"

"You don't remember?"

"Um . . ." I searched through the memory of the last time we talked. I'd told him about my tutoring session but I hadn't agreed to meet afterward.

Luca smiled. "I'm just kidding. I was walking by and figured you could use a break. Also, I got your phone." He pulled a package from the sack I hadn't noticed he was carrying and handed it to me.

"Thank you." He would never understand how grateful I was — for the cell phone and for getting me out of that studio.

Luca picked up my painting by the edges and held it up to the light. "You never told me you could paint."

"I didn't think it was a big deal." *And then there's the fact that I'd never painted before.* I opened the package, glanced at the instructions, and tossed everything but the cell phone into the garbage can.

"Well, Gonzales was right about this being good work. It is as if I'm actually there. You could teach a class on this stuff."

"Okay, now you're just making things up. I think we'd better leave before you start comparing me to anyone." I tucked the new cell phone in my back pocket.

Luca set the painting back on the easel. "I can't."

"Can't what?" I started to reach for my school bag, but Luca beat me to it.

"Can't compare it." He threw my backpack over his shoulder and followed me out of the studio.

"Okay, seriously stop it."

When we reached the stairs, Luca glanced down to the first floor. "I know I promised you a date tonight, but do you mind if we take a rain check? I just remembered something I have to do."

"It's okay. I wasn't actually planning on a date."

"Let me help you upstairs and then I can . . ."

"No, I'm fine. I need to learn to do this on my own anyway." Luca reluctantly handed me my backpack, which I managed to loop over my arms without dropping a crutch.

"See you tomorrow, Dana."

"*Adiós*."

I made it halfway up the stairs before glancing back. Luca had already vanished down the stairs to the first floor. The lobby was empty when I reached the dorm level. I also didn't hear any sounds coming from the boys' hallway. Now was my chance. I wanted answers—answers I wasn't going to get with the CIA's suggested line of questions.

After I retrieved my nail file kit (aka breaking-and-entering tools, courtesy of Millard) from my backpack, I left the pack on the lobby couch with my CIA necklace tucked inside. I crept—or whatever you would call trying to move quietly on crutches—down the hall to the boys' dorms. Every ten feet or so, I stopped and listened. When I didn't hear any voices or movement, I continued to Luca's room. His roommate might be home, but I figured I could always come up with an excuse for sneaking in. I put my ear to the door. With no sound on the other side, I started for my nail file kit.

"It was insane!" said a boy around the corner. I bit my lip and held my breath.

"He did a three-sixty right off the rail and then kept walking like he was on a stroll," another male voice said.

"Man, I wish I could have seen that." A door opened.

"Maybe you should try it," replied the first boy. Someone else spoke, but I couldn't make out the words before a door closed and the hallway went silent again. I started to reach again for my kit when the door handle, which I had been holding onto for support, turned. I tumbled right onto the floor inside Luca's dorm, my crutches clanging to the tiled floor. *So much for being quiet.*

I scrambled to my feet and closed the door. The dorm was nearly a copy of the one I shared with Sofía, except the layout was the exact opposite, as if the room had been flipped. The entrance to the kitchen was on the right instead of the left, and the couches faced the opposite wall.

I moved as quickly as possible to the bedroom that was most like mine. Clothes were piled on the floor, and photographs covered nearly every inch of one wall. A glance at several selfies told me it was Luca's roommate's room. I peeked under the bed, in the dresser drawers, and through the closet. He might not have been a suspect in Amoriel's disappearance, but since I was there, I decided to leave no stone unturned.

After finding nothing in the roommate's room, I headed to Luca's. I expected to find a room in a similar state as the last one, but it wasn't. The walls were bare, except for a large painting of the ocean. The bed was made and there was nothing on the dresser or nightstand. The clothes and shoes in the closet were organized and lined up perfectly.

I searched through the dresser drawers, where the clothing was, not surprisingly, meticulously folded and arranged. Even Luca's socks had been separated into color columns. *Who is this guy?*

Next I lay on my back on the floor to look under the low bed. Nothing. With nowhere left to search, I was about to roll over and stand up when something underneath the dresser caught my eye. Taped to the bottom of the last drawer was a large manilla folder. I carefully removed it, making sure to keep the tape intact.

The folder had no markings on the outside. I carefully opened it and found a photograph of a teenage girl, and then another, and another. The photos weren't inappropriate in any way — in fact, some of them looked like school pictures. I thumbed through the stack and counted nine. I leafed through the photos to see if I recognized any of the girls. When I saw the second-to-last photo, I gasped. It was Amoriel. She wore a school uniform in the photo, and her hair was shorter than in the picture Agent Denisovich had shown me, but it was definitely her.

I closed my eyes and used one of Itosu's meditation techniques to stop myself from screaming. *I was right about Luca from the start! Why did I think I could trust him?*

Furious, I wanted to take the folder straight to the CIA, but something held me back. I knew enough about their policies now to understand what would probably happen. They would take Luca into custody and question him on the whereabouts of Amoriel. If they were lucky, he would break and disclose her location. Most likely, though, he would refuse to talk, and if that happened we might never find her. No. I needed to come up with a more foolproof plan.

I returned the folder to the bottom of the dresser and secured it with the tape as best I could.

As I headed to the lobby, my mind flipped through memories like it was shuffling a deck of cards. Hiding things from The Company on my last mission had nearly cost me my life. If it hadn't been for the CIA, I wouldn't have saved a Van Gogh painting from being stolen, and a terrorist organization wouldn't have been shut down.

In my dorm room, I dropped my backpack and crutches and sat on the bed. I had to tell the CIA what was going on. Didn't I?

I pulled a cell phone from my back pocket and made a call.

19

Chickadee

"Thanks for meeting me," I told William. We sat side by side on a wooden park bench, watching birds eat the small pieces of bread we threw at them. The expanse of bright-green grass and large, bushy trees reminded me of the Northwest.

"You bet." William tossed a piece of bread in the air. A bird sailed down and caught it before it hit the ground. "I needed an excuse to take a break from the piles of paper on my desk. Don't get me wrong, I'm loving the research. I just didn't realize how much time I would be spending alone, organizing and analyzing everything."

"If you ever need a hand looking at the stuff, let me know. I may not be able to draw anything more than a sad stick figure, but this brain of mine" —I tapped at my temple— "likes to record and organize information."

"So you're still struggling with that sketching class?"

"Sketching yes, but I might have made a breakthrough with another medium."

"Let me guess . . ." William bit the side of his lip. "Painting. It has to be painting."

I threw a handful of crumbs onto the grass. "How did you know?"

"Just knowing you and your background, I guess. And then there's Paris and your mom's addition to the painting in Golkov's office. Honestly, I'm kind of surprised you hadn't painted before."

William's words reminded me that I didn't have to hide from him anymore. It was a relief to sit next to someone who knew who I was but wouldn't treat me differently. I hadn't given him the details of my Mexico mission, but he knew all about St. Petersburg and Moscow, and Elijah and Ivan, and how my mom had worked for the CIA and The Company. I'd explained about Tanner's coma and how he was now awake.

I scratched at the top of my cast, just under my knee. "There's still a lot of things I've never tried—skydiving, climbing Mt. Everest, roller skating, caviar—"

William smiled. "You've never had caviar?"

"Have you?"

"No. I just figured with what you do, you'd be wining and dining all the time."

"Nope. Still just mostly hamburgers and sandwiches, I'm afraid. Or more like enchiladas and beans here."

William plopped a large piece of bread into his mouth and started chewing. I laughed. He put his hand over his mouth and said, "What?" The word came out muffled.

"I thought the bread was for the birds. It was hard to get, you know. In Mexico, they are more into tortillas."

He finished chewing and swallowed. "The birds would have eaten tortillas just fine. I just didn't eat much for lunch." William took a second bite of bread.

"If you're hungry, we can meet another . . ."

"No. You wanted to talk. So talk." He brushed crumbs off his T-shirt and shorts. He had jogged over to meet me at the park. I missed our runs together in Providence but knew there would be no running for me until my leg healed.

"As you know, I can't tell you the specifics about why I'm here in Mexico."

"I get it. Wait, are they listening right now—the CIA?" William glanced around as if to make sure no one was eavesdropping on us.

"I left their transmitter back at my apartment," I said. "They won't be happy about it, but I needed some time to think."

"About what?"

"About why I'm really here, who I trust, and what information I should divulge." My eyes fixed on the birds waiting for more bread.

"You can trust me." William put a hand on my arm. "You know that, right?"

"That's why I called you." I shifted position so his arm fell away. His touch was a distraction and I needed a clear mind. "I have information the CIA wants, but if I give it to them, it might compromise the mission."

"Let me get this straight. You're worried if you give certain information to the CIA, they might do something that could make the mission fail—the one they recruited you for in the first place?"

I tossed a piece of bread to a bird that had wandered away from the others. "Exactly."

William frowned. "Don't they want the mission to succeed?"

"Yes, but they don't totally trust me anymore or believe I can do more than pose as a student." I turned to look at La Academia behind me, though the stone fence and large trees hid the actual building. "I know how they'll respond to the information. It's part of their policies. And they are all about their policies."

"So show them yours," William said.

"What?"

"Alex, from what you've told me, The Company and the CIA have different ways of doing things. They both have their own rules that make them run a certain way. I know you care about Professor Golkov and about completing this mission for the CIA. But you've also mentioned not knowing what would happen when you returned back home to Providence . . . about where your place would be. Have you ever considered that you might be struggling with this decision because you haven't been true to yourself?"

I shook my head. "I don't follow."

"Do you see those birds over there? In the tree?"

"Yeah." I glanced up to the small birds that had gathered in a tree about fifty feet away. They were gray and white with a black head, and probably only the size of my hand.

"Do you notice how they aren't coming down with these larger ones to eat our bread?"

"Yes."

"Those are Mexican Chickadees. They could eat the bread pieces, but they aren't coming. They prefer seeds and berries."

"So . . ."

"So, the chickadees are doing their own thing. The bread wouldn't necessarily hurt them, but knowing what is good for them, they remain where they are. When someone comes with seeds, I can guarantee you they will come down and feed on the seeds."

"But what does that have to do with me?" I tossed some small pieces of bread toward the tree. The chickadees ignored the bread, while the other birds quickly pecked at it until it was gone.

"You're like a bird," William said.

"I'm a bird?"

His smile revealed a dimple in his cheek. "You're being offered pieces of bread from different sources. But maybe bread isn't what you need. A bird who only eats bread will become malnourished."

"Are you saying I shouldn't work for The Company or the CIA?"

"No." William grabbed my hands and turned me to face him. "What I'm saying is that you don't have to accept it."

"I don't know what that means. If I'm supposed to be like the chickadee, I should look for seeds, right? Like another place to do what I do?"

"No, Alex." William dropped my hands and reached for my shoulders. He shook me gently. "You don't need to find a new place. You don't need to look outside of yourself or change who you are. Have you ever considered that maybe *they* are the ones who need to change?"

"You think The Company should change?"

"Not exactly." William let go of me but stared at me with such intensity that I couldn't look away. "Can you honestly tell me that things wouldn't have turned out differently with Red Eye and Paris if you had gone to The Company right from the start, right after that Ivan guy made those threats? Something held you back, and it wasn't just the threats against people's lives. From what you've told me, The Company would have found a way around it."

"Maybe things would have been different," I replied. "I'm not really sure."

"I know you were trying to be independent and take care of it yourself, Alex, but if you'd realized you had a choice in how The Company responded, you could have worked together to come to a conclusion without so much risk."

I sat back against the arm of the bench and thought about the Paris mission. I'd been so worried about Ivan's threats that I hadn't asked The Company for help. Now I realized such thinking was faulty. If I had told Golkov about my plan, he could've used some of the organization's extensive resources to support me at the Louvre. Maybe that is what William meant. All this time I'd thought of myself as an agent for The Company, yet I didn't have to be their agent. The CIA might consider me to be their agent as well, but I didn't have to be.

"I need to be an agent to myself," I said.

William's broad smile told me I finally understood what he was trying to say. I thought back to the conversation with Daly a few nights before. Is that what he had been saying, too? He had told me to find my own way. Maybe this was it.

"Do you mind if we call it a night?" I asked, pulling the CIA phone from my pocket.

"Sure. Got big plans?"

"Maybe. If I'm going to be my own agent, I need to start with this current mission."

William stood and stretched his arms. "You know how to reach me." He started to turn, then stopped and moved closer. "I'm proud of you, Alex. I just . . . I just wanted you to know that." His fingers brushed my cheek before he turned and ran down the sidewalk, the sound of his footfalls moving nearly as fast as my heartbeat.

I reached up and touched my face where his hand had been. I wasn't ready for the emotions warring within me, or for the phone call I was about to make.

20

Undercover

The taxi carried me down the street, not as fast as I wanted, but I'd already yelled "*mas rapido*" into the driver's ear—twice. I'd be fine as long as we didn't lose the taxi that was two cars in front of us. Right after our design class, I'd overheard Luca on the phone, mentioning something about the Palacio de Bellas Artes. I didn't know why he was going there, but after what I found in his room, I wasn't about to let him go anywhere without me. Maybe he would lead me right to Amoriel.

The taxi driver revved the engine and sped up. The CIA necklace swung back and forth in front of me as I leaned forward in my seat. Five minutes later, Luca's taxi stopped in front of a white marble building just ahead. He jumped out of the vehicle and ran up the steps.

"Right here!" I told my driver, who immediately slammed on the brakes. I handed him several pesos and thanked him, then shoved my crutches out of the car and scrambled onto the sidewalk. I tried to look casual as I moved as quickly as possible to the entrance of the Palacio de Bellas Artes. My eyes barely had time to record the large golden dome at the top of the building, which really did resemble a palace.

Inside, I searched the first floor, passing murals painted by Diego Rivera and David Siqueiros, and architecture that deserved better study. No sign of Luca.

Heading toward the stairs, I ran into William. "What are you doing here?" I gasped. It was like seeing him at the Louvre all over again. Scenes of him and Daly in Paris ran across my vision. It was amazing how the people I'd tried to protect from my spy life managed to get right in the center of it, even when I was thousands of miles from home.

"I'm here like everyone else, to see architecture and art." William rubbed a hand over the side of his face and then shook his head. "That's a lie. I knew you'd be here."

"What? I barely knew I'd be here less than an hour ago."

"I stopped at the school. Your roommate told me where to find you."

"Sofía?" I'd mentioned where I was headed when I told her I was skipping our next class. She'd thought I was meeting Luca at the palace. She didn't realize who he was and why I was following him.

"I told her it was important."

"William, I can't talk with you right now. I'm in the middle of a mission." I still couldn't believe that the CIA had accepted my terms after I told them what I had found on Luca. They had agreed to give me forty-eight hours to get closer to him while they did their own research on him. After forty-eight hours, they would take him in.

Wondering where he'd gone, I glanced behind me and then to my left and right.

"He's on the third floor," William said quietly.

"Who?"

"The guy with the black hair. The one you called Luca."

"Luca? How . . ." I shook my head and moved in the direction of the stairs, but William caught my arm.

"Listen, Alex, I'm not trying to get involved in your mission, and I don't care who you're dating, but I had to warn you."

"Dating?"

"You and the Luca guy. Sofía told me you are going out. It's okay that you've moved on. I get it."

"I'm not dating him," I said. With what I knew about Luca now, the thought of being alone with him repulsed me.

William's shoulders relaxed a bit. "Then why are you . . . Wait, is he a part of the m—"

"What did you come to warn me about?" I broke in. "About Luca?"

"That's the thing. I don't think his name is Luca."

"What do you mean?"

"That first day I saw you in Mexico, at the cathedral, I thought I recognized him but wasn't sure. Then I noticed him near the university campus, talking with a gray-haired man. As I walked by, the man called him Juan."

"Are you sure?" I was nearly a hundred-percent sure Luca had been involved in Amoriel's disappearance, but learning he was pretending to be someone else solidified everything.

"Yes. What are you going to do?"

"You can't be involved in this, William. The CIA already suspects Luca. I'm here following him."

William stared down at my crutches and then at the stairs in front of me. "Let me just see where he is headed. I'll make sure you don't lose him."

I should've sent William home, but he had a point. It would take me too long to go through the building. "Here." I unfastened the CIA necklace from around my neck and shoved it into his hand. "Just keep this facing in front of you and watch him. I'll check the exits on this floor. I don't think he can get out unless he comes back down this way."

William eyed the arrow pendant of the necklace, then took the stairs two at a time. I didn't wait for him to reach the top before I proceeded down the hallway. My crutches bumped against a ridge of tile and I nearly fell forward, but managed to grab the stair railing. In a flash, I saw the back of a man who looked like Señor Gonzales. When I glanced up again, he was gone. I reviewed the memory in my mind. The hair looked similar, but I couldn't be sure. Why would Gonzales be here instead of teaching his other classes at La Academia?

The crowd that had gathered in front of a large mural parted as I moved down the hall, peering into each room. The back of the palacio had exits, but they were for emergencies only, and an alarm would sound if Luca tried to escape through one of those doors.

I paused in the hallway. Why would Luca come to the palacio? Was he meeting someone here? Another victim?

A hand gripped my upper arm and pulled me into an alcove just a few feet to my right, making me drop a crutch against the wall of the space. Thinking it was William, I turned to ask if he'd found Luca.

Dark, shiny hair fell over the eyes of the good-looking guy—Luca or Juan, or whatever his real name was.

I opened my mouth to speak, but he covered it with his hand.

"Shhh." He peeked out of the alcove and then returned his gaze to me. "Don't make a sound. He's here."

Luca's grip tightened on my arm as I tried to move. He had the advantage of weight and strength, but I hadn't been training with Sensei Itosu for several months for nothing. Though one of the crutches had fallen out of my reach, one still remained in my hand. I whipped it at his shin. The sound of metal against bone echoed through the alcove. Luca grunted and released his grip on me. I swung the crutch into his knees, sending him farther into the alcove. Not waiting for him to fall, I hopped from the alcove and searched the crowd. No William.

Using my remaining crutch, I limped to the nearest room to find a place to hide. A door in the corner looked promising, so I hobbled over and turned the knob. The door opened and I stepped into a janitor's closet about three or four feet wide and across. I shut the door, which I discovered did not have a lock. A line of light trickled in from under the threshold. I searched for a light switch, but the only things my hand found were a broom handle and a bucket of cleaning supplies.

I pulled my phone from my pocket and texted William to explain what had happened. I waited for a response. Muffled sounds on the other side of the door kept me on alert, but no one neared the door. I called William's phone. No one answered. *Where is William?*

After about two more minutes, I pulled out the CIA phone. Just as I was about to press the call button, the door in front of me swung open. It took a second for my eyes to adjust and recognize the silhouette standing in the light.

"What is wrong with you?" Luca said. He bent to rub his leg. I took my chance and pushed into him, kicking his other shin with my cast. From the scream that came from his mouth, the pain in my leg couldn't have been as bad as the pain in his. I stepped around him, but he grabbed for my shirt and pulled me back in his direction. "Stop running from me," he said through gritted teeth.

"What is wrong with you? Where is Amoriel?" After I said the words, I realized my mistake. I shouldn't have admitted I knew what Luca had done. I pushed at his chest and tried to shake free from his grasp. He wrapped an arm around my middle and pinned both of my arms at my side, pushing me back toward the closet.

"That's what I'm trying to figure out, if you'd stop moving long enough to let me talk," he said. I struggled, trying to elbow him in the ribs. "Seriously, Dana, hold still or he might see us and then my cover will be blown."

I stopped moving. "Your cover?" I twisted to look into Luca's eyes. The honest expression on his face gave me pause.

"Yes." He pushed me back to the closet and looked over his shoulder. "I'm PFM. Now get back in there before you're seen."

"The Policía Federal Ministerial?" I paused. "Why should I believe you?" I managed to get one arm free and grabbed for the doorframe. There was no way Luca was part of the organization in Mexico that was comparable to the FBI in the U.S. He seemed too young, plus I simply couldn't believe he was capable of solving crimes.

He threw up his arms. "You know what? Fine. I saved you yesterday and probably again today. Don't believe me. I don't care."

"You saved me?" I stepped back until I stood in the closet again. I thought back to Señor Gonzales in the art studio. Luca had rescued me from an awkward situation, but he hadn't truly *saved* me. And how was he saving me today?

He peered in at me. "I know you're smart, Dana, and extremely talented, but seriously, don't you get it?"

I rewound and fast-forwarded everything I knew about Luca. I'd never seen him hurt anyone. If anything, he'd always been helpful. But the pictures in his room—all those photos of girls, including Amoriel. I had assumed he was targeting the girls. But what if he was trying to rescue them?

"Those photos in your room?"

His eyes widened. "What were you . . . Who *are* you?"

"It doesn't matter. What does matter is that I find Amoriel."

"I'm trying to find out what happened to her and the others, and—" Luca suddenly ducked inside the closet, pushing into me until I stumbled back into the wall. He slowly closed the door and put his finger to his lips. I could barely make out his face in the dark. We waited for several minutes, the heat of his breathing warming my face. One set of footsteps passed by, and still we waited. Just when I was sure we were clear, someone approached the door. I tried to still my panicked breaths, but I had to cover my mouth to keep quiet. I was sure the stricken look on Luca's face matched my own.

He turned his back to me and put out his hands, as if to protect me. I widened my own stance and clenched my fists, ready to fight.

The door opened. As light flowed into the dark space, Luca rammed into the figure in front of us. They both fell to the floor and struggled. I heard a few punches before my eyes adjusted to recognize a pair of penny loafers and a head of curly brown hair.

"Stop!" I stumbled forward until I could shove into Luca's shoulder with my good knee. He fell to the side. "Stop it. This is my friend William."

Luca got to his feet and tried to pin William, who promptly kneed him in the gut, sending him to the floor right in front of me. "Dana, this guy has been following you," Luca said. "He's probably in on everything. He may even be working for Gonzales."

"Gonzales?" I stared at Luca. "What are you talking about?"

William jumped up. "You're following her and pretending to be someone you're not. Right, Juan? Are you even Mexican?"

I hopped in front of William and put my hand on his chest. "He's PFM. He's trying to figure out what happened to Amoriel."

With confusion written in his brows, William looked between Luca and me.

"You're--" He stopped when I gave him a look. "And he's—" William threw his hands in the air. "I'm living in a telenovela."

"I'm here to find answers to what happened to all of the missing girls," Luca finished. "The ones you saw in my room, Dana. PFM put me undercover last year when the second girl vanished."

Everything was starting to come together. Luca disappearing at strange times, watching out for me, and now, I realized, keeping his eye on all the girls at La Academia, but not for the reasons I had previously thought.

"So the man I saw you with on the university campus . . . he was PFM too?" William asked.

"You saw me?"

"Yeah, yesterday."

Luca closed his eyes and let out a sigh. "Yes, I was with my handler. He's the one who helped me figure out that Gonzales is involved. That's why I'm here today. I heard him tell a girl in our class to meet him here today. It didn't sound at all innocent."

"So he's here?" I asked.

"Yes." Luca bent over with his hands on his knees.

"And you think Gonzales is involved in the disappearance of those girls?"

My mind played the movie of me walking down the hallway earlier. It must have been Gonzales I saw. Then my brain flashed to a scene from the week before. Standing on the top of the Pyramid of the Sun, I had felt eyes on me. I slowed the memory down as I searched behind me. The same long dark hair. The familiar walk. Señor Gonzales had been in Teotihuacan and had lied to me about it. But why? Had he been following me since I arrived? Was he following other girls from La Academia? Why was he outside the school so late the night he saw me fall out of the tree?

Luca and William stood in front of me now, waiting, as if I had all the answers.

"Why not just arrest him?" William asked Luca.

"We have no proof he's done anything illegal. We only know he had contact with the missing girls."

"Isn't that enough to question him?" I asked.

"No, but even if it was, we could lose the girls if we can't get evidence to hold him indefinitely."

"So how do you know he's involved?" I continued. "I mean, he is a teacher at the school. Lots of teachers had contact with these girls." I reached into the closet and found my crutch and then shifted my weight onto my good leg.

"I don't have proof exactly, just what I've seen and what others have told me. Gonzales' contact with the girls, it wasn't . . . like . . . you know . . ." Luca's face reddened.

"The contact wasn't all teacher-student appropriate," I guessed. I thought back to the art studio and Gonzales' hands on me. A shudder rippled through me.

"What did he do?" William stepped closer to me, his jaw set and his eyes a sliver of darkened blue.

"Nothing. Nothing happened." I touched William's arm. "Luca came before . . ." I didn't know what would have happened if he hadn't arrived when he did, though the thought of Gonzales doubled over from a knee to the gut wasn't entirely unpleasant.

"Listen, Dana," Luca said. "Gonzales might suspect I know something. I'm sure he saw me here today. But he doesn't suspect you."

"Did you see him? The day at the pyramid when we first met. Was he there?"

"I . . . I don't know," Luca replied. "But he's obviously had his eye on you since you first arrived. He probably knew your records had been transferred here."

"But why me? Why the others? Those photos I found in your room—all of those girls couldn't have attended the academy. Wouldn't everyone at the school wonder why girls keep leaving?"

Luca looked over his shoulder toward the hallway. Then he turned back to William and me. "Amoriel was the third girl to disappear from La Academia, and as far as everyone there knows, she packed up and left, just like the first two. The other six missing girls went to private schools here in the city, but they all disappeared under similar circumstances. I got involved because the second girl who disappeared from La Academia was a state official's daughter. The family has been keeping everything on the down-low, but the PFM put me undercover here because of her."

I wanted to ask Luca more about Amoriel and if he had been dating her because he suspected she might be next, or if their relationship had been an unexpected part of the mission.

"So how are you going to prove this Gonzales character is a sleazebag?" William said the last word in English, but Luca seemed to get the gist of it.

"First, let's get out of here." He looked between William and me. "Separately. If you see Gonzales, text me his location and try to act natural, especially if he interacts with you." Luca pointed to me.

"Okay, but if he tries anything again, I'm not afraid to use this as a weapon." I lifted up my crutch.

"I believe you," Luca said. "But if my plan is going to work, you might have to hold off on inflicting so much pain. We need proof, and I have an idea on how we can get it."

"How's that?" William came to stand beside me and crossed his arms over his brown-plaid vest.

"Dana, how would you feel about doing some undercover work?"

21

Work in Progress

A few hours after returning from the Palacio de Bellas Artes, I stretched out on my bed, then picked up my cell phone and called my brother. Hearing his voice soothed me like nothing else. Tanner was awake and he was still okay.

"How are you?" I asked him. "And don't just say 'good.' I've heard that enough from Daly."

Tanner laughed a little. "It's been slow going, Lexie, but my strength is returning. I'm not going to lie, though. It's been hard."

I hated not being there while he struggled. "But you're feeling good and you can move better now?"

"Yeah. My arms don't spasm like they used to. I won't be bench-pressing my weight any time soon, but it's getting better."

"What about your head? Do you feel like yourself?"

"Kind of." Tanner cleared his throat. "Except I keep having the same dreams over and over. It's actually kind of freaky."

"What do you mean?"

"I don't know. Everything happens so fast and the colors are too bright, but I'm supposed to do something, maybe find something—I just can't remember what. And nothing slows down long enough for me to get more than pieces."

"That is weird."

Tanner hesitated. "And Mom is there, too."

"Mom?"

"This will sound strange, but it doesn't seem to be a dream. It's like it's a memory."

My heart went out to Tanner. For nearly a year, I'd had memories of our mom. They were bittersweet reminders of what we'd lost . . . what we'd never be able to get back.

"I just wish I could remember." He let out an exasperated breath.

"I'm sorry, Tanner. Don't stress about it. I've come to understand that my involuntary memories surface for a reason. If you're supposed to remember something, you will. Just give it time."

"I guess." He sighed again. My brother had never had much in the patience department. "And since you brought up time, when are you coming back, Lexie?

I'd known the question would be coming; I just wasn't prepared to answer it yet. I still had to make Luca's plan work. "Not much longer. I'm hoping by this weekend."

"Wow. This Golkov professor better be paying you a lot to traverse the globe for him. Daly says you guys were in France a few months back. Next time you go someplace cool, I'm coming."

I started tracing the embroidery on my comforter. "Now that sounds like a plan, though honestly I'm tired of being away. I'd live off ratty cafeteria food and sleep in a smaller-than-twin bed, just to have you and Dad and Dal . . ." I cut myself off. I hadn't realized how much I missed Daly until his name began to leave my lips.

Tanner laughed. "Speaking of James, he wants to talk to you."

"I wasn't talking about . . . wait, he's there?"

"Are you kidding? He's like my wingman now."

"No, I'm not." Daly's voice carried over from the background.

"Bye, Lexie," Tanner said with enough playfulness that I knew this wasn't the end of our conversation about Daly.

"Bye, Tanner."

I heard the phone being handed off and then Daly's voice. "Tanner doesn't need a wingman. He does fine on his own."

"I'll bet."

"On the other hand, I do a lot better when I'm with someone."

Catching the inference in Daly's tone, I wished I could see his face. "So, Tanner is doing better?" I asked.

"He's great, Alex. Really. You don't need to worry about him. What I'm interested in is how . . . how the work is going." Daly's voice sounded tight, so I assumed he was still in Tanner's room.

"If by work you mean mission, I'm pursuing a lead right now. I'm not sure how it will pan out, but it's probably my only shot."

"You know I'm going to need more information than that. You aren't going to go off on your own again, are you?" Daly was referring to my semi-solo mission to the Louvre, and though things had worked out in the end, it was only because he'd followed me and I'd accepted his help.

Doing things on my own was probably a knee-jerk reaction I would always have to fight. But I'd learned my lesson, and after Luca had explained his plan to me, I had taken William's advice. I'd already spoken with Denisovich and the CIA and even received permission from them to bring in my own resources, aka The Company. The CIA had even returned my Millard-enhanced phone, which I was now using.

"No, those days are behind me," I told Daly finally. "You were right before about me finding my own way. I think I've figured it out now."

"You have, have you?" he said, and I pictured his wry smile in my mind.

"Yeah, it took William to help me see it, but I know where I want to go from here."

"Oh," Daly said quietly, and I sensed something in the silence that followed. Disappointment, maybe.

"What is it?" I asked.

He cleared his throat. "Nothing. I'm just glad you figured it out."

"Well, I don't have everything worked out, and I need to complete this mission first, but once I come home I can figure out the details. William even said he'd help me."

"He's coming back to Providence?" Irritation edged Daly's words.

"You're the one who sent him to help me, remember?"

"Yeah, I know. I just . . ."

"He's not coming back right away," I said. "His grant will keep him here until late this year, but it's not like we can't communicate. You and I have been doing that the last few weeks."

Daly let out a breath. "That's true. I just thought . . . never mind." A door closed and I heard the faint call of a siren in the distance. "Now tell me about this mission."

I stood just outside the classroom. Juan—who would always be Luca to me—was late. I wasn't about to enter Gonzales' class without him, no matter how many students had already filed into the room. I wished I could tell Sofía about the mission and warn her about Gonzales, but doing so would force her to be involved in something dangerous. Every day I better understood my mom's choice to hide her secret life from me. Growing up oblivious to her dangerous adventures had allowed me to experience an innocent and carefree childhood. If I could've had my mom back, even for a minute, I would thank her for that. Sofía deserved the same chance as I had. As it was, my roommate had already found her seat in the classroom and thought I was waiting for Luca because I had fallen for him.

A student walked past me and I peeked through the doorway. At the front of the room, Señor Gonzales sat at his table, leafing through sketchbooks. It amazed me that a person involved in several abductions could look so normal. I patted at The Company phone nestled at my side. The CIA had insisted on adding their own untraceable technology to Millard's wizardry. Denisovich said everything else was still functioning, though I had yet to try out the taser. I wouldn't have minded using it on Señor Gonzales right then and there.

"You ready for this?" Luca said, suddenly standing beside me. Maybe he was better at this spy thing than I was.

"I don't think I'll ever be totally ready, but I'm here."

"You're wearing the GPS tracker I gave you?"

"Safe and hidden." I patted at my neckline, where I'd attached the tracker under the collar of my dress, close to the CIA necklace.

Luca still didn't know I was working with the CIA. It's not that I didn't believe he was a PFM agent; I just didn't trust him enough to keep my secret after this was over.

"Then let's do this." He reached for my hand. I held up a crutch in response, so he put his hand on the small of my back and escorted me into the room. I tried to ignore the stares that followed us as Luca led me to my seat, but I couldn't hide the blush rising up my cheeks. He took my crutches and helped me into my chair.

"We have to make it look real," he whispered in my ear as he leaned down to set my crutches next to my sketching table. Before I had a chance to respond, he lightly kissed my lips. I was so taken aback that I dropped my sketchbook to the floor. Luca bent to pick it up, a wide smile on his face. If we hadn't been undercover, I would've responded with a slap to his perfectly chiseled cheek. Our fake relationship was part of his plan, but his expression made it clear that he was enjoying this far too much.

A few hushed whispers broke out behind Luca and me before my gaze returned to the front of the room. Gonzales' eyes caught mine for a few seconds before he cleared his throat and started the lesson.

Luca played his part well for the rest of class. He got up several times to sharpen his pencil and managed to loop around my table, even though the sharpener was in the opposite direction. Each time he smiled and winked before returning to his seat. Gonzales was nearly seething when I chanced a look in his direction.

When class ended, Luca escorted me out of the classroom the same way he'd brought me in. Sofía looked over her shoulder and raised her eyebrows at us before I headed to my next class. If all went as planned, I would be gone for good before she returned from her classes. Then I wouldn't have to explain myself or dignify Luca's actions with any kind of response.

"Do you really think it worked?" I said quietly to Luca before we arrived at the door of my next class.

"Did you see his face?" Luca whispered next to my ear. "I'd say it definitely worked."

"Do you think Gonzales suspects anything?"

"What could he suspect? And seriously, your acting in there was spot on. How can you make yourself blush on cue like that? If art doesn't work out for you, maybe you should look into the secret service. You're a natural at this undercover thing."

You have no idea. "So we'll meet here at noon?" I asked.

"Make it 12:03. We have to time this just right."

"Got it."

Trying to retie my belt, I dropped one of my crutches. Luca snagged it before it toppled to the ground. He handed the crutch to me and said, "I'll see you in a few hours."

During my sculpting class, I couldn't concentrate. Plus, clay was almost as sketching. Itching to paint again, I wanted to sneak out and find myself a brush and canvas.

As I sat my bowl—or was it a plate?—on the kiln tray, a female student I'd talked to only a few times came up to me.

"So, you and Luca, huh?" She tossed back her fluffy brown hair.

I picked up my bag. "Yeah."

"Just be careful of him. He's a real heartbreaker."

"Aren't they all?"

She smiled for a second and then got serious. "Guard yourself, okay?"

I looked at her quizzically, but she left before I could ask what she meant. It was already noon anyway. I needed to get to Luca.

A minute later, I paused on the bottom step that led to the lobby. Luca stood near the center of the room, facing the other direction. Mara, a girl from my design class, was talking animatedly to him, her hands waving. She spoke loudly enough that I could hear her words from across the lobby.

"Pelé is the best fùtbol player of all time," she said. "Have you even seen footage of his playing?"

"Yeah, he's good. You should meet him sometime."

"I wish." Mara tucked her too-perfect-to-be-real auburn hair behind her ear.

"I could arrange a meeting." Luca grabbed her hand and pulled her close to the wall, right next to Gonzales' classroom.

"You know him?" she asked.

"I have friends that do. If I arrange for you to meet him, you and I could do something before the meeting or afterward." Luca's tone was so telenovela-ish that I had to hold in a giggle.

Mara's eyes met mine then and she smiled over Luca's shoulder. *Okay, Alex, it's now or never. Prove how good you can be.* I narrowed my eyes and moved close enough that I could smell the girl's passion-fruit perfume.

"What is this?" The words burst out of me in a quick rush.

"What?" Luca put up his hands in feigned innocence.

"You're asking another girl out?" I yelled.

He crossed his arms in front of him. "Does it matter?"

"I thought we were dating." I looked the girl up and down and channeled my inner "mean girl" glare.

"You actually thought I was only dating you? Have you even met me?" Luca's pretentious smirk was totally over-the-top.

"You are such a pig!" I pushed at his chest with my hand, dropping a crutch in the process. If anyone in the vicinity wasn't paying attention to us, they were now.

He stepped back. "I thought you knew we were just having fun."

"Fun! Fun?" I felt my face go red, but it wasn't enough. If I was going to make this real, I needed more raw emotion. I needed to think of something sad, something that forced me to feel. The memory of the accident and the funeral afterward pushed into my mind, but it didn't stop there. I pulled on the memories until there was only one left that I hadn't let myself face.

"Is that everything?" my father's hollow voice carried from the front door into the empty living room, where I stood motionless. I wondered if he would ever sound like himself again. The small moving van outside held everything we'd decided to keep. Most of our furniture had already been donated to a local charity.

"Just a few more boxes," I said. "They're in the studio. I'll get them."

"I can help."

"No. I need to do this on my own."

"Okay." Dad sounded unsure but didn't press me. He stayed where he was, and I headed to Mom's studio. My mind played memories of me standing in the doorway, telling her about my day. Sometimes she would continue to paint, but usually she would set down her brush and listen.

Most of her finished pieces of artwork had been framed and hung in the house, and those had already been packed up. The drawers had been emptied and the easels given away. All that was left were two large boxes with the words "Work in Progress" written in Mom's flowy script across the sides.

The tops of some larger canvases peeked out above the top of the boxes. I stared down at the edges of twenty-five or thirty pieces of work that would never be hung. All the canvases would remain incomplete, with no artist to finish them. The strain of the last few weeks shattered my façade. I collapsed to the carpet of the studio and let tears wash down my face. There would be no more paintings, no more late-night talks, no more family vacations to Cannon Beach, no more nights making homemade ice-cream. Most of all, though, there would be no more of Mom's smiling face, the look in her storm-gray eyes reassuring me that everything would be okay. Now things would never be okay.

When I had no more tears left, I stood and placed a hand on one of the canvases. I started to remove it but stopped when I saw the purple and blue and white on the edges. The subdued colors and lines reminded me of the impressionistic brush strokes of Monet. The painting fell back into the box when I let go. I didn't want to see what hadn't been completed, because then I would be constantly reminded of my mother's incomplete life. The memories playing on a constant loop in my head were reminder enough.

I stood and stared down at the paintings for another minute. "Goodbye, Mom," I said before I walked away, trying desperately to shove memories of her away in the recesses of my mind.

The tears falling down my face while I stood in the hallway at La Academia weren't pretend. I had already cried for Tanner. I had cried for what had changed and what had been lost. But in the last year, I'd never really let myself cry for my mom.

"Dana?" Luca's grimace disappeared and he started to step forward. Mara reached for his arm and I saw his composure waver for a second. Did he sense that my tears were real? Either way, it didn't matter. We had a mission to complete.

"Stay away from me," I said loudly so my voice would travel into the adjoining halls and classrooms. I looked to Mara. "If you had any sense, you'd stay away from him too." Movement behind them caught my eye. Señor Gonzales stood in his open doorway, with what looked like confusion drawing his brows down over his dark eyes.

I picked up my fallen crutch and exited the back door of the school. I kept moving past the spot where I had fallen the week before, then continued around the pool and didn't stop until I reached the outermost portion of the school grounds. Tall bushes covered in pink roses lined the bottom of the stone fence. As tears poured down my cheeks, I wasn't thinking of Luca, the mission, or my family and friends back home. I played memories of my mom, periodically wiping away the tears and mascara with the back of my hand.

"Here," Gonzales said from behind me. I turned to see him holding out a tissue. I accepted it and dabbed at my face. He had responded quicker than Luca and I had planned, but that was a good thing, because it meant we would get answers sooner. I took a deep breath, trying to regain my composure.

"Teen boys can be cruel," Gonzales said, stepping to my side.

"Yeah."

"If it makes you feel better, he was never my favorite student."

I gave a weak smile and faced the bushes again. Playing an innocent, heartbroken girl should've been easy, but I wasn't sure what to say next. I'd never let myself let go like that before. I'd always tried to be strong, no matter how weak I felt inside.

"It must be difficult being at a new school, away from family and friends, especially when . . . well, when things aren't going as you would like." Gonzales' voice sounded so comforting, as if he was genuinely interested in my problem. If this is how he had treated Amoriel, I could see how she might have trusted him.

A small breeze rustled the leaves and flowers of the bushes, sending a few pale-pink petals to the ground, and the scent of roses through the air. "It is hard," I said. Feeling a bit lightheaded, I wondered if I'd eaten breakfast that morning.

"I bet I could make it easier for you," Gonzales said.

"How's that?" I asked. Teachers definitely weren't supposed to talk to their students like this. A flash of bright-blue eyes filled my mind. William had been my teacher once, and *he* had talked to me like this. I blinked away the memory.

"What if I could take you away from this place for a while? Make you forget your worries?"

I smiled at Señor Gonzales. Apparently I wouldn't have to use my acting skills to get closer to him. Maybe I would find Amoriel before the night was out . . . if I could get rid of the pounding in my head.

"Here, for your nose," Gonzales said next to me, but his voice sounded far away. I took the other tissue he offered and wiped my nose. I hadn't even realized it was running. The aroma of the rose bushes around us was intoxicating. My limbs tingled and my vision blurred. Feeling dizzy, I started to sway. Gonzales gripped one of my arms.

"Something is wrong with me," I said, looking up at him.

"It's okay, Alexandra. Everything will be okay." His voice was so soft and nice. I felt like I was floating, being lifted up on a cloud.

Wait. Alexandra? Did he just call me by my real name? The world around me began to spin. The last thing I remembered was a strong, sweet smell filling my nostrils.

22

Shipped

I lay on the hard metal floor, my entire body aching. The pressure in my head was excruciating. Seeing only blackness, I reached for my eyes to remove whatever covered them. All I felt was my sweat-damp hair on my dirty face.

I tried to think back to what had happened. I'd been standing next to Gonzales, enjoying the scent of roses, and wiping my face with a tissue and then . . . then what?

"Ether," said a weak female voice.

"What?" I managed to answer. My throat felt raw.

"It was ether. That's what he used on me, anyway. I didn't realize he was doing it until it was too late."

"How do you know? What's going on?" I tried to sit up, but a wave a nausea came over me. I turned to the side to vomit, but only bile rose to my throat. *How long was I out?*

"Gonzales, right? You were with him?" she asked after I stopped gagging.

"Yeah, but I was . . . I was trying to trick him. I was . . ." I stopped myself before I told her who I was. For all I knew, this could be another trap.

"My dad taught me about chemicals—ones that incapacitate people. Ether is one of them, but it's different than chloroform and more easily accessible. It also has more of a sweet smell."

A sweet smell? Ah, I thought it was the roses.

"Why would he do that?" I asked the girl.

"Because he's a psycho. From what I can tell, he targets girls who have some kind of government association. At least that's what I got from the others who were here."

"There were others?" I laid my head back down to try to calm the nausea.

"Yes. But they're gone now."

"Gone?"

"I'm not sure where, but he acted like they were useful for whatever he needed them for."

"Were they hurt?" I asked, not wanting to know the answer, but needing to.

"I'm not sure." Something in the girl's tone made me believe her. It didn't necessarily mean I was safe, but there was comfort in feeling I could trust someone who happened to be in the same predicament.

"I'm Dana," I said. I lifted my head, as if I could see her in the dark. A pounding at the base of my skull made me groan.

"It'll pass," she said. "It took two days for me, but feeling like I was going to throw up went away, along with the headache."

Two days? There was no way I could lay in wait for two days or more. I had to make a plan. *My phone!* I reached for my back pocket, only to find it empty. *Of course.* I felt at my neck for my camera necklace. It was missing too. At least Gonzales wouldn't have seen the GPS tracker Luca gave me. I slipped a hand under the collar of my shirt. The tracker was gone. "No," I whispered.

If this girl was right and Gonzales was targeting the families of government officials, did he know who I really was? Even if he did, my dad was just a college professor, and my mom was gone. How would holding me hostage benefit this guy at all? Since the tracker was missing, maybe Gonzales knew I was working for someone.

"I'm Amoriel," she said.

Amoriel. This time I sat up, regardless of how awful I felt. She was still alive and well! I smiled, and my mind flashed to Agent Denisovich's face. I'd made a promise to him, one that I had to keep.

"I have been searching for you. I know your father." I spoke in Russian instead of Spanish, partly as a test for her, but also to prove I really knew who her father was.

"Was he okay?" Amoriel's voice shook as she replied to me in Russian, her accent flawless like her father's.

"Yes. He's been doing everything he could to find you."

"How did he know where I was?"

I debated how to respond, but finally settled on a form of the truth. "He didn't know where—just that you'd been taken. I've been posing as a student at La Academia de Arte de Santa Catalina, hoping to figure out who might know where you were."

There was movement on her side of the room. Amoriel's feet barely made a sound on the cool metal beneath us as she neared me. "Gonzales is still there? At the school?" She sat just a few feet away now, close enough for me to catch the faint scent of sweat and dirt.

"Yes." I reached out until I found a metal wall behind me. My cast scraped against the floor as I scooted back to lean against the wall.

"What was that?" Amoriel asked.

"Plaster on metal. Sorry. I broke my leg last week trying to sneak into Luca's room."

"Luca?" Her voice tightened when she said his name.

"That's right. You two dated, right?"

"I thought we did." Amoriel stopped and took a deep breath. "But then I found out I was just a pawn in his game."

"His game?" I frowned, wondering if the ether was still affecting my ability to think clearly.

"I found out he'd been talking to all the girls at the school. Always asking questions. Then I found this notebook in his backpack where he had all their names and details about their lives. It was kind of creepy. After I broke up with him, I was going to tell the headmaster, but Gonzales got to me first. I never had a chance to tell anyone."

"Luca's not—" I stopped myself. *You can't tell her, Alex. It's not your secret to share.*

"He's not what?" she asked.

"He wasn't . . . He's not creepy, at least not in the way you think. He was getting information for the authorities. There have been other missing girls—a few more at the school and others in the area. He was trying to help find them."

"You mean he's not working with Gonzales?"

"No. Luca's been trying to find you."

"He has?" There was a relieved sigh behind her words. "What day is it?"

"How long have I been here?" I asked.

"He brought you in last night, or at least I think it was last night. It's always dark in here, and they don't bring food regularly."

"Well, if it's only been one day, today would be the 30th."

Amoriel shifted next to me. "I've been here over three weeks?"

"Yes."

"I didn't think it had been so long."

With my head starting to clear, I realized I had no idea where we were, or what type of space we were in. The metal floor felt cool, but the air was hot and stuffy. My hands fumbled on the metal wall behind me. There were deep ridges every six inches or so. I had a feeling I knew what we were inside, but I had to ask just the same.

"Do you have any idea where we are?"

"No," Amoriel replied. "Whenever they leave food, a little light is let in, but it takes too long for my eyes to adjust. All I know for sure is that we are in some kind of shipping container."

I let out a slow breath. I'd been taught how to jimmy a lock, climb a drain pipe, and break a window with just my shoe, but so far The Company hadn't taught me how to escape from a metal shipping container. I could add it to my list of things to learn, along with how to detect whether or not someone is drugging you before you black out.

"You aren't Mexican, are you?" she asked.

"No." I wondered if my accent wasn't very good.

"Are you from Russia? Is that how you know my father?"

I paused, not wanting to disclose too much. "I'm American. Do you know where your father works?"

"He does some kind of ambassador stuff between Russia and Mexico," Amoriel said. "I don't know all the details. I hadn't really questioned what he did for the government until I started talking with the other girls. We all tried to figure out why we were abducted and brought here. Obviously, we were all teenagers. And girls. For a while, I kind of thought . . . well, that maybe . . ."

"It was for human trafficking," I finished the sentence for her. The thought had crossed my mind too, until she had mentioned the government connection. But why had Gonzales taken me?

"Yeah, but when a few of the girls mentioned their parents' professions, we put it together. Two girls' fathers were senators. One girl said her mother worked closely with the Secretary of State. The last girl that came in had a father who worked for the CISEN, but she didn't know much about what he did."

It made sense. The Mexican CISEN was similar to the secret service of the United States. The girl's father could have been involved in espionage or analysis of intelligence, both of which dealt with sensitive information. He wouldn't have shared any of that with his family.

"So what does your dad do?" Amoriel asked me.

"He's a history professor at Brown University."

"No government connections?"

"Not unless you count his obsessions with past American presidents."

Amoriel gave a weak laugh. "So not him, then. What about your mother?"

It had been a long time since I'd answered questions about her. Fortunately, the ache wasn't as incapacitating as usual. "She died last year in a car accident."

"Oh. I'm sorry." After several seconds of silence, Amoriel added, "Then maybe my theory isn't right."

"No, I think you're right." *How did Gonzales know I wore a tracker, unless he was searching for it? And my name. He knew my real name.*

"But what about—" Amoriel began.

"It's me," I broke in. I couldn't tell Luca's or Denisovich's secrets, but I could share part of mine. "I have the government connection. At least partially." There was still a possibility Gonzales didn't know who exactly I worked for. Even if he knew my name and my association with Brown, he couldn't have known about The Company or my work with the CIA. Maybe he just thought I was an informant for PFM or something. That had to be it.

"You work for the U.S. government?" Amoriel asked. "But you don't sound much older than me."

"I'm not. It's a long story, but right now, we have to find a way out of here. Have you felt all along the walls?"

"I spent the whole first day trying to escape. There are no gaps or places that can be pried open. The only way out is the door. Some of the other girls and I tried pushing and kicking it when we didn't think anyone was on the other side, but it was no use." She banged against the metal behind us with what sounded like her fist.

"You said they bring in food. How does that go?"

"It's not Gonzales, at least not just him," Amoriel explained. "Because it happens so fast, I don't see them really, but I can hear their voices. I think there are two of them plus Gonzales. They bang on the door and tell me to go to the back. I'm not sure how they know, but they don't open the door until I'm touching the back wall. Then the door cracks open just long enough for them to push a bag of food through."

"Wait. What do you do about garbage? Or what if you need to go to the bathroom?" I tried not to think about the fact that I would need to soon.

"There's a bucket in the corner. It's actually more of a portable toilet with a seat and lid. There's some kind of sanitizer in it because it doesn't smell horrible like it should. They've emptied it twice since I've been here."

"And the garbage?" I needed to learn our enemy's habits to see if there was a possibility of breaking out when they opened the door.

"They tell me to leave it by the door and they take it away."

I moved to my side and attempted to push myself up, but my stomach lurched and I dry heaved again.

Amoriel said softly, "It will probably be a few more hours until you can stand. What are you trying to do?"

I cleared my throat, desperately wishing for water to wash out the sick taste in my mouth. "Have you checked the ceiling?"

"Yeah, maybe not as carefully as I checked the rest. It's about eight feet high and I'm only five foot two. The other girls checked and couldn't find anything."

"Have you tried standing on the bucket?" It was what I wanted to do if I hadn't been forced to sit down again.

"What do you think I'll find?" Amoriel asked.

"I'm not positive, but I think they have a camera in here."

"But how could they see anything? I can't even see my hand in front of me."

"Infrared cameras can see in the dark."

"So he could watch us all the time?" Amoriel sounded as disgusted as I felt. Gonzales had creeped me out since his behavior in the art studio, but this was worse because I couldn't fight him from in here.

"Maybe," I said. "Can you check again for me? The ceiling and maybe the tops of the walls?"

Amoriel moved across the container. "What am I looking for?"

"Any holes in the metal or ridges that seem out of place. It might just feel like a bolt in a strange place."

"Okay."

The bucket scraped against the floor as she moved around the enclosed space. I could hear her hands brushing the surface of the upper walls and ceiling. I closed my eyes and listened to my breathing. In and out. In and out. Just as Sensei Itosu had taught me.

After a few minutes, Amoriel gasped. "I . . . I think there's something here. It's above the door, on this side. It feels like a bolt like you said, but the edges—they're smoother. How did I not notice this before?"

"Okay. Get down. Move away."

"Why?" I heard her step down.

"With any luck, they didn't see you notice the camera. Now put the bucket back."

She started to move across the container, then stopped. "I don't get it. Shouldn't we cover it up or something?"

"Oh, we will. Just not yet. I might have an idea how we can get out of here."

A loud banging woke me with a start.

"Get to the back," yelled a deep man's voice from the direction of the door.

"Dana, come on." Amoriel found my upper arm in the dark and pulled me to my feet. Though the nausea had passed, my head still pounded. Each hop toward the back of the shipping container pressed harder at my temples. Once we reached the wall, Amoriel let go of my arm and I lowered myself to the floor.

"You ready?" I asked Amoriel.

"Yes." Her voice was calm.

"Good," I said before I slumped to the side and didn't move.

"Dana? Dana?" Amoriel shook my arm.

Chains rattled and hinges creaked. I opened my eyes just enough to see a sliver of light around the edges of the door. The door opened about a foot wider and a paper bag was thrown into the container.

"Wait!" Amoriel yelled. The person at the door paused for just a second longer as my eyes adjusted to the light. "There's something wrong with the new girl. I think she might be dehydrated."

"I don't care," came the answer through the open doorway before the man slammed the door. Chains rattled again on the other side of the door. I still didn't move.

Amoriel shook me again before she moved across the container and grabbed the bag. She came back and sat in front of me. "Come on, Dana, wake up." Though I was pretty sure the camera had no audio capabilities, I wanted to make sure everything looked like I had passed out and wasn't coming to. Amoriel placed the bag between us with the camera at her back. As she started to pull food out of the bag, I smelled bananas. After several seconds, she shook my shoulder again.

"She's not waking up!" she yelled. When there was no response, she moved to the door. "Help. She needs help!" She pounded on the door and jumped a few times. I prayed my plan would work.

When there was no answer from the other side of the door, Amoriel returned to me and the food. She said in a low whisper, "Might as well eat up. The camera's covered, and as far as they know, you are still passed out."

"What food did you use?" I whispered, sitting up.

Amoriel handed me a bag. I pulled it open and inhaled the scent of corn chips. I shoved some in my mouth, grateful no one could see me.

"Smashed banana," she said with a mouthful of food. "It was the only thing that would stick."

"Good job." I continued to eat the chips and found a water bottle to sip on.

"Now what?" she asked as she crunched down on some chips.

"Now we wait. Once they realize the camera is no longer working, someone will have to check it out."

"But what did you see?" Amoriel asked. "I tried to peek through, but everything was so bright."

My mind flashed to when the man threw in the bag of food. Like Amoriel, I couldn't see anything at first. When she yelled, though, he had paused long enough for my mind to capture what was on the other side of the door. I hadn't realized before what I was seeing. It was like viewing a picture you had taken and discovering a photo bomber in it.

I had imagined we were in a warehouse or some kind of old shipping yard, since we were in a metal container, but the scene in my mind was far from it. All I saw was blue—a brilliant blue, and a horizon line in the distance. I listened in the memory. It was faint, just a whisper of a sound, but there was no mistaking it. Usually the sound of waves brought about a calming peace. This time it brought panic, because it meant two things. First, we were no longer in Mexico City, which was miles from any ocean. Second, I was on my own. There would be no CIA rescue. Luca wouldn't be there with PFM agents to help me complete the mission. No one in The Company could swoop in and save the day. I was alone.

"Dana?" Amoriel said in the darkness. "What did you see?"

I thought about Tanner's words that had brought me through my first mission: *You're strong enough to take care of yourself.*

My mom's elegant handwriting from her last letter to me burned through my mind: *I know you have the potential for great things, and not just because of your exquisite mind, but the strength you carry within you.*

Daly's voice from my memory filled the silent darkness. *I knew from the very moment I met you that you would choose this life . . . You would sacrifice yourself . . . to save someone. It's just who you are.* I may not have known Amoriel, but I would protect her and get her home to Denisovich. My memories gave me the strength to realize exactly who I was.

I was Alexandra Stewart. And I was a spy.

23

Swim

"I don't know if I can do this," Amoriel whispered, crouching over me in the dark.

"Yes, you can," I reassured her.

"But what if I can't? And what if it's too far down?"

I found her arm in the darkness and squeezed. "I know this is hard, but we have to be strong. It's our only chance."

"How do you know the plan will work?"

I closed my eyes and relaxed my body against the metal floor. I had to appear unconscious if we were going to get out of here. "I'm not sure," I said.

"Then why are you so calm?" Amoriel's voice trembled.

There wasn't time to explain about the movies in my head of the people I loved. I'd used my memories on missions before, but now I realized they were my greatest weapon.

"Because I know what I'm fighting for and who I want to return home to when this—"

A pounding started before I could finish. The fists on the door were louder than before, and an obviously angry man yelled, "What's going on in there?"

I squeezed Amoriel's arm once more, then dropped my hand and went still.

"She's not moving," she shouted. "Please hurry. I think she stopped breathing." The desperation in her voice sounded real.

"Stand back," a deeper voice yelled. Neither man sounded like Gonzales.

The door burst open, and light flooded through my closed eyelids. I remained motionless while two sets of feet moved in our direction. Their heavy breathing and loud footfalls told me these were large men. What they didn't know was that Amoriel and I weren't exactly at the back of the container. We were about three feet from the back. Three feet closer to the exit.

"What's wrong with her?" One man asked as he leaned toward me, his exhales laced with the stench of onions. I didn't flinch when his fingers dug into my neck to feel for a pulse. I couldn't stop my heart from pounding, but I held my breath for a few seconds until I was sure both men were near.

I'd watched the move several times in my brain since the first time I saw Sensei Itosu use it on Daly. Now it was my turn. I opened my eyes just enough to see where both men stood before I spun my body as fast I could in a circle on the ground and used my cast as a weapon, sweeping at both men's legs. The men tumbled over me and onto the metal floor at the back of the container.

"Go!" I screamed at Amoriel. I scrambled to my feet and moved as quickly as I could with the pain in my leg and the cast on my foot. My fuzzy vision registered that she was several feet ahead of me in front of the container, and getting farther away every second. I pitched myself in her direction, hoping to get to the dock where she stood before the men reached me. The door of the container rattled as I stepped outside. I limped along the concrete, so close to freedom now that I could smell the ocean. Just a few more steps to the dock.

A hand gripped my shoulder when I was less than ten feet away.

"Where are you going, Alexandra?" asked a furious voice behind me. My eyes had already adjusted to the light when I turned around. Gonzales' too-perfect smile almost made me falter. *Who is he and how does he know who I am?*

I gripped his forearm and twisted it. He screamed in pain as I pushed away from him. I only made it a few more feet, right where the concrete met the faded gray wood of the dock, before arms wrapped around my middle and tried to pull me down. I spun around and elbowed Gonzales in the jaw. A searing pain bit at my wrist as he yanked me down to the concrete. I tried to pull memories forward in my mind of the moves Itosu had taught me, but the scenes blurred from all the motion—I still hadn't yet recovered from the ether.

Gonzales crouched above me, his red face dripping in sweat. He dropped to thrust his knee into my stomach. The air escaped my lungs in a loud huff and I couldn't pull any back in.

"You came to my school, got all nosy, and thought you could ruin my operation? Government officials will pay a great deal of money to keep their families safe—and even more to keep their *secrets* safe. I would've cut you in on the deal if you hadn't ratted me out to the Federales." His hands pressed my biceps to the ground. I twisted but could barely move under his weight. "Yes, I know Luca works for them."

"You actually believed I would help you?" My vision blurred as he pushed his knee deeper into my middle. "You're sick."

"No. I'm smart. Smart enough to do my research. It only took me a few hours to find out who you really are, Alexandra Stewart." His knee cut off my breath again. I shifted until I could inhale. His hands twisted my arms back down.

"And who do you think I am?" I knew my strained voice could barely be heard over the ocean waves around us.

"A stupid little girl who couldn't mind her own business."

I let my body go slack. Maybe he only knew my name. He probably had no clue about my personal life or that I worked with The Company and the CIA.

"And a father who works at the university. I wonder how much he would pay to keep his daughter safe."

No! A rush of energy burst through me. I thrust my right leg into Gonzales' side with such force that he let go of my arms. He groaned as I scrambled out from under him and got to my feet. I hobbled forward, only glancing over my shoulder once at his hunched-over frame, before I reached the edge of the dock and jumped feet-first into the ocean.

The cool water shocked my skin and enveloped me as the momentum from the jump took me deeper in the sea. I tried to kick but it was no use; my casted foot was a dead weight beneath me. My lungs burned as the sunlight shining through the water's surface began to disappear above me.

My mother's face flashed in my mind as blurry spots filled my vision. At least I would see her again—and not just in my head. Salty water filled my mouth after I released the last bit of air in my lungs. This was it. This would be my final mission. An overwhelming sadness swept over me at the realization. There would be no more racing across campus to replace the missing arm of the Caesar Augustus statue with one made of pink duct tape. My mind would no longer be used as a photographic tool to unveil a terrorist's plan. No more last-minute science experiments to help rescue a father and daughter from a terrorist organization. I wouldn't get to rescue myself with the aid of a Millard-enhanced device. No more disguises involving wigs and glasses to save a Van Gogh painting. The Mariinsky Theatre, the Superman building, the Louvre—my stories would disappear, along with my memories.

Light had vanished around me as the ocean swallowed me. I'd been unable to save a helpless girl from her evil kidnapper.

In the darkness I heard Daly's voice, clear and strong, almost like he was there. *Don't give up. Fight. Push yourself. Alexandra Stewart can make a masterpiece out of any canvas.* He was right—I couldn't give up.

Adrenaline coursed through me, sending my good leg into a flutter beneath me, and my arms in wide, powerful strokes. When light poured through the water onto my face, I gave one more strong kick with my good leg. My head surfaced and I gasped for a breath, but coughed out water instead. A documentary I'd once seen pressed through the spots in my vision. It was about a pilot who had ejected himself from a flaming plane. He'd landed in the ocean and had to swim for two days. The man had said that when his arms and legs were spent, he would float on his back. I turned onto my back and tried to float. My cast still weighed me down, but I found if I paddled with my arms, I could stay afloat.

Once I stopped coughing, I did a visual search for Amoriel. Half a minute later, I spotted her tiny frame clutching one of the pillars holding up the dock. The dock was ten feet above us. Gonzales was nowhere to be seen, though I had a feeling he hadn't given up yet.

I motioned away from the dock and then attempted to swim the breaststroke toward Amoriel. She shook her head. When I reached her, I yelled over the roar of the waves, "I know you're tired and scared. So am I. But if we want to get out of here, we need to swim." Her glossed-over eyes began to focus. "Do you want to get home?" I urged. "To your family?"

She nodded. "Then let's go," I said as firmly as I could. She released the pillar and began a crawl stroke in my direction. I floated on my back for a few seconds until we were side by side, and then I pushed my already worn-out limbs. I wasn't sure where we were heading, but it didn't matter as long as we got away from Gonzales.

"Where are we going?" Amoriel asked after several minutes of swimming.

The salty water had made its way into my throat several times, and my stomach felt bloated and sick. The dock was hundreds of feet behind us, but there was nothing on the horizon and I didn't dare head back. "Just keep moving," I said, trying to sound sure of myself.

After another ten minutes, my leg was cramping and I told Amoriel to stop so I could float for a few minutes. A rumbling motor sounded in the distance and I began to panic.

"Amoriel, they're coming for us. They must have a boat." A wave splashed over my face. I spit out the salty liquid and blinked away what remained in my eyes.

"No, no!" she screamed. "I can't go back."

"I know." I coughed. "Listen to me. As soon as they get close enough and shut off their engine, I want you to swim underwater. Rest now. When it's time, swim as long as you can before taking a breath, and then push yourself as fast as possible back to shore. If he's here, he's not there and you can make a run for it."

"But what about you?" Amoriel's tiny voice sounded raw. She wiped her eyes and continued to tread water.

"I'm going to create a distraction," I said. "Don't worry about me. Remember, I'm a fighter." The sound of the engine got louder and my heart beat even faster. "Just swim, Amoriel. You got it?"

"Okay." She took a few deep breaths.

The roar was upon us now, blaring in my ears. Then the engine cut and I grabbed Amoriel's arm. "Go!" I yelled. She disappeared under the water.

The glossy white surface of a twenty-foot boat reflected in the bright afternoon sun. It was less than ten yards away now. I didn't make a sound or try to escape. Instead, I swam directly toward the boat . . . directly toward danger.

Gonzales watched me from above. A thick man—one I remembered from the shipping container—stepped to his side and crouched down, then yanked me out of the water and tossed me into the boat. My shoulder slammed against the floor, and my cast vibrated against my leg in an eruption of pain. *I should have swum away. Maybe I could've made it.*

"Where is she?" Gonzales yelled, pulling me up by my arm.

"I don't know," I said between clenched teeth.

He threw me back down.

"Search the marina. She's the valuable one. Find her!"

"I should have let you drown." He hovered over me. I could see in his eyes that he wasn't sure what he was going to do with me, but I had a feeling I wouldn't make it if I remained on the floor. There was only one way to get out of this predicament.

"Please," I said quietly, trying to sit up. "I can't . . . I don't feel . . ." And then in what would have been an award-winning performance, I fainted. Or at least, I pretended to faint. My head hit the hard plastic of the bulkhead, but I didn't open my eyes, call out, or move. I let my entire body go slack.

"Is she . . ." asked his minion.

"No, you idiot." For the second time in less than an hour, fingers pressed at my jugular to feel for a pulse. "Just passed out. She can't help us now. Let's get the plan back in motion."

"What about her?"

"Focus, Hector. We don't need her anymore," Gonzales said. "She's just a professor's daughter. Toss her in the ocean, for all I care. We need Amoriel." The motor revved and the boat began to move, flopping my head against my chest.

Just a professor's daughter. Hearing that phrase gave me added strength. This guy didn't know who I was or what I was capable of.

I remained limp as hands reached under my arms and dragged me a few feet. When I was sure Hector was about to heave me off the edge of the boat, I opened my eyes, pushed my feet against the floor, and shoved him backward with all my strength. A splash sounded behind me. I looked over the edge of the boat to see a large lump of a man floating behind us. Had it not been for our increased speed, Gonzales might have heard his yells over the motor. As it was, Hector's voice was muted by the engine.

Gonzales had his back to me, but was too far from the edge for me to push him off the boat. *Think, Alex, think. What would Itosu do?* A memory played on fast-forward of my first fight with Daly, involving a broom and a cookie sheet. Yes, I needed a weapon.

The first thing I saw was a beach towel lying in a heap on the floor of the boat. I picked it up, put one end in each hand, and lunged toward Gonzales. He looked over his shoulder just as I reached him. His hands flew from the steering wheel in my direction, but I already had my arms raised above me. I threw the towel over his head, crossed my arms and pulled. He yanked on the terry cloth, trying to get it away from his neck. Keeping my grip tight, I let my weight fall forward. Just as I hoped, Gonzales held his ground, making the towel tighten even more on his neck. Anger flared in his eyes, but he couldn't speak—I'd cut off his air supply. Ten seconds more and his eyes would roll back in his head and he would never regain consciousness. He deserved it. He'd been ready to kill me, and I had a feeling it wasn't his first time. The faces of the girls in Luca's file flipped through my mind. If the girls were still missing, they had probably been murdered. All I had to do was hold on, and Gonzales would get his deserved punishment.

Suddenly, my mom's face filled my mind, the unbidden memory forcing itself upon me. I tried to shake it free but couldn't.

"Hold on, Yuri." My mom's voice carried down the hallway and into the kitchen, where I was getting a glass of water. I started toward her office to ask if she wanted me to start dinner. I'd been famished since starting a karate class at a local studio, and I still felt a little guilty about not telling my parents. "Yes, I can talk," she said in Russian. I still had a lot of work to do on my own pronunciation, but I understood just about all of the language.

I stopped outside her office and finished my drink. I'd wait to ask until she was off the phone. I sat my glass on the hallway table and began stretching my legs and arms, hoping to prevent the buildup of lactic acid caused by some new techniques I'd learned at the studio.

"The Monet?" Mom's voice had raised an octave. "I can't believe I was right." She paused. "I'm not sure if this weekend is . . . No, no, I understand. As long as I'm back by next Friday. It's Tanner's final game of the season." There was a rustling of paper. "Just a minute. I'm going to put you on speaker. I just dropped my entire 'To Do' pile on the floor."

"Some things never change," an older male voice said through the phone speaker.

"What is that supposed to mean?" My mom sounded serious for a moment before she began to laugh. "Ha, yes, I get it now. Some of us are just clumsier than others."

"We all have our strengths, and I'm sure Director Williams was able to get that stain out of his shirt from your drink last month."

My mom cleared her throat. "Yuri Golkov! That's enough about my lack of grace. I want to hear about the painting."

"Our sources have confirmed its location. Though Monet had done several similar scenes of Waterloo Bridge, your initial analysis seems to be accurate."

"I still can't believe it. It's been nearly five years since the heist, and after the rumors of it being burned by the accomplice's mother . . ." My mother rhythmically tapped her papers against the top of her wooden desk.

"Let's not count our chickens before they hatch. You get the painting and then we'll celebrate once we turn it over to be officially authenticated."

Papers rustled again, and one of them slipped under the door and into the hall. "Officially authenticated? Turn it over?" My mom sounded panicked. I gently kicked the paper back under her office door.

"Yes. Our client is a private wealthy Frenchman who has claimed ownership since the beginning," Yuri replied. "Even though he still believes the painting lost, it is our duty to return it to the last rightful owner."

My mom blew out a slow breath. I imagined her closing her eyes and biting on her bottom lip, a definite sign she was trying to keep her anger in check. "Yuri, what about the French government? Or the Dutch government? It was on display at their museum. Can't they fight for it?" My mom's passion for art was even more profound than Tanner's passion for football, or Dad's for history. I wished I had something that meant that much to me.

"As you are well aware, the painting had been sold several times over the years to private owners and was only on loan to the Kunsthal to begin with."

"I know. I know." The creak on my mom's old wooden office chair was loud enough to muffle her next words. ". . . just worried that if it gets back into an individual's hands, it will never be on display again. How sad would it be for a painting as great as Waterloo to be hanging in some private home, never to be seen?"

The man cleared his throat. "I understand. I'll look into other options, but for now, we have to do what's right."

"Even if it's wrong?" My mom's voice reminded me of my own. I'd never realized before how similar our cadence and tone were.

Yuri's hearty laugh carried through the door. "The dichotomy of life, I'm afraid. Sometimes following rules and laws, even if they don't seem quite right, shows strength of character."

"*Are you quoting that sensei of yours? What's his name again? Tosu?*"

"*Itosu. And I think he'd probably add something about balance and the universe.*"

My mom heaved a sigh. "I hate it when you're right."

"*Sometimes I hate it too.*"

I released the towel, and Gonzales pitched backward. His head met the steering wheel with a *thwack* and he toppled to the floor, unconscious but still breathing. Golkov's advice to my mother had traveled from one generation to another. No matter what Gonzales had done, the right thing to do was to turn him over to authorities.

I clumsily moved forward and pulled him to the back of the boat. After I stripped the rope from the life preserver, I began to tie his feet and hands together. I shook uncontrollably, probably just chilled from my wet clothes. I used a tow line to fasten Gonzales' hands to one of the rails toward the back of the boat. When he was secure, I made my way to the steering wheel. I placed my hands on the rubber handholds and stared at the controls. As I realized I'd never driven a boat, the events of the last day finally hit me. I crumpled to the floor, emotions washing over me. I'd been kidnapped by a man who was supposed to be my art teacher. I'd escaped from being locked in a shipping crate. I'd nearly killed a man.

As I sat there, unsure what to do, the rumble of a motor came to life in my ears and then died out just as quickly. I shot to my feet. The fast movement caused my vision to blur and my head to feel light. I grabbed the edge of the boat to keep my balance.

"Alex!" a voice called from right in front of me. My head cleared and I stared in disbelief at a pair of bright-blue eyes and windblown, curly brown hair.

"William?" My voice was tired and hoarse and his name came out in barely a whisper. "What . . . how are you here?"

He looked me over, no doubt noting how terrible I looked, and then stared at the back of the boat, where Gonzales' limp body lay.

"You didn't think we were going to let you have at the fun, did you?" said Luca, now standing at William's side.

"James called me while we were trying to find you," William said.

"We thought maybe you'd gone rogue or something, but La Academia's camera picked up Gonzales carrying you from the school." Luca reached out his hands to keep his boat from knocking into mine. He peered over at Gonzales. "Looks like you didn't need our help after all."

I stared over at the teacher's still body. I had done it on my own. No, that wasn't true. That was the thing about my eidetic mind. I was never entirely alone. My mom had been there in my mind, giving me strength. Golkov's and Daly's words had carried me through. Every memory had been a tool—a weapon against my enemy.

The fog in my head was clearing. "Wait! Amoriel!" I pointed out toward the dock. "She's swimming in that direction."

"We found her." Luca's calm voice soothed my panic. "PFM agents are with her now. Her father is in route. She will be fine."

"How did you find me?" I asked.

"Like I said" —William put his hand on Gonzales' boat to help Luca— "James gave us GPS coordinates of your location."

"But how did he know?"

"He said something about Millard, and a bug in your ear."

I touched my head. I hadn't forgotten about the coms-unit nanochip near my eardrum; I just didn't think it worked from so many miles away or that it had GPS capabilities. "That Daly," I said under my breath. I should've known he'd always keep track of me.

"You ready to get out of here or what?" Luca asked.

I stared at both men, who looked at me expectantly. Despite my exhausted body and throbbing leg, a laugh rippled through me. William and Luca looked at each other, lifting their eyebrows as I continued to laugh. I put a hand over my mouth.

"Are you okay, Alex?" William asked.

A slight breeze tickled at my exposed skin. I breathed in the salty ocean air. "Yes. Yes, I'm fine." I smiled weakly and shrugged. "I just don't know how to drive a boat."

24

Impression

I set my suitcase on the bottom step of La Academia and turned around. The white stone columns still rose the same distance above my head, but the mansion seemed smaller than when I'd arrived three weeks ago.

Sofía burst through the school's big white doors and rushed down the stairs to stand in front of me. "You weren't going to leave without saying goodbye, were you?" She put one hand on her hip. She carried a large framed picture under her other arm.

"Of course not." I kissed both of her cheeks. Actually, I hadn't planned to say goodbye to anyone at La Academia. A stealthy exit was more my style.

"I still can't believe all that stuff about Señor Gonzales," Sofía remarked. "I should have known his looks were the only good thing about him."

"Yeah." I wished I could tell her about my role in his capture and how messed up he really was. News had spread quickly, so everyone at the school knew Gonzales had abducted Amoriel, though the students were unaware of the details. In a search of Gonzales' apartment, the PFM had discovered artwork from the other missing girls, confirming his involvement with their abductions. In addition, the PFM had arrested his accomplices, including Hector, the man I had pushed into the ocean. So far, two government officials had come forward and revealed how Gonzales forced them to help pass certain laws in exchange for their daughters' freedom. While no money trail had been found, the PFM and CIA were hopeful that information provided by the other missing girls' families would lead to sufficient evidence to convict Gonzales. Six of the nine missing girls, including Amoriel and the other two from La Academia, had been recovered in similar shipping crates. The remaining three girls had yet to be found.

"It's a good thing you're returning to school in the U.S." Sofía lifted the frame she was holding and hugged it so that the back was facing me.

"It is?"

"Amoriel is going to be coming back in a few weeks, and I told her on the phone this morning that she has to be my roommate again."

I smiled at Sofía. Even though I wasn't a real student at La Academia, I would miss being her fake roommate.

"What's that?" I pointed to the framed picture in her arms.

"Oh yeah, I almost forgot." She handed it to me. "I wanted to keep it, but then I realized it would be the perfect way to help you remember your time here and what you're missing out on."

I turned the canvas around and saw my painting of the pyramids at Teotihuacan. A simple black frame surrounded the canvas, drawing out the dark tones of the shadows. I still couldn't believe I had painted it.

"Don't forget us when you go back to your big school in the States," Sofía told me.

"I won't." I touched her arm, but she pulled me forward and squeezed me into a tight hug, nearly making me drop the painting.

She let me go and stared at my outfit—a simple, black butterfly-sleeve dress with a flared skirt. I'd bought a few more dresses to wear, since I still couldn't fit my leg into a pair of jeans, even with my new walking cast. "And you should keep wearing black," she said. "It's a good color on you."

"Thanks." I felt a blush creeping up my neck.

Sofía pulled forward a lock of red hair from my faded streak. "But this" —she tugged at the hair— "is not really you." She dropped the hair and proceeded up the steps, her skirt swishing back and forth until she disappeared inside the doors.

Facing the driveway again, I waited for my ride to the airport. A figure emerged from the front gate and moved down the walk. Even if I hadn't seen his face, I would've recognized that gait from a mile away. William slowed as he neared me and stared down at my suitcase. He'd known I was leaving, and I guess I'd secretly hoped to sneak away from him too.

"This is the second time, you know." His voice sounded spent.

"Second time?" I stared into those blue eyes—the ones that had helped bring me back to life after I lost my mom and Tanner. If it wouldn't have been for William and The Company, the last year would've been unbearable. I'd always be indebted to him for that. I had thought I'd never feel again, but he had showed me how.

He studied my face as if he was trying to memorize it. "It's the second time you're leaving me. I know this is goodbye." He paused. "Goodbye for real."

"What? Why would you . . .We'll still see each other."

He smiled at me—the playful one from memory, but now filled with regret . . . or maybe defeat. *He means a different kind of goodbye.*

"I guessed it the first time I saw you two together, but I hoped I was wrong. Then when I saw you a few weeks ago, I knew."

"What?"

"It's okay, Alex. I get it. It's not meant to be. I'm not the one. Or some equally cliché line."

Realization dawned. "You saw Daly and me?" I wasn't playing dumb, but the thought of William seeing me without my knowledge had sent my brain flying through scenes, searching for moments when it could have been possible.

"The morning before I left for Mexico," William said.

My mind searched that day, slowing down time. I watched a scene in my head—the moment when Daly had seen me off to the airport in Providence. At that moment my only thought had been my complete trust in him. He had promised to stay in Providence to help my brother because I had asked him to do it. Daly's promise told me something I was only now beginning to understand. He would take care of me, no matter what. I'd thought it then, but now I recognized how much it meant to me.

I searched through the moment again. My mind had never left Daly's face. I had no memory of William being there, because I'd been completely focused on someone else.

"I didn't know, William. I'm sorry."

He stuffed his hands into his pockets. "When I found out you were in Mexico, I hoped . . . but when I saw your face after I told you Daly had asked me to help you . . . well, it kind of solidified everything." William looked down. "He's a lucky guy."

Neither of us spoke as a couple of female students rushed down the stairs. They joined the residents and tourists moving down the sidewalk on the other end of the gated entrance. I should've been rushing too, but I didn't want to say goodbye. That was the hard part about having memories of William scrolling across my vision—I would always be connected to him. Normal people could probably bury their feelings and eventually forget and move on. Long ago I'd discovered I wasn't capable of that. He'd always be a part of me.

"Thank you. For being there for me here and for keeping my secret," I told William. There was no need to elaborate, because I knew he'd never say anything about my eidetic memory, or my work for The Company and the CIA. That trust made it harder to say goodbye, but easier at the same time.

He pushed back the brown curls that covered one of his eyes. "I'm not going to stay in Mexico forever." He was trying to make this easier for both of us.

"I want to read that book of yours, when you finish it," I said.

"Okay. It might be a year or two. I'll let you be the first to read it, if you promise to tell me about your latest mission when you do."

I almost asked what he was talking about, but stopped myself. I wouldn't end things by lying to him or lying to myself. There would be more missions. There would *always* be more missions. It was a part of who my mom was, and a part of me too.

"It's a deal." I put out my hand. He hesitated before reaching out and clasping it. We shook hands slowly until he squeezed my fingers one last time and let go.

"Good luck, Dana." He gave me a one-sided grin, a duplicate of the first one he'd given me in the Marston building hallway. Then he turned and joined the crowd. I followed him with my eyes until his figure was a distant memory.

My phone, the original one the CIA had recently recovered, vibrated in my pocket. I pulled it out and saw Tanner's name, so I answered the call.

"Hey, Lexie," he said, nearly out of breath.

"Are you okay?" My mind raced at what could be wrong. Maybe his lungs weren't working properly.

"Oh yeah, doing great. I just finished my set of lat pull downs. I'm waiting for James to finish his bench press so I can do mine."

"You're working out? Already?"

"Dr. E. gave me the go ahead. Don't worry, I'm taking it easy. James wouldn't let me do more than forty pounds. It's ridiculous."

"Dr. E.?"

"The same one that woke me up. You know . . . Dr. Elijah Ser—. Actually I don't remember his last name. That's why he's Dr. E."

"It's Elijah Serben, but I like Dr. E." I sat on the bottom step and rested my arms on my suitcase. Two days had passed since my swim in the Gulf of Mexico, and my arms were still sore.

"You sound tired. Did I call too early?" Tanner said.

"No, no. I am tired," I admitted. "I'm ready to come home."

My brother blew out a breath. "It's about time. You've been gone forever. We were just talking about flying out there and dragging you back. What professor needs you away from school for three weeks? Seriously, aren't you missing a bunch of classes?"

"I know, I have a lot to make up, but this was important."

"Yeah, that's what James keeps saying. Dad misses you too, you know." I heard what sounded like metal weights being stacked on a weight bar, on Tanner's side of the line. "Just a sec, Sis." More clanging of metal against metal. "So when will you be here?"

"I should be in tonight."

"Great," Tanner replied, but his voice sounded strained.

"Are you sure you're okay?"

"Yeah. It's just—" He paused and I imagined him brushing his hair from his eyes and chewing his cheek, a nervous habit we shared. "I remembered something. It's what Mom wanted me to remember."

"You did?" I sat up straight and held tightly onto the phone. "I told you it would come. What was it?"

"The weekend before the accident." Tanner swallowed, and I sensed what he was feeling. Only weeks ago, he had learned of our mom's death. I'd had nearly a year to deal with it. Even though it was still hard, it didn't ache as much as it used to, but Tanner hadn't had the time to heal. "I'd gone to Mom's office to ask her something," he continued. "I didn't knock. I kind of just barged in."

"Sounds like you."

"Yeah, well, she was standing in the middle of the room with a painting in her hand. When she turned to face me, she was crying. I had looked at the painting in her hands—it wasn't one of the lifelike ones she often painted, so I was pretty sure it wasn't hers. And honestly, it wasn't that great of a painting either, so I had joked with her about it. She'd laughed for a few seconds and then got serious again. She set the painting down and tucked her hair behind her ears, the same way you do when you're frustrated."

"I don't—" I froze with my hand in midair, involuntarily headed toward my ear. I placed my hand back on my suitcase. "Fine. Maybe I do."

"Anyway, I braced myself because I'd remembered my room was a mess and I'd never taken out the garbage."

"That sounds about right."

"Hey!" Tanner let out a little laugh. "Now stop interrupting me."

"Okay, I'm zipping my lips. Continue."

"I don't have your gift for memory, but she mentioned never giving up and talked about doing the right thing. Honestly, I was so focused on the possibility of getting grounded that I didn't pay attention."

"Tanner."

"Yeah, I know. But I remember what she said next. She said we should always put things back where they belonged. I thought she was talking about my bedroom until she picked up the painting again, slid it into one of her boxes, and said she'd find a way."

The skin on my arms prickled.

"I wouldn't have even remembered it," Tanner went on. "But there was a look in her eyes, like this was important and I shouldn't forget it. I still don't know why she wanted me to remember it, but I'll figure it out."

"Tanner, what was the painting she was holding?" The sun had risen and its rays beat down on my face. I wiped at the sweat on my forehead.

"I don't know, Lexie. It wasn't that good and it looked kind of old. It seemed like the person painting it wasn't putting enough paint on their brush, because their brush strokes were all really short, like they had to keep going back for more paint."

"Like an impressionist?"

"Impress . . . what?"

I rolled my eyes. How could the son of an artist not know what an impressionist painting looked like? "Anything else you recall?"

"It was blue and purplish. I think it kind of looked like an overpass or maybe a bridge. Yeah, I think there was water."

I slowly rose to my feet, a painting surfacing in my mind—one with short brush strokes, blue and purple paint, and a London bridge across the middle. "The Monet," I whispered. "She actually found the Monet."

"The what?" Tanner asked.

"She was on a . . . It's a . . . " I couldn't do this over the phone. Last fall I'd discovered Tanner had found out about my mom's work as a spy. The memories were in my mind, but it wasn't until Elijah told me of my mom's involvement with The Company that I had realized what Tanner knew. I'd never told Tanner I was aware that he knew our mom was a spy. And not just that. I had never told him about my work as a spy, except when he was in his coma, but that didn't count. If I told him how I knew Mom found stolen paintings and how she often went undercover to retrieve them, I wouldn't be able to hold back that I had done the same thing and more.

"I've got to get going, Tanner. I'll talk to you tonight."

"Okay. I'll . . ." There was a loud grunt and more metal banging on metal. Tanner exhaled. "I'll see you then."

A bell sounded and I glanced over to see Luca riding up on a bicitaxi, from the side of the school. He motioned to the back seat. *My ride.*

After he hopped down from the bike, he grabbed my suitcase and offered me an arm, which I accepted graciously.

"We've got enough evidence on Gonzales now to keep him indefinitely. He's going away for a long time."

"What now for you?" I asked. "You headed back to . . . well, whatever you did before?"

Luca lifted my suitcase into the back basket. "I'll tell you what. You tell me and I'll tell you."

"Good point." I smirked at him.

"But I'll remain here undercover the rest of the semester."

"You will?"

"The PFM wants me to stay while Gonzales is under investigation. Besides, I got involved in PFM fairly young. If I'd discovered art years ago, maybe things would have gone differently for me."

"You wouldn't have become an agent?"

"Nah. I think I would have eventually found my way there, but at least now I can enjoy a few more months with people my age."

"And maybe with a particular someone, too." I thought of Amoriel and how she spoke of Luca once I told her he was, indeed, good guy.

"Well, you ready to go home?" He smiled, but I saw the regret in his eyes. Though Luca would never know everything about who I was and whom I worked for, we'd helped each other fulfill a mission. We would always have that bond.

I nodded. "I've never been more ready."

25

Waterloo Bridge

I stood at the doorway of Golkov's office, watching him stare up at the electronic displays on his back wall. His gray hair seemed lighter now, almost a snowy white along his neckline. Some of the screens in front of him played national and foreign news channels. Others showed maps or scrolled through lists of data. The information helped him keep track of The Company's agents on current missions throughout the world. I knew he worried about the agents. And even though Golkov's gray suit was freshly pressed, something about the tired way he stood told me he probably hadn't been home to sleep in days.

I knocked on his open glass door and he glanced back. Wearing a big smile, he rushed over as if he might hug me. Instead, he put his hands on my shoulders. "Welcome back." His eyes were shining.

"Thank you for your support on this mission. I couldn't have done it without your collaboration with the CIA and PFM."

Golkov motioned to the couch in front of his glass desk. He walked to his chair on the other side and sat down. I followed, moving more easily now with the walking cast, and sat across from him.

"Agent Helm called." Golkov shuffled a stack of papers and moved them to the side of his desk. "She told me about the CIA's offer. Congratulations." He wouldn't look me in the eye. He might have taught me about beating a lie detector, but he wasn't good at hiding his tells.

I thought about my mission debriefing that afternoon. A CIA car had picked me up from the airport. Agent Denisovich was staying in

Mexico with his family, but Julia Helm had insisted on a face-to-face debriefing with me. After I shared the details of the mission, she had offered me a permanent job with the CIA—one with substantial pay and an opportunity for as many missions as I wanted. And I could remain at Brown to finish my degree.

I had promised to get back to her with my answer. Then I'd dropped my suitcase off at my car and come straight to Golkov's office. I'd already made my decision.

"I'm not going to work for them." I leaned forward and placed my hands on the glass of his desk.

He raised his head. "You're not?" He said the words in English, not in the Russian we always spoke.

I shook my head. "No."

"You've accomplished a lot in your short time as an agent. This clandestine world will miss you."

Does he think I'm going to give up being a spy altogether? "I was hoping there still might be a place for me here," I said.

The pen in Golkov's hand slipped onto his desk. "I thought . . . Well, of course, yes. You know you're welcome here any time."

"I want to continue my mother's work. I'll still go on other missions, but I want to continue hers."

Golkov's eyes focused on me, speaking more than words could convey—he missed her too.

"There was a painting that she was looking for, a Monet."

"Ah, yes. *The Waterloo Bridge.* Stolen from the Kurlich Museum in 2012. We thought we'd found it, but the mission failed and your mother never recovered the painting. The only one she never found."

"I know."

Golkov's small eyes widened. "How do you . . ."

"Tanner had a flashback about it, which brought forward some of my own memories I hadn't thought about since I'd experienced them. I don't recall much, just a phone conversation she had with you, and some conversations she had with my father."

"It was the strangest mission." Golkov shook his head. "I thought for sure she'd found it, but she returned empty-handed."

Once more I flashed through the scenes of my mother that referenced the Monet. Then I remembered what Tanner said. If his memory was accurate, my mom had found the painting. I was sure of it. *But she would've told Golkov, right?*

"Alexandra, what is it?" Golkov said.

"I think . . ." My mind kept coming back to Mom's home studio. The box of her works in progress. The colors of the edge of the painting I saw sticking out over the brown box—short blue and purple brush strokes. "Is it possible she did?"

"Did what?"

"Found it. What if she actually found the painting?"

Golkov stroked his beard. "I would have known."

"There was a box. In her old studio before we moved." I scanned through the memory. "I think I saw it. And Tanner may have, too."

Golkov stood. "Why wouldn't she have told me?"

"What if she never had a chance to tell you, or to hand it over?"

"It's possible. But if that's the case, where is it now?"

"I'm . . . I'm not sure." My mind raced through the possibilities. I'd left the box in our old house, which had been sold soon after we left Wenatchee. The new owners probably either tossed it or donated it to Goodwill. Unless . . .

"Alexandra?"

"Golkov." I got to my feet. "I'll be back."

"Where are you going?"

"Across campus. There's a history professor I need to see."

"Alexandra, wait."

At the doorway, I paused and turned. There was fear on Golkov's face. I took a few steps back into the room. "Golkov? What is it?"

"I need to show you something." He bent down and reached under his desk to the black file drawers on the right side. The beeps of pressed buttons filled the silence of the room.

"I wasn't sure when it would be the right time. But now—now I think you're ready." He lifted a manila envelope from a deep drawer and closed it.

"Another mission already?"

"No." He came around his desk and held out the envelope. "Just open it."

I accepted the envelope, half expecting a silver wax seal with the impression of the bittersweet nightshade. There was only a metal clasp. I carefully pulled back the silver tabs and lifted the flap. "What is it?" I slid out a stack of paperwork, all in Russian.

"Your father didn't know. She wanted to complete the final exhibit before she told him. It was kind of a pet project of ours. She helped design it and put it in motion."

She? I scanned the top page. It was a title to a building in Moscow on Petrovska Street. Petrovska Street? My mind flashed to my first visit to Moscow, my first mission. On the drive from the airport to my apartment, we had passed a building on Petrovska Street. That same building held the Rembrandt painting my mom had rescued. I leafed through the rest of the pages, passing building specs and architectural renderings, until I saw it. A logo and a name.

The Rejnikov Museum of Art logo wasn't new to me. I'd seen it when I visited the museum last fall. But now I studied it with new eyes. A small rectangular frame surrounded a line drawing — ocean waves and a simple ship with a sail. If I stared at it long enough, it reminded me of the Rembrandt painting my mom had found — *Storm on the Sea of Galilee*. The museum name was typed in bold print below the rectangle that framed the line drawing.

Pride filled me as I stared at the logo on the bottom of the page.

"She left the museum to you and your brother," Golkov said.

"It's ours? The museum is ours?" I held the papers against my chest and let the news sink in. "But how? It had to cost a fortune."

A mischievous grin filled Golkov's face. "It's not all work and no pay here." He held out his arms to motion around him. "Your mother located many priceless works of art. Some individuals gave handsomely for their retrieval."

I tucked the papers back into the envelope. I owned a museum. A real museum with pieces of art. "What do I do with it?" I asked.

"Nothing." Golkov sat down and leaned back in his chair with his hands behind his head. "Or everything."

26

Home

I opened the old wooden door on the third story of the Peter Green House and let myself into my father's office. Pinstriped yellow wallpaper covered the walls. The side table was so full of books that the oak top was no longer visible.

"Alexandra." My father removed his thin-rimmed glasses and set them on an antique-looking map on his desk. "How was the mission?"

My mouth fell open. We hadn't talked about my spy work since we were at Tanner's side in the hospital, when my father had admitted he knew about my mom and me. He'd also said he didn't want to know anything more about what I did, so I wasn't sure how to broach the subject now.

"I realize you can't share details, but we can be honest with each other about how things went and how you are," he said.

I took a few steps forward and he peered down at my casted leg.

"A mission casualty, or are you as uncoordinated as your mother?" There was a bit of worry behind my father's smile.

"How about we say it was a little of both." I sat down in an antique chair at the side of his desk.

"I'm glad you made it back." He put his glasses on again. "Your brother needs someone to talk some sense into him. Did you know he wants to try to walk on for the Bears next season? He just woke up from a coma and already thinks he's going to be donning shoulder pads and a helmet."

"Dad, we both know that no amount of convincing can change Tanner's mind. That would be like telling you to stop studying your maps and books." I tugged at the corner of my father's map, which I now noticed was a replica from the fifteenth century.

"Rightly so." He pulled the map back toward him.

"Hey, Dad, can I ask you something?"

"Mmm-hmm." He nodded with his gaze still on his map.

"After we moved, did you come across any paintings of Mom's?"

His back stiffened and I wondered if I shouldn't have asked. He removed his glasses again—bifocals, I now realized—and held them in his hand. "I hung the ones you've seen at my apartment. Do you mean those?"

I'd already considered this, but I'd been to his apartment dozens of times and had never seen a Monet. "There were two boxes in her studio before we moved. They were things she hadn't finished—her works in progress. I left them there."

"Oh, those." He replaced his glasses. "The new owners called about those last fall. They'd been holding onto them, not sure what to do. But I'd already gone through them before we left and taken all of the ones that weren't duplicates of what I already had. Those are hanging at my apartment."

"So what did you tell the owners?"

"I said they could toss them. I'd planned to do it myself anyway."

"They're gone?" My voice cracked.

My dad came to his feet and moved around his desk, knocking two books onto the floor in the process. "Hey, Alexandra, it's okay. They were just canvases she was planning to paint over. We have all the ones she was proud of."

Except one. But I couldn't tell him. I couldn't let him know that he'd thrown away a painting that was probably worth more than half the university. The Monet was gone. It was over.

I put on a brave face. "I guess I just still miss her."

"We always will. But she'll always be here." He touched the side of my head at my temple. "And here." He placed his hand over his heart.

"I know." I felt lucky to always have memories of her in my mental library. I just wished I could've done one last thing for her.

I rose and gave him a hug. "Thanks, Dad."

"For what?" He squeezed me back before letting me go.

"For being here. For making Providence feel like home." *Home isn't a place. It's the people.* William's words from Mexico echoed in my mind.

"Well, you know what Holmes said."

"Sherlock Holmes?"

"No. Oliver Wendell Holmes, Sr. 'Where we love is home, home that our feet may leave . . .'"

"'But not our hearts,'" my father and I said together, my voice not quite as animated as his.

I smiled. Holmes was right. Where we love is home.

"See you Sunday for dinner?" my dad asked, looking at his map once more.

"I wouldn't miss it."

As I left his office, I tried not to think of the painting that would never find its home again.

27

Remembrandt

I wished I could run away my frustration at the lost painting, but all I could do was limp back to my dorm. At least the walking cast allowed me to forgo using crutches.

"Hey, Casey," I said to my roommate when I arrived in our tiny dorm in Wayland House. I would definitely miss the living arrangements of La Academia.

Casey looked up from her textbook. "You're back!" She rolled off her bed in a kind of acrobatic move before she fell awkwardly into me and grasped me with her petite arms. I'd never been a hugging person before, but it was nice to know I'd been missed.

"Is your cousin better?" Casey asked after releasing me from her tight hold.

Ah, the cover story of my sick cousin. "Yes, but I was worried for a while there." I thought of Amoriel and Denisovich as I pulled off my jacket and draped it over the bottom of my bed. "But she's home now and on her way to healing."

"Wow, that dress!" Casey tugged at the black chiffon flowing skirt. "I'm taking you shopping with me next time. Your eye for fashion has definitely improved."

She meant it as a compliment and I took it as one. I'd arrived at Brown University in jeans and a T-shirt. Things had changed for me, in more ways than she knew.

"Thanks," I said.

"But I don't approve of your choice of shoes." She pointed to my cast and then tapped her lips with her finger. "Let me guess . . . tightrope walking?"

"Something like that." I smiled. "Or it might have involved a clumsy me and a plain old sidewalk." At least it was partly true.

She motioned to my dress. "So is this for Mr. James Daly?" She said his name with a British accent, but her Southern drawl got in the way. "Have you seen him since you got back?"

"No. I had to check in with Professor Golkov first. Now I'm on my way to meet Daly and my brother."

"I still need to meet this brother of yours." Casey winked at one of the photos of him on my collage wall beside my bed.

I punched her lightly in the arm. "I thought you had J.R." She and Millard seemed like the perfect couple.

"I do, but that doesn't mean I can't get to know your brother. You and I are like sisters, so that makes him family." She sat down on my desk chair.

Her comment made me smile. I'd always wanted a sister.

"Something came for you while you were gone." She leafed through a stack of mail and handed me a thin white envelope with the Brown logo printed on the back.

I'd nearly forgotten about my application to the Slavic Studies master's program. No wonder I'd never gotten an email. With the mission and everything, I had pushed the application to the back of my mind. I tossed the envelope on my bed.

"You're not going to open it?" Casey stared at the envelope.

"I will when I get back," I replied, not wanting to face more disappointment right now.

"You got in."

"What?"

"They accepted you into the Slavic Studies Program."

"They did?" My hand came to my mouth. *I made it.* "Wait. How do you know?"

"Oops." Casey smiled sheepishly. "You were gone and I had to know! Sorry. Millard has this cool little tool that can X-ray through things. You should see some of his gadgets. He could totally make things for 007."

I laughed. Maybe I should've been mad at her for snooping, but it wasn't as if I hadn't snooped before. Besides, sisters did stuff like that all the time.

I reached over her and grabbed my car keys.

"Aww, you're taking the car back?" Casey said.

I patted her on the shoulder. "Don't worry. It's a family car." I winked.

She flashed a bright smile and spun around on my desk chair. "I won't wait up," she said in a sing-song voice. "Tell James hi."

The news of my acceptance to the Slavic Studies Program only distracted me long enough to walk to my Jetta. On Elmgrove Avenue, I drove quickly toward Brown Stadium. Fortunately, the football stadium was off campus and allowed me a few good miles of speeding to try to clear my thoughts of a Monet painting rotting away in a dump somewhere. The loss of such an important painting was mortifying, but what really upset me was knowing I had let my mom down.

I screeched to a halt in a stall up front. The public parking area was empty except for a few utility vans on the opposite side of the lot from Daly's ostentatious BMW. I parked my car exactly five spots away from his—no need to make it easier to compare the two vehicles. That would have been like deciding between gelato and ice cream—both were the perfect dessert, but one would always come out on top. I didn't want my Jetta to be pitted against gelato.

I rolled down my windows to let in the cool air suffused with moisture from the Seekonk River. I shut off the Jetta's engine. The parking-lot lights cast harsh shadows inside the car as the scene of saying goodbye to my mom's works in progress played on repeat in my head. Why hadn't I just grabbed those boxes? There was no one to blame except me.

I pounded my palms against the steering wheel until they stung. Then I rested my forehead on the wheel. I wouldn't cry over a lost painting, but I wanted a moment to mourn what could have been a final tribute to my mom.

"Lexie?"

I lifted my head. Tanner stood at my passenger door, his face flushed. Clearly out of breath, he rested his hands on the door and leaned in through the open window. His blond hair was nearly an inch long now and spiked on top.

"I remembered," he said.

"You're up? And walking?" I stared in disbelief. I knew he'd been working on it, but I hadn't expected it so soon.

"Yeah, yeah. Beside the point. But didn't you hear what I said? I know the rest of what Mom really wanted me to remember."

I sat up straight and peered into his eyes, which looked just like my mom's. And mine. "There's more?"

"That painting I told you about." My brother took a breath. "The one that was an impression or whatever you called it."

"Impressionist," I corrected.

"Yeah. Well, she said she was supposed to give the real one to the owner, but she hadn't yet."

"Yeah?"

Tanner opened the car door and slipped into the passenger seat. His skinny legs showed under his cardinal-red athletic shorts. He wore a brown T-shirt with the word *BROWN* written in bold white across the front. "She had tried to find the painting's owner to allow a museum in Moscow to borrow it." As my brother pulled the door closed behind him, his foot hit my backpack on the floor, and metal clanged from inside it. I hadn't unpacked from the mission yet.

"She was?"

"But the owner had died and another museum had it on loan when it was stolen. So Mom was working with them to get the rights to have it on display or something. I don't remember specifics. I just know that whatever she did, it worked. You know how good she was at getting people to do things."

"It worked? So she was giving her museum in Moscow the painting? That's why she had it?"

"No. See that's the thing. That was why I kept thinking I was supposed to remember something. It was the Remembrandt."

"You mean Rembrandt?"

"Yeah, whatever. It sounds like remember."

"The painting with the bridge was a Rembrandt?"

Tanner shook his head vigorously. "No, that's why I was so confused about the memory. We all can't think like you can." He shifted his position so he sat with his back against the passenger door. "It's where the Rembrandt is."

I shook my head. "I have been to the Rejnikov Museum. It's not there." I thought back to last November when I visited the Rejnikov, right after Elijah disclosed that my mom was a spy too. That's when I saw the museum in Moscow and remembered it from architectural drawings I'd seen as a child in my mom's office. At the museum, I discovered that my mom had recovered the *Storm on the Sea of Galilee* by Harmenszoon van Rijn Rembrandt. That painting had been the clue to finding a letter my mom had left me—a letter telling me of her work as a spy. It felt like so much time had passed since that winter day. "Tanner, the Monet was in the boxes. The ones I left behind."

He frowned in confusion. "Boxes? What are you taking about?"

"You said she put the Monet in the box in her office. I saw the boxes before we moved here. We didn't bring them with us, and now everything that was in them is gone." I couldn't hide the despair in my voice.

"Lexie, the painting was never at our house."

"But you said . . . the painting she had when you went into her office—"

"That painting? No, that was her attempt at a replica. I guess some museums keep fakes in the place where the real ones are whenever the paintings have to be cleaned and stuff. The real painting was too valuable to be left sitting around at our house. She had to find a safe place to keep the Monet. That's what you called it, right?"

"Yes." I was thoroughly bewildered. If the painting my brother had described wasn't the real Monet, then where was it and what did it have to do with Rembrandt? "So, where is it, Tanner?"

"It's with the Rembrandt!" His eyes were bright now, his wide smile the one from my memories. "Like literally. She said she put it behind the Rembrandt in that Moscow museum. Isn't that awesome?" His arms came up to his sides, his hands animating his words.

"At her museum?" I'd been there not six months before. I pulled on the memories of the Rembrandt and Monet. *Waterloo Bridge* would have fit perfectly behind *Storm on the Sea of Galilee*. Was it really possible?

"She said it was hiding there at the museum she designed. No one else knows. Wait, why did you call it *her* museum?"

I'd left the papers with the title Golkov had given me at my dorm, but I figured it was time to at least come clean about one thing. "She didn't just help design the museum and procure paintings for it. She owned it, Tanner." Since she owned the museum, it made sense that she could hide a painting there. If my brother hadn't woken up from his coma, no one would have ever known about the hidden Monet.

"The whole museum? But how?" Tanner grabbed my forearm and I put my hand on his.

It was time for the truth. "I think you know," I said.

Tanner went still. "You know?"

I nodded my head, but I wouldn't be the first to say it.

He released the breath he'd been holding. "Did she tell you she was a spy?"

As he said it, everything clicked. "I didn't know she was a spy before the accident. I'm not sure why I never considered it when we were growing up. I was probably too caught up in my own life."

"Me too, Lexie. I didn't even believe it until too many overheard phone conversations didn't make sense and her overseas trips seemed beyond her work at the museum back home. When I confronted her about it, though, she didn't deny it. Maybe she was tired of living that part of her life alone." Tanner released my arm and turned his body so he could lean his head back against the passenger seat. "Such a cool job, and she couldn't even talk about it with anyone." He stared out the windshield.

I thought about my work for The Company and the missions I'd been on. I had so many stories I wanted to tell Tanner, so many secrets.

"She did it to protect us, you know," he said.

"Yeah. I get it."

Tanner rubbed one of his arms up and down like it was sore before he looked up. "I miss her."

"Me too."

"I never really got a chance to say goodbye." His eyes glistened but he didn't cry. We'd already done that together. He deserved a chance to say goodbye and honor her, just like I wanted to do.

I smiled. "If what you said about the Rembrandt and Monet are true, I have an idea—one that would give you the chance you missed and make her happy at the same time, but I'll need a day or two."

His right eyebrow lowered over his gray eye, just like our mom's did whenever she was confused. "Okay."

"Okay?"

"I trust you, Lexie. If you say it, I believe it." He reached for the door handle and his foot hit my bag again. The metal inside jangled. "What is that?" He started to unzip my bag, exposing my running shoes.

"Oh, just a puzzle the professor gave me. I haven't had the time to figure out how to separate the rings." I bent over and searched inside one of my shoes. My fingers found the puzzle and I pulled it out.

Tanner snatched it from my hand. "Let me see that." He started twisting the two metal rings around. "By the way, Dad wants us there for dinner on Sunday."

"I'm only coming if you bake the brownies," I said.

"From scratch?" Tanner held the rings up to the faint streetlight and started shaking them.

"I wouldn't have it any other way." I smiled.

"So" —he looked through his window toward the stadium— "James is waiting inside. We have something to show you."

"Okay." My insides flip-flopped at the mention of Daly's name.

Tanner lifted his hand and nonchalantly dropped the metal puzzle between us. I threw a hand out and caught it before it landed in the space between the seats, where I could've never retrieved it.

He started climbing from the car. "Oh, and that puzzle" —he pointed to the rings in my hand— "can't be solved."

"What?" I stared down at their silver surface. "Why not?"

"Because it's not a puzzle. Those rings are like two links to a chain. They were made together. You'd need a metal saw to get those babies apart."

I stared at the puzzle again with renewed eyes. Why didn't I see it before? Each ring was a perfect circle, no seams or blemishes. Tanner was absolutely right. I could yank and twist all I wanted, but some things weren't meant to be separate.

As we walked through the gates into the stadium, I couldn't help but stare at my brother in awe, marveling at his transformation while I was in Mexico. He was talking and walking and moving just like he did before his coma.

Tanner led me to an empty football field lit with huge stadium lights that brightened the field and all sides of the twenty-thousand seat arena. Even though the night sky above us had darkened, it felt like nearly midday.

"Stand here." He pointed to the sidelines not too far from one end zone. Pink and blue sparkly hulu hoops hung from the horizontal cross bar that ran between the goalposts. "Don't laugh. It was James's idea, and those are the only hoops we could find at the store."

"What is it?" I folded my arms and shivered as a cool wind blew across my skin.

"Just watch." Tanner jogged to the ten-yard line. He jogged! He limped a little and moved slowly, but he was moving. I was still in shock as he bent over and picked up a football, one of about ten lined up along the ten-yard line. Then he began to throw. My brain flashed to scenes from high school football games as Tanner pulled back his arm and released the football. It shot through the air about thirty feet before it sliced right through the center of a hula hoop. The hoop swayed slightly from the action. Tanner immediately picked up another ball and did the same thing. Down the row he went, throwing footballs with ingenious accuracy, like he'd never been in a tragic car accident or a ten-month coma.

When he finished throwing ten footballs, my loud clapping echoed through the stadium. Tanner jogged back over to me, smiling with beads of sweat dripping down the sides of his forehead. The look on his face reminded me of how I felt after each mission. Even though it was hard and at times I wondered why I was doing it, the rush of accomplishing a goal was worth it.

"Did you see that? First time I haven't hit a hoop. Brown Football, here I come." He put his hands behind his head and glanced up at the dark sky. I'd missed his confident smile. He might not be the exact same Tanner who left me last year, but he was well on his way.

I rushed forward and wrapped my arms around him. The laugh from his chest rumbled against my ear and I squeezed him tighter. "Don't ever leave me again," I said.

"Lexie, you're choking me!"

"Oh, sorry." I dropped my arms and stepped back. "I just missed you."

"I'm not going anywhere." He stretched his arms. "Except back out on the field. I still have five more sets before Coach Daly will let me go." He motioned to the other side of the field to a figure standing in the opposite end zone. "Just leave him intact. He's my ride home."

Daly stood across the field. Even with my walking cast, it was hard not to run to him. My heart was so full it surged with anticipation. Each step forward sent another wave of heat through me. When our eyes met, his steps in my direction were cautious and guarded. Even as he passed his twenty-yard line, I couldn't read his expression. It was as if he hadn't decided if he wanted to smile or grimace. Had I made a mistake in leaving him like I had? Was our timing off again? Was I too late?

We met at the fifty-yard line, both of us within feet of the faded white center line, but neither of us crossing over.

"You're home." His deep voice filled the space between us. To hear the sound in real life, not in memories or from thousands of miles away over the phone, soothed me to the core. I'd missed him, even more than I had realized.

"Yes, I'm home."

What he didn't realize was that I wasn't talking about the place anymore. Providence had become a kind of home for me, but after all my travels—from Washington to Rhode Island and Spain to Russia—I realized Holmes was right, just like my dad said. The place could never replace the people.

Wearing the most vulnerable expression I'd ever seen on him, Daly looked down at the center line and rubbed the back of his neck. "I wasn't sure . . . I didn't know if you'd want to see me."

"See you? Of course I'd want to see you."

"I just thought . . . after Mexico . . . after William. . ." Daly's words trailed off.

My hand broke the invisible wall between us. I grasped his forearm and pulled him toward a bench at the sidelines. The warmth of his skin against my palm sent a steady flow of tingles from my fingers to my toes.

Tanner continued to throw footballs through the hoops hanging from the crossbar. Two of them sailed through the center again, not even touching the hoop. I still couldn't believe he was standing there. After nearly a year of him gone and then lying in a coma, I never thought I'd see him on a football field again. It was right where he belonged.

"I figured it out." Daly's voice was lighter as we both sat down on the bright-silver bench. I adjusted myself on the cold seat so I could put my casted foot out in front of me on the ground. The sides of our legs touched, but neither of us moved away.

I frowned to myself, wondering what he had figured out. Us?

"Cannon Beach." A kind of hopefulness filled his dark-brown eyes.

"Cannon Beach?" Why was he talking about the West Coast vacation spot I went to growing up?

"That's where you should go."

"Me? Why would I go there?"

"When you're ready to escape, to run away. That's where you should go."

Again I thought of all the places I'd traveled to. All the wonders of the world I'd seen in Mexico and Europe and the United States. But of everything I'd ever seen, the quiet Oregon ocean was the one place where I would always feel close to home—the place where I could clear my head and only think of the present instead of always reliving the past in my mind.

Daly knew me all too well. But what he didn't know was that I would never run away—at least not on my own. Because if I had learned anything in the past year it was that I didn't want to be alone. If I really needed to, I could survive on my own; Mexico had taught me that. But I didn't want to. And if I wasn't on my own, there was only one person I wanted to be with.

I turned to face him. "I love Cannon Beach. That would be the place I would choose if I ran away. But I don't need to." I shook my head. "I don't want to. At least . . . I don't want to run away unless it's with you."

Daly shifted next to me and I glanced up to find his eyes wide with surprise for just a flash before a bold smile filled his face. "Run away? Who says I want to do that?"

My racing heart slowed in my chest and an overwhelming disappointment filled me. "Oh, I just thought . ." I guess I'd believed things would just turn out, that I'd come home from Mexico and we could pick things up where we'd left them. That he would feel the same way I did.

"Alexandra, look at me." I felt Daly's hand on my chin as he tilted my head toward his. "Following you would never be running away." His eyes glistened in the overhead football stadium lights. "Because that's where I would always want to be."

A smile found its way to my lips as his hand moved to the back of my neck, pulling me closer. The stadium disappeared. This moment . . . this moment I would relive many times in my mind.

"Barcelona, Moscow, St. Petersburg, Providence, Cannon Beach. It doesn't matter where you go, Alexandra. I would follow you on any mission to anyplace." He kissed my forehead and leaned back. "You okay with that?"

Overcome with the emotions bursting within me, I nodded.

He grabbed my hands and pulled them up to his lips, then gently kissed my fingers.

"Thank you," I breathed out in a whisper.

"For what? For this?" He kissed my hands again.

"For staying. For taking care of my brother." I peered over Daly's shoulder to watch Tanner walk to retrieve his footballs. It might take some time for him to regain his speed, but I had a feeling his new coach would get him there just fine.

Daly's hand found my face again and his thumb brushed my cheekbone. "I'll always be there for you, even if that means you need me to stay thousands of miles away."

I wrapped my arms around his neck until our faces were only inches apart. There was one more thing I needed from him. "How would you feel about staying right by my side for a few days, thousands of miles away?"

He scooted toward me. "A getaway?" A sly smile turned up the left corner of his lips.

I lifted a brow and scooted back, dropping my arms to my lap.

His smile grew wider. "Another mission?"

"Not for me."

He looked at me questioningly.

I thought of my mom and of Tanner's revelation about the painting. If he was right, I knew exactly where we all needed to go.

"If it's not your mission, then whose?"

"My mom's." I swallowed the emotion rising in my throat. Daly found my hand and squeezed. "Her final mission," I said.

"The painting? The one Tanner remembered. Do you think the Monet is really there, in Moscow?"

I nodded and embraced Daly again. He always knew more than I gave him credit for.

"So, you in?" I asked.

"Maybe." His hands looped around my waist and stopped at the small of my back. "I do have one stipulation."

"Oh, and what's that?" I pulled him an inch closer.

In answer to my question, he pulled me forward and his lips found mine. Our first kiss had been unexpected, our second and third had been an admission of our feelings, but our fourth was a commitment. It held a promise, one both of us shared. We'd all found a place—my father at Brown University, William in Mexico, Tanner on the football field. And me. It wasn't in those vivid memories of the place I'd lived as a child. It was here. With Daly. I'd finally found home.

28

Final Masterpiece

The Rejnikov Museum of Art hadn't changed from the image in my head. The four large columns in front still gave it the appearance of an ancient Greek temple, standing out against the Russian architecture. The half moon in the sky cast bluish shadows across the exterior. I patted the duffle bag at my side. Daly had offered to carry it, but I had insisted on doing it myself. It was part of my last gift for my mom—the last puzzle piece to her final mission.

Tanner walked beside Daly and me, his limp barely noticeable now. His arms were still thin, but his cheeks had filled out a bit in the last month and his light-blond hair was back to its usual messy-cool style. The three of us walked up the concrete steps and joined Golkov, who stood by the front doors. He didn't need to be there, but then neither did anyone else.

We waited for my dad, who was meandering up the stairs in his typical tourist attire— khaki pants and a loud shirt, with a camera around his neck. Apparently U.S. history wasn't his only passion. It had taken us twice as long to get from the airport to the museum just so Elijah could pull the car over at each and every historic sight. We'd already stopped at the Menshikov Palace and St. Isaac's Cathedral. For the remainder of the drive, we had let my father sit in the front with Elijah and take pictures out the window. We all decided to let him in on the Monet painting. He already knew what my mom had been doing, and the knowledge that she had left behind one last legacy had brought a happiness to his eyes that I hadn't seen since before the accident.

Wearing a dark tailored suit and overcoat, Elijah jogged up the steps and stopped at my side. "I remember the first time you saw this place," he said.

"Me too," I replied. It felt like years had passed since the Moscow mission when Elijah had driven me around. So much had changed since then.

"I still can't believe this place is yours." Daly's hand found mine.

"It's mine too," Tanner said, bumping into me. "Do you think we could add a game room?"

Daly and I stared at him in disbelief. Golkov let out a laugh that was soon followed by Elijah's.

Tanner shrugged. "I'm kidding, guys. Seriously."

"You sure you want to do this?" Daly asked me. "You have a key and you know the security codes. We could all just walk in." He said this last part in Russian. Since Tanner was the only one who didn't know about my work as a spy and also didn't speak Russian, it was like our own secret code.

"It's my museum, so I have to know," I said. When I'd told everyone, minus Tanner, about the mission I'd planned to break into the museum, they all thought I was crazy — at least until I explained I was doing it all as a tribute to my mom. No one could argue with that. What they didn't know was that this was also a test. If I could break into my own museum in the middle of the night, it meant other people could, too. Now that I was continuing my mom's work in recovering paintings for The Company, I felt it was my mission to keep the paintings in my care as safe as possible.

Out of breath but beaming, my dad finally reached the top of the stairs. He stared up at his wife's masterpiece. He'd known she was working on a project in Moscow, but she had kept the museum a secret, waiting for the Monet mission to be complete. Now it would be.

Tanner stepped in front of everyone and turned to face us where we stood in a row, admiring the museum. "I don't know about you guys, but if we're going to have to wait for Lexie to play spy and complete this mission of hers, I say we go to that restaurant I saw a few streets down. It looked like it was one of those twenty-four-hour places. I hear Ptichie Moloko is like having s'mores in cake form. Who's in?"

Everyone stared at Tanner. No one had told him I was a spy, had they? I glanced at Daly, who shrugged his shoulders. Nobody spoke, but they all seemed as surprised as I was.

"Seriously, guys," Tanner said. "I'm the one who found out my mom was a spy. Do you really think I'd be the last one to know Lexie is in on it too? And you." He turned to Daly. "You're a terrible liar."

I laughed "I could have told you that. But really, how did you find out?" I thought we'd all been so good at keeping the secret of The Company and my involvement as a spy.

"You told me." He leaned against a column and pretended to polish his nails on the shoulder of his shirt.

"I did not." Unless . . . My mind played the movie of my visit to Tanner while he was still in the coma. I'd talked to him about everything. Daly. William. The Company.

And being a spy.

"You remember stuff from when you were asleep?" A few weeks before, we'd started referring to his coma that way. It made it all seem less serious.

"Maybe I have superpowers too." Tanner tapped his temple.

"Why didn't you say something?" I asked.

"It was too much fun watching you guys try to hide things. I was actually kind of impressed. You're a pretty good spy."

Apparently not that good.

Golkov stepped forward. "Well, I think Tanner may be onto something, at least about eating. It's been a while since I've had some real Russian food. Besides, even if everyone here is asleep, that seven-hour difference doesn't mean we shouldn't get a proper dinner. Let's allow Alexandra to take it from here." He patted my back and winked. There was a youthfulness to his face now that I hadn't seen since the first time I solved that cupboard word puzzle in his office months before. The anagram message from the letter cubes flashed in my mind—*Quid est veritus? Est vir qui adest.* What is truth? It is the man who is here.

Golkov's puzzles were always more than just mental games. I slipped a hand into my pocket and retrieved his metal puzzle. "This is for you." I pressed it into his hand. He looked down at the silver rings, still intertwined. A large smile spread on his bearded face.

"Figured it out?" he asked.

I nodded my head. "Some things are meant to be together."

Golkov tucked the puzzle into the pocket of his coat, put a hand on my shoulder, and said quietly, "Your mom would be proud." His weathered hand squeezed my shoulder once before he let go and started down the steps.

"Give us a call when you're ready for us," Elijah said and then followed Golkov down the stairs.

"Hey, wait for us." Tanner grabbed our dad's arm and pulled him down the stairs too. Dad mumbled something about a memory card for his camera before they caught up with Golkov and Elijah on the sidewalk.

"I guess I'll leave you to it," Daly told me. "You want me to wait here?"

"No, it's okay. I've got you right here if I need anything." I pointed to my ear, where I still had my coms unit.

"Okay. But I do have something you need to take with you."

"I've got everything right here." Lifting the strap on my shoulder, I hoisted up the bag Millard had prepared with the tools I would need to break into a highly secure art museum.

"Not everything." Daly reached into his jacket pocket. "Close your eyes."

I did as I was told, trying not to peek as he lifted my left hand. His fingers traced around my ring finger in slow motion. My racing heart cut off my breathing. *What is he doing? He couldn't possibly be—*

"Oh wait. Wrong hand." He dropped my left hand and lifted my right one. I felt something smooth and cool slide onto my ring finger. "Now you can look." He held my hand up between us.

I stared down at the ring Daly had placed on my finger. The Company ring fit perfectly there, like it was right where it should be. Finding paintings and discovering truth—that was exactly where I wanted to be, too.

"So what do you think?" he asked.

I stared up at my museum and then back at the man who'd been there at the start of this journey.

"I think" —I unzipped my duffel bag and pulled out my new grappling-hook gun— "I have plenty more memories to make."

I grabbed the collar of Daly's leather jacket and pulled him toward me, while my other hand aimed the gun high above us. I cocked my head to the side and smirked at his raised eyebrows. Then I gave him a kiss he would never forget before I pulled the trigger.

Dear *Memory of Monet* Reader,

Thank you for going on Alexandra's mission with me. I hoped you love reading her story as much as I enjoyed writing the series. Readers are what keep authors in business, so I thank you for your support.

If you enjoyed *Remembrandt, Van Gogh Gone* (Remembrandt #2), or *Memory of Monet* (Remembrandt #3), please consider leaving a review on Goodreads.com, Amazon.com, DeseretBook.com or any ebook store you purchase through. Reviews and word-of-mouth are what keeps an author writing.

As a thank you to my readers, I wrote and recorded a song (yes, I sang!) that accompanies the series. You can listen to "Remembrandt Song" and download your free copy online (https://soundcloud.com/author-robin-king).

I love to attend book clubs, conferences, and school assemblies. Please email me at authorrobinking@gmail.com to schedule your event.

Also, if you would like to keep up-to-date on my books, author events, or giveaways, please sign up for my quarterly newsletter (http://eepurl.com/bzMItL) or send me an email and I'll add you to my list.

Thanks again,

Robin

About the Author

Robin M. King received her bachelor's degree in education from Brigham Young University and has been instructing children and young adults for over ten years. When she's not writing or helping her students remember the quadratic formula, she leads a clandestine life as a wife and mother of six. Don't tell anyone, but she's also an undercover marathoner, photographer, singer, seamstress, baker, and household-appliance repairman.

Robin's first novel, *Remembrandt* (2014), introduces readers to Alexandra Stewart's world of crypic codes and covert missions. The second novel in the Remembrandt series, *Van Gogh Gone* (2015), tests Alex's limits as she searches for a stolen painting.

Learn more about Robin and her books at AuthorRobinKing.com or on social media @authorrobinking.

Remembrandt

Robin M. King

Alexandra Stewart doesn't just walk down memory lane, she lives on it. Her eidetic memory records and plays back her experiences, DVD style. It's great when she aces a test, but not so great when she topples over a cute guy. Talk about an endless loop of humiliation.

When her Russian professor gives her an impossible puzzle, Alex discovers he has a secret—one that will catapult her into a life of cryptic codes and covert missions. Of course, conducting secret ops would be easier if she weren't trying to impress her handsome new running partner. As if love weren't hard enough already, now Alex is trying to find it while dodging bullets and going undercover.

One thing is for certain—whatever happens will be forever etched on her memory. And some things are better left forgotten.

Espionage isn't just her job. It's a work of art.

Van Gogh Gone

Robin M. King

Alexandra Stewart's eidetic memory won't let her forget anything, ever. And finally she has a life worth remembering—a Spanish tutor who gives *perfecto* a new name, a roommate that could double as her sister, and a special role in a spy organization with secret headquarters at Brown University.

When Alex's colleague Daly returns from a covert mission in Moscow, he is accompanied by a man she hoped she would never see again. He claims he can bring back to her a loved one she'd thought was gone forever. But the price he demands could be impossible to pay: Alex must find and retrieve a stolen Van Gogh painting.

From Barcelona to Paris, Alex and Daly's friendship is stretched as they uncover a truth neither one of them saw coming. Alex's unusual gift may help her protect the people she cares about, but will her choices compromise everything else that matters to her?